MY FAKE FIANCÉ

A NAVY SEAL ROMANCE

ODETTE STONE

ODETTE STONE PUBLISHING INC.

My Fake Fiancé, The Navy SEAL Series, Book 3

Copyright © June 2018 by Odette Stone

www.odettestone.com

ISBN: ISBN: 978-1-9990538-9-5

First edition, June 2018

This book is a work of fiction. All names, characters, locations and incidents are products of the author's imagination. Any resemblance to actual persons, things, living or dead, locales or events is entirely coincidental.

PROLOGUE

PORTER

MY EYES BURNED, struggling to stay open, and my body worked to hide its aches and sores, but I was thankful to be stateside again. After a deployment in a country not fit for humans, a sixteen-hour flight to Virginia to pick up my suit, and another flight to New York, I felt punch-drunk tired as I walked through JFK.

"You made it." Jackson assessed me while I fell into step beside him. "We're parked this way." He eyed my bag. "Did you bring your suit?"

"Emily texted me twice."

A ghost of a smile traced his lips. "Figured she would."

At his truck, I tossed my bag into the back and hopped in beside him. "When did you get into New York?"

"We drove up yesterday." He turned and checked me over. "You look like shit."

That's what happens when life kicks you in the nuts.

"The bowels of hell will do that to a person."

He laughed as he started the engine. "Beer and steak?"

"Wouldn't say no."

"We gotta make a pit stop first." He merged out of the parking lot.

"I have all of Theo's diapers, and Emily is living on a prayer right now."

I glanced over my shoulder at the baby blue bunny diaper bag sitting on the back seat. In the field, Jackson was one of the most ruthless and skilled operators I'd ever worked with, but around Emily and Theo, he became a different person. A better person. Better than I'd ever have the chance to be.

I needed to share my news, although I dreaded it. After three back-to-back deployments, my recently approved leave of absence would come as no surprise to anyone, but I felt like I was letting down the team. After this weekend, I'd have just four more weeks in the field, and then I was free.

I couldn't remember the last time I had taken more than a week off.

"I took a L.O.A."

"How long?"

This was where it got tricky. Most approved L.O.A.s lasted six weeks. I'd requested an open L.O.A., which meant I could take up to six months off without needing to be retested.

"It's open."

He hit me with his green eyes. "You good?"

"Just need to take care of some personal shit."

Translation: my life was a mess.

No. My life was a fucking mess.

I'd pushed off dealing with any of my shit by simply signing up for deployment after deployment, but my body had started to protest. I needed to rest. The other night, my mind had wandered, and I'd almost gotten my head blown off.

Fuck me.

I cleared my throat, feeling a need to explain. "I found Felicia. She's in New York."

"You talk to her?"

"Just a text."

He pulled his truck up against the curb and reached behind us to grab the diaper bag. "Give me a minute."

As he jogged across the street with Theo's diaper bag over his huge shoulder, I fought my first smile in a month. Hell, the only thing that made me smile these days was time spent with Theo. It was an honest-to-God honor to be his godfather. Emily and Jackson knew I'd guard that kid with my life.

A tall, leggy blonde stepped out of the building and stopped in front of Jackson. He handed her the diaper bag. She laughed at something he said, and her entire face radiated warmth and such pure fucking happiness, it almost hurt to watch.

I held my breath as the wind whipped her thick shoulder-length blond hair over her wide eyes. She wasn't a classic beauty like Emily, nor was she a siren like Felicia, but for some reason, I couldn't take my eyes off her.

She spoke with animation and pointed at something down the street. Her own story made her laugh and, in response, my dick twitched.

Hard.

Which didn't make sense. She wasn't my type. She was too girl-next-door. She looked too happy. But she did also look like a good dose of trouble. Exactly how I liked it. Exactly what I didn't need.

But my brain and my cock were rarely on the same page.

Hard cock or not, I needed to get my act together. What I didn't need was to get tangled up with a chick who looked like she could lead me around by my dick with one mischievous smile.

I forced myself to look away.

Jackson jogged back towards me. "Ready for that steak dinner now?"

"I could eat." The question ripped out of me before I could stop it, "Who's the chick?"

I could feel Jackson's scrutinizing glance, but the bastard took his time answering. Long enough that I turned to see if he'd heard me. His green eyes looked amused.

"Her name is Beth."

CHAPTER 1

BETH

MY TOES WERE KILLING ME. Judging from the amount of circulation cut off by my insanely high and pointed Louboutins, you'd think I would've lost all feeling in my phalanges by now. Instead, they screamed in pain.

The church felt unusually hot for a Wednesday afternoon. I stood at the front and tried not to sweat as the minister droned on in front of empty pews. This was the exact spot Emily had announced, in front of all her wedding guests, that she was pregnant with Jackson's baby.

Now, today, we were here to celebrate that baby.

All five of us.

Jackson and Emily.

Theo.

The minister.

And Jackson's friend, Porter.

I shifted my stance for the third time in a minute, trying to be discrete, but a set of eyes shifted to my body. Like their owner, they were dark and broody—grey eyes, fringed with thick, sooty lashes.

Porter was as tall and built as Jackson. He wore a black suit, and his shirt collar sat so tight around his thick neck, it gave the appearance that he was being strangled. The rough biker facial hair that covered his face made it difficult to tell what he looked like under the fuzz. His un-styled and messy hair was a beautiful, dark blonde with natural highlights that would make my girlfriends envious. Even the best salon couldn't produce those highlights.

His intense eyes continued to hold my gaze. Feeling judged, I lifted my chin at him a fraction. In response, he shifted that all-knowing gaze away from me.

I didn't like him. I know you're not supposed to judge people before you get to know them, but something about him dug under my skin. I couldn't decide if it was his x-ray vision that seemed all-knowing, or if it was the fact that the guy hadn't spoken or cracked a smile since he'd arrived. Christenings were supposed to be joyous occasions, but he acted like he was attending a funeral. Theo deserved more from his godfather.

The minister glanced up at us. "Would you like to gather around Theo as I bless him with the holy water?"

I stepped forward, conscious of the fact that Porter matched my step. I could feel him close beside me. Despite my five-inch heels, he still loomed over me, like some gargantuan hulk.

I smiled at Emily. The minister said some words, then slowly poured water over Theo's head. Theo's eyes widened. Shocked. And then, when I expected the kid to scream bloody murder, he rewarded us with an infectious giggle. Emily and Jackson shared a look.

I never cry. Not at weddings. Never at funerals. But that look was filled with so much love, so much tenderness and heartfelt expression, it choked me up. I raised my eyes upward to blink away the surprising, unwanted tears.

We made eye contact again. Me and the grey-eyed soldier. Except, I leaked weepy emotion, and he was utterly blank. Devoid of emotion. No expression. Just observing me. His lack of expression made me feel oddly vulnerable, which only made me dislike him more.

The minister asked us to bow our heads in prayer. I tucked my chin down, staring at our feet. The prayer was taking forever. I wavered slightly and stepped sideways to catch my balance. I hit a wall. A solid, hard, muscular wall that didn't budge. Using core muscles I didn't know I had, I managed to shift my balance, so I no longer leaned against him.

Face flaming, I focused on one spot on the floor. His fresh, clean scent surrounded me. A subtle hint of sporty, masculine soap and male pheromones. I wanted to lift my head in the air and sniff like a hound catching a scent. That's how good he smelled.

I gritted my teeth. Why did this guy get under my skin so bad? I couldn't take his unwavering gaze, his knowing eyes, his emotionless heart. He had no business being a godfather. Theo needed love. Not some wary, cold robot-man watching over him. Although maybe that's why Jackson had picked him. He wanted Theo safe, and what better way to do that than to assign a solider to watch over him.

The prayer ended, and the service was done. We took photos, I fussed over Theo, Jackson shook hands with the minister, and we made our way to the front steps of the church.

"Now the fun part." Emily smiled up at Porter.

To my surprise, he gave a small smile back. It didn't quite reach his eyes, but his lips did move.

She placed a hand on my shoulder. "Jackson and I'd like to take you both out for dinner."

"Yay, I'm starving. Can't wait." I hooked my arm around hers. "Where to?"

Emily gave me an apologetic smile. "Bayswater."

Oh, fuck.

I beamed a tight smile at her. "That's a perfect place for dinner."

"You're sure?" She chewed her bottom lip. "I thought it'd feel like my grandma was here with us today if we went there."

"You're not going to hear any complaints from me," I assured her.

But then again, she could drag me to Hell's gate, and I wouldn't complain. Emily was the kind of friend I'd do anything for. No matter what. But if you asked me, I'd choose Hell's gate over Bayswater any day.

She unhooked her arm from mine, expertly slung the diaper bag over her shoulder, and shifted Theo in her arms. "Beth, do you mind taking Porter in your car? It's a bit tight in the back with Theo's car seat."

"Of course not," I lied through another smile. "There's lots of room in my car."

Her smile radiated. "Thank you so much. I'm so excited! Okay. See you guys there."

I tilted my head at the silent stranger standing beside me. "I'm parked over here."

We walked in complete silence to my car. My heels clicked decisively on the pavement. We got in my twelve-year-old Corolla. With his big knees against the dash, Porter looked like he was sitting in a go-cart.

"You can put the seat back." Sighing in relief, I reached down to take off my shoes and toss them in the back. *Fuck heels.*

Without speaking, he pushed the seat back as far as it would go, looking only marginally more comfortable. Then he took off his tie, stuffed it in his pocket and unbuttoned the top two buttons on his dress shirt.

I started the engine. We drove in complete silence. I wanted to turn on the radio, but that felt like conceding defeat. If he could sit through awkward silence, so could I.

"Why don't you like Bayswater?" His question caught me off guard almost as much as his deep voice—smooth as a fine scotch.

How did I answer this question? I had attended weekly dinners there, twice a week, for my entire childhood. It was a stuffy, extravagant country club, built solely for the purpose of allowing wealthy, pompous people the opportunity to flaunt their affluence in front of each other. In other words, it represented everything I didn't want to be as an adult. Self-absorbed, selfish, and greedy.

"I don't like some of the people that hang out there." I glanced at him. "But it holds some good memories for Emily, so that's all that matters today. Our job is to focus on making more good memories for Jackson and Emily."

I added that last part for good measure. To prompt him to think about Emily and Jackson's experience today. Perhaps he could crack another smile or partake in some conversation.

More silence.

"So, how do you know Jackson?"

"We did BUDs together. And now we're in the same unit."

I glanced at him, stating the obvious, "You're in the Navy."

He barely nodded. His eyes were on the road. Observing everything.

"What's with the beard and long hair? I thought everyone in the military had to be clean cut."

"Social camouflage."

I processed that for a moment. "You don't want to look like an American soldier."

He paused so long, I wasn't sure he would answer. "Nope."

Huh. Okay. Maybe he didn't want to talk about his job. That was fine. I didn't like to talk about my job either, because as far as careers went, mine was circling the drain.

"So, where are you originally from?"

Nothing. We drove almost a block before he begrudgingly said, "Montana."

I inwardly rolled my eyes. Trying to talk to this man was like pulling teeth.

I concentrated on driving but got distracted by his big hands. Those rough and strong hands rested on his knees, and they moved with nervous energy.

I liked a man with big hands. The metrosexual men of New York tended to get manicures, and nothing made me feel more unfeminine than a man who took care of his nails better than I did. What would it feel like to have those calloused hands touch me? Would he be gentle or rough?

"Look out." One of those hands reached out and grabbed the wheel, swerving my car into the next lane.

A high-pitched scream escaped out of me while I slammed on the brakes. Thanks to my surly passenger, I managed to avoid side-swiping the car in front of me.

A lone horn sounded long and impatient from behind us.

"Are you okay?" his voice sounded irritatingly calm.

In a panic, I grasped the steering wheel with both hands and managed to wrap my fingers around his.

"Sorry." My fingers fluttered, releasing my hold of his fingers.

He scanned behind us. "You're okay to drive."

I did a three-point check, then slowly merged back into traffic. The adrenaline made me feel quivery and uncertain.

"I'm a good driver," I lied, feeling a need to explain myself.

He didn't respond.

"Okay," I modified. "I'm not a terrible driver."

Still no response. Would it kill him to make some polite conversation?

I snuck a peek at him, and his direct grey stare jarred me. I forced myself to focus on the road in front of me, feeling more self-conscious by the moment. This car felt like a pressure cooker, and I blamed him. His hands distracted me. His intensity threw me. He took up too much space. Too much air.

"Say something," I demanded.

He paused so long, I wasn't sure he'd answer. "I don't think you should drive if Theo's in the car."

Irritation needled under my skin. Who did he think he was?

"Well, there are lots of things I don't think you should do where Theo is concerned."

"Like what?"

I wracked my brain and came up blank. "I don't want to be rude."

"Go for it."

"You're a guest in my car."

"I don't mind."

"Just... look out your window and stop bothering me." That might have been the rudest thing I could have said.

He did just that.

A long sigh escaped out of me. I hated my sharp tongue. Why couldn't I be gentle and kind like Emily? Why did I have to rise to the bait every single time?

I glanced over at him, my eyes taking in his long, muscular legs.

He focused his attention forward. I should have said something and tried to ease the tension between us. But what would be the point of that? The guy obviously didn't want to be friendly. So, why should I keep trying? Bayswater promised to be stressful enough. I didn't need to concern myself with this man.

I flipped on the radio to mask the uncomfortable silence, but I couldn't help but notice those big fingers, tapping to the beat of the music.

CHAPTER 2

WE PASSED THE MASSIVE, iron-and-stone gate and drove down the long driveway to the parking lot. Not wanting to pay for valet parking, I slowly cruised my car through the lot. If Porter noticed that there wasn't a single car that sold for under six figures in the parking lot, he didn't say anything.

We got out, and I reluctantly reached into the back seat to retrieve my heels and the big silver-and-blue-wrapped gift. Juggling keys and my purse, I turned around and almost ran into his chest.

He didn't speak, instead he lifted the huge gift from my arms. I averted my eyes from his flexed muscles, cursing the world for gifting that body to Porter. Where were the ripped nice men of the world?

I shifted my weight onto the tips of my toes as I walked over the hot asphalt of the parking lot barefoot. We walked up the wide stone steps of the building, looking odd beside one another—a barefoot, former socialite and a bearded giant.

"Hold on." I hopped on one foot, then the other, while I shoved my now dirty feet into my $900 shoes. I didn't care. I hadn't bought these shoes, nor would I ever be caught dead buying shoes for this amount of money.

Porter held the door open for me. We walked across the expansive, regal foyer and down a massive hall until we reached the club's fine dining restaurant.

"Good evening, Miss Beth." A hint of surprise colored the maitre d's voice.

"Hi, Gerald." I didn't know whether to smile or wince. "We're here for the Hunter dinner."

It seemed like he wanted to say something more, but instead, he nodded and led us to a round table in the corner. After a low bow, he walked away.

I glanced up at Porter, who stood, holding the gift. He was appraising me in context of this place. To think he thought I was part of this place was laughable. Every move I'd made in my adult life had been to remove myself from this world.

"You can put that on a seat." I pointed to a random one.

"Beth," a cool voice spoke from behind me.

I turned, taking in my mom's lavender suit, perfectly coiffed hair and a string of pearls. Classic.

She placed a delicate hand over her chest. "Darling, you haven't been here in ages. Why didn't you tell us you'd be here tonight?"

We leaned towards each other and did two fake air kisses, not touching. We never touched.

"Didn't know. Emily planned this. Today is Theo's baby christening."

She didn't seem to hear me or care. Her eyes were narrowed on Porter. Probably focused on his open collar. Damn, I should have told him the dress code here was suit and tie. God forbid anyone should dress like a normal person in front of rich people.

She focused her attention back on me. "I meant to call you. Yates has been fairly begging us for information about you."

My entire body stilled. Typical... the only reason Mom would call was to get information for my ex-boyfriend. Mom loved Yates. When I'd dumped his cheating ass, she'd been inconsolable.

She knew I didn't want to talk about him. She knew this was off topic.

I crossed my arms and lifted my chin. "Well, you know what message you can give him for me." My middle finger itched.

Must. Not. Raise. Finger.

"Beth," her voice trailed like she held the weight of the world on her thin shoulders. "He'd love to talk to you. You should give him a chance to explain his side of things."

Rage blurred my vision, but I held my tongue. Mom and I had extremely opposing views on cheating. In her book, as long as a man was well-spoken and knew which fork to use, infidelity was something that one should overlook. We'd already had this exact conversation before. Many times over. It always ended in disappointed sighs from Mom and unshed tears from me.

This day was not about Yates or me, so I nodded. "Thanks. I'll think about that."

It was sad how much that comment made her brighten. "Splendid. Well, enjoy your night."

"You, too."

I took a few deep breaths before looking over at Porter. A gentleman would have pretended he hadn't seen or heard that conversation. Instead, he watched me fight my emotions with the first flicker of interest on his face since we'd met.

"That was my mother." I forced my voice to stay light. Like explaining it made it better.

He held my gaze but didn't say a damn word.

"Yates is my asshole of an ex, who thought it was appropriate to cheat on me. Then, he couldn't quite understand why I took issue with that. His pedigree is impeccable though, so no one, not him nor my parents, can understand why I would take issue with him fucking my now ex-boss."

I was so mad, I could feel tears well up in my eyes. I stood up, and he shot to his feet. "Excuse me." Even to my own ears, my voice sounded strangled.

In the washroom, I splashed cold water on my face. This place. It killed me. There were too many memories, too many triggers here. It didn't matter how much I worked to be my own person. The moment I stepped back into this building, I became the same person I worked so hard to grow out of. Bayswater wanted to suck me back in time.

I squared my shoulders and stared at my reflection. I would not let my emotional issues ruin this day for Jackson and Emily. This was their day. I had to do everything in my power to make it about them.

When I returned to the table, Jackson was holding Theo and Emily had grabbed the seat beside mine.

I took a deep breath as I sat down. "The service was beautiful, Emily. Truly, it was. I loved how Theo giggled."

"He's a really cheerful kid." She grinned. "I lucked out."

"He's the cutest kid I know."

"I think I saw your dad?" The hesitation in her voice soothed me. Someone cared, and I was glad that it was Emily.

"Yes." I gave a little laugh that sounded so real, even I was convinced. "I ran into my mom. She says a big hello and congratulations."

"How is she?"

"She's doing great. We talked about how we need to catch up."

Emily squeezed my arm. "That's so great, Beth."

I flushed when I made eye contact with those knowing grey eyes. The way he watched me sent shivers down my spine, and I wasn't sure what to make of them. I wanted to lift my chin up and challenge him with my stare, but I couldn't.

Nothing like being caught in a lie.

⸻

I cursed as Emily deliberately steered the conversation back to me. Jackson and Porter had been talking amongst themselves, and I thought I'd been doing so well at keeping the conversation about Emily.

She tucked a loose strand of hair behind her delicate ear. "Have you heard from Yates?"

"Almost every day, but it's more of a one-way conversation."

"He still wants you back?"

"Who wouldn't?" I playfully flipped, to cover the true dismay I still felt over that entire situation.

She leaned forward and whispered. "What do you think of Porter?"

He unsettles me.

I couldn't say that, though, so I squinted. "You mean the mute caveman that looks like he recently walked out of some bush?"

"He's really quite handsome," Emily said with a serious face that only Emily could pull off. "And he's such a great guy. Jackson and Porter go way back. And Theo adores him."

That I needed to see to believe.

"Are you trying to set me up?"

She bit her lip. "No way."

"You're such a smooth liar."

She laughed. "Come on, he's really great."

"Emily, you know I draw the line at *Duck Dynasty*."

"Beth." Her laugh turned into a snort that had Jackson smiling her way. "Wait until he shaves."

"I'm not holding my breath."

"He's really quite breathtaking."

"Still doesn't help me if he doesn't speak."

"What happened on the drive over?"

I decided to omit the details about me almost rear-ending a car. "I think I managed to pull ten words out of him."

"I was hoping he'd open up to you."

"You overestimate my power of charm."

"But you're so funny and interesting."

I leaned forward and dramatically whispered, "Pretty sure I'm not his type."

"I think you are."

"You're adorable, but trust me when I tell you, we didn't jive."

"He needs some time."

"He needs something," I muttered when Emily turned away. "But it's not me."

Theo woke up, and while Emily lifted him into her arms, I used the time to look over at the man in question. He could possibly be hiding some good looks beneath his crazy biker look, but that wasn't the issue. I could never be with someone as silent as him. It would drive me bat-shit crazy.

Emily passed Theo to me, who squirmed in my arms. I watched in dismay as she and Jackson left the table to do God knows what. Theo seemed equally dismayed as he watched his mom disappear from sight.

"Shhh," I urged, anxiety tinging my voice. "She'll be right back."

"I can take him," that whiskey-smooth voice said from beside me.

I held Theo protectively, not sure I wanted to pass this small human being off to someone who looked so scary. Porter held his big hands open, and I reluctantly handed Theo to him. I watched as he expertly lifted Theo high above his head. Theo cooed with delight and kicked his legs.

Our eyes met again. It kind of pissed me off that he was winning the baby race by a mile. Who knew he would be the baby whisperer in the group?

"No one likes a showoff," I said under my breath.

"What's that?"

"Nothing."

But his lips turned up a bit, telling me he had heard exactly what I had said.

CHAPTER 3

ONE MONTH LATER...

"GOOD EVENING, MISS STIRLING," the maitre d' said as I stepped into the large, opulent dining room. "Your parents are already seated at their usual table."

I had been summoned back to Bayswater. Summoned, like I was a dog my parents could whistle for when they needed me. Except they hadn't even given me the courtesy of calling me themselves. My dad's butler had telephoned me and informed me that I was expected for dinner tonight.

"Thanks, Donald."

"Would you like your usual drink to start?"

"Yes, please." I spotted my mom across the room. "Make it a double." That would undoubtedly piss her off.

I walked across the room. The Bayswater Country Club was the epitome of luxury with its high, painted ceilings and antique chandeliers, red velvet chairs, and floor-length, white tablecloths.

I recognized every single person seated in the restaurant. It was the same members every week, dining at the same tables, eating the same food. Like every other time I came here, I felt like I was slowly being suffocated by the ostentatious wealth and judgmental stares coming from every direction.

"You're fifteen minutes late," Mom reprimanded me as I approached the table.

"Sorry." I leaned down to air kiss her on both cheeks. "Traffic was bad. Where's Dad?"

"He's talking on the phone on the terrace."

When was my father not talking on the phone?

"How are you?"

She shrugged her thin shoulder. "Beth, really, that dress is so last season."

She should know. She'd bought it for me. Mom hates my taste in clothing and regularly has high-end clothes and shoes delivered to my apartment. I struggle to keep a roof over my head, and my car is being held together by duct tape and prayers, yet Mom fills my apartment with designer shoes and bags so expensive, they could pay my rent for months. The polarity between my old life and my new life staggered me. I was reminded of this every time I stuffed my size-four ass into these stupid Mulberry silk dresses.

I schooled my face to remain passive. I thought my sundress was cute. "How are you, Mom?"

She gave a long-winded sigh. "I've had a very challenging few months."

"Oh. What's going on?"

"You know I'm on the board for NYTA, and Kelly Brockers was the chair, but her husband recently got transferred to London. It's been complete chaos. The in-house fighting on the board has kept me awake for weeks. I can't handle it."

I blinked. The board of the New York Tennis Association was stressing Mom out. This world sometimes felt like an SNL parody.

"I'm sure you're doing great."

She sniffed. "It's been exceedingly stressful."

Mom was stressed. Something was bothering her. Something

real. Something was keeping her awake at night, but God forbid she ever talked about it.

Mom was the queen of hiding the truth of her life away from the world but used something frivolous as a surrogate reason to vent. How many times had I wished that we could be closer? In the end, I couldn't handle her cover story no more than she could handle my truth.

The waiter came forward with my gin and tonic, placing it in front of me with a small bow. The only redeeming thing about dinner at Bayswater was the expensive booze.

The pointed look mom sent my way as I drank at least a finger's worth didn't escape my attention. I ignored her, though. It was easier that way.

Unused to being ignored, she pursed her lips and fussed with the expensive linen cloth on her lap. "Where are you working now?"

Dad approached the table, saving me from answering. I studied him behind the rim of my glass. His hair was beginning to grey at the edges of his forehead, but he pulled it off in a George Clooney type of way. Still, he wore his mid-fifties well and carried himself with presence.

He sat down across from me. "You're late."

I took another sip of the gin. "Nice to see you, too, Dad."

He didn't bother responding as the waiter immediately approached the table. We ordered our food, then sat in silence for a moment.

"Your father has a family announcement." Mom turned to my dad, benignity written all over her carefully made-up face.

I could never quite tell what she was thinking.

"I'm running for mayor." Dad met my eyes. "We're announcing it at the gala next week. Saturday."

Mayor of New York? Geez. I shouldn't have been surprised, but I was. My father was already an extremely wealthy businessman, but he also craved power and control. Always had.

The neutral expression never left my face. "What brought you to that decision?"

"New York is the greatest city in the world. It needs stronger leadership."

Dad's idea of leadership was closer to dictatorship.

"I'm very excited for you," I lied.

Was it too late for me to leave this city? Maybe I could move out west. Perhaps Hawaii.

"I'd like your support during my candidacy."

"You know I'll always support you," I relented. "Just like you've always supported my choices."

Mom cleared her throat. "We want you to move home. We'll clear out the guest house for you. You can live there. Rent free."

Her offer wasn't even tempting. I'd left home when I'd turned 18 for a reason. Hell would freeze over before I returned to that gilded cage.

"Mom, as much as I love living with you and dad," I lied, "I'm too old to move back home. I have my own life that I'm living."

"Beth, why be difficult about this? You have no idea how important optics are during a political campaign. Plus, it'll make things so much easier for you to be at home for all the campaigning events we need to attend."

I ignored her and focused on the food a server dropped off. One mouthful at a time, I chewed and swallowed, not tasting a single bite. I felt a sense of panic that my parents had even suggested I move back home. My independence meant everything to me. Why did my parents want to keep dragging me back under their wing?

"Are you listening to me, Beth?" Mom's voice pulled me from my thoughts.

"Sorry, I was thinking about work for a moment."

She rolled her eyes, her frustration thinly veiled. "I was saying that I called Donna, and she can see you anytime this week."

"Donna?" I swirled my mostly empty glass in my hands. I really wanted another drink, but since I was driving, it was a bad idea.

"My personal shopper."

I paused. *Personal shopper?* "Why do I need to see Donna?"

"Haven't you listened to a word I have said?"

"Tell me again."

"Your father is entering the campaign late in the game. So, we have to make up for lost time. We have a very tight schedule of canvassing that includes grassroots fundraising, membership drives, galas, dinners, parties, baseball games and BBQs. Your father has something scheduled practically every single night."

I raised my head and met Dad's eyes. They shone with hope, and I had to swallow to ease the guilt that wrapped around my throat, suffocating me.

I averted my eyes, preferring Mom's disapproving eyes. "What does this have to do with me?"

"Beth"—her exasperation was apparent—"Because you're going to be front-and-center of this campaign."

"Why would you say that?"

I wasn't the front-and-center type. Never had been. It was part of the reason such a big rift had wedged its way between Mom and me. She wanted a daughter she could show off, and I wanted to be my own person.

"Because you're part of this family, and we need you to help with the campaign."

Oh, fuck.

Fuck no.

Fuck me.

Fuck.

She continued, oblivious, "It's going to be fun. We're going to go shopping together, and I'll buy you lovely outfits."

I needed to stop this runaway train. Now. There was no way I'd do this. It wasn't even an option. "Dad, I'm very happy for you and your career plans, but I don't think I should be campaigning with you."

"Why won't you help your father?"

"I have my own life. I have work and commitments."

Okay, that was a lie. Kind of. Lately, my life had been reduced to watching a whole lot of Netflix—sans chill. But that sure as hell didn't mean that I wanted to commit to spending every waking hour for the next seven months alongside my parents, pretending to be a happy family.

That was *never* going to happen. Mom and I could barely stomach each other's company, and Dad always deferred to Mom for everything. I hated fighting with my parents. I really did. But there was no way I would take any of this lying down.

"What's it going to take?" she finally asked.

Negotiations. Mom truly believed everything had a price. She'd never been able to realize she couldn't buy my love or attention. All she had to do was care for me, and she'd get it for free. The whole thing made my stomach churn.

I rubbed my forehead. God, why was everything such a battle with Mom? Every single time we got together, it was some sort of negotiation. Nothing was ever about what was right. It always came down to what I could do for them. Of course, I wanted to support my father, but if I got dragged into this, Mom would own me for the next several months.

I carefully set my cutlery down on my plate, and a waiter instantly appeared to whisk it away. "I am not sure I can commit to anything at this point."

"Yates thinks it necessary."

I tilted my head slowly, taking in her posture. "Why does my ex-boyfriend have any say in this private matter?"

"He's my campaign manager." Dad sounded bored with this conversation.

My jaw dropped open. "Please, tell me you're joking."

"He's completely qualified," Mom rushed to tell me. "He has a bachelors in marketing and an MBA from Yale."

"I know where he went to school, Mom. I dated him for three

years. What I can't wrap my head around is *why* you hired him when there are thousands of other candidates."

"He's the best."

I swallowed. Did Mom even care about my feelings? Didn't she know it crushed me when she put Yates and his needs before my own? He was the cheating ex. I was the daughter. The math should have been easy.

Mom droned on about Yates' accomplishments and the things he had planned for our family, but I was officially done entertaining this conversation. I had to protect myself. I *deserved* to protect myself.

My eyes skimmed the room, not surprised to see Yates shaking hands with someone at the end of the room. He was like a prince here, loved by all. He was the all-American boy with his boyish good looks, perfect blond hair, dazzling white smile and bright blue eyes. In faded pink slacks, a crisp white dress shirt and his standard navy blazer—a jacket I knew cost no less than five grand—he looked like he stepped off a GQ summer shoot.

Dating Yates had been easy. Too easy. He was charming, witty, and carefree. He had a lot of money and knew a lot of people. And to be honest, I had cared for him. Deeply.

When he'd cheated on me, he'd hurt me more than I wanted anyone to know. I remembered the day I had ended it with him. It was the only time I'd actually seen him scared, but his panicked words erased any doubts I'd had: "Who cares who I fucked? I'm with you. Doesn't that count for something?"

He couldn't understand why I played by different rules than anyone in this world. Our fathers cheated on our mothers. It was par for course on the Upper East Side. My need for fidelity would never be something he could wrap his mind around.

Mom reached out and uncharacteristically touched my hand. The small gesture made tears prick the back of my eyelids.

"You look tired, Beth."

I *was* tired.

Since I had broken up with Yates, I'd lost my home, security, and job, which had become such a living hell, I'd quit it in a fit of rage. My parents may have been rich, but I was broke, and I couldn't catch a break to save my life.

I was working as a temp for peanuts, and I was barely able to make rent and feed myself on anything other than instant ramen. My savings were drained, and I needed a real job, but it wasn't from a lack of trying.

"Let me think about it," I said, unwilling to commit to this.

Mom and Dad exchanged a look until Dad finally nodded. "I'll be expecting your call."

CHAPTER 4

MY HANDS STILLED on my keys as a text buzzed from my old friend, Janet.

Janet: Hey, Beth! What r u up to tonight?

Me: On my way home

Janet: Come out with us

Me: No, thanks. Not tonight

Janet: But it's my birthday

Wow. I was such a shit friend. I laid my head on the steering wheel. Janet had been my friend since grade school. We weren't close anymore, but that, in part, was my fault. She ran with a fast crowd, while I preferred spending my nights watching Netflix.

Me: Happy Birthday!

Janet: You're coming out.

Me: Can I take a rain check? I have nothing to wear.

Janet: I'm coming over with clothes for you

I groaned and stared unseeing at the parking lot. When was the last time I had gotten drunk? Maybe a night out would cure how shitty I felt.

Me: Nothing revealing

⊏▭⊐

My phone rang, as I walked in the door.

"Hey, Em."

"What's wrong?" At my hesitation, Emily continued, "I can hear it in your voice."

I released my frustration in a pent-up breath. "Couldn't be better. Tonight I had dinner with my folks. And then I got sucked into going out with Janet."

"What? Why?"

"Today's her birthday. She texted me and guilted me into birthday drinks, and I caved." A long paused filled the line.

"It's not Janet's birthday. Her birthday is in December."

I worked to unlock my apartment door. "Are you sure?"

"Absolutely." One of Emily's gifts was remembering this kind of stuff. She had to be right.

I leaned my head against my front door, closing my eyes against the smooth wood. "That brat. She totally conned me."

"Are you sure you want to go out with her?"

I paused. "Why? What do you know?"

"It's probably nothing, but I've heard that she's been wrapped up in some bad stuff lately."

"Really? Where have I been?"

"Be careful, okay?"

"I'm not going to stay out that late. I'll go for a couple drinks and be home before midnight."

"Will you text me when you get home?"

"You're sweet, but you don't need to worry."

"I'll worry if you don't. Besides, I'm up twice a night with Theo."

I stopped walking. "Really?"

She laughed. "Yes."

"Why?"

"He gets hungry."

"It scares me how little I know about kids. Are you sure you picked the right person to be his godmother?"

"He only needs love from you."

"Well, he's got it."

"Remember to text."

"I promise. It's going to be a really tame night. No antics."

I could almost hear the world laughing at me.

***

"Turn around," the cop demanded, ice in his tone.

Oh fuck.

Fucking fuck.

I turned around but not fast enough for him. He shoved hard against me, causing me to topple against the metal table. I cried out as he jerked my arms back, twisting my left elbow.

"Please." I gasped in pain.

"Shut up."

The pressure on my wrists increased while he removed the handcuffs. I exhaled as they came off. He yanked hard on my shoulder, hauling me back to my feet.

"Sit down."

Stunned, I staggered to the cold metal chair beside the table. He exited the room, shutting the door behind him without sparing me a second glance. Pain vibrated down my arm, and panic laced its way across my chest.

Holding my injured arm against my body, I took stock of the interrogation room. The brick walls were painted puke-beige. Other than the one-way window across from me, the room was eerily windowless. A plain clock ticked loudly in the silence.

12:47 AM.

There was nothing to look at but my reflection in the mirror. My hair was wild. My dark lipstick looked too stark against my pale skin.

In the harsh fluorescent light, my heavy eye make-up made me look cheap.

I'm drunk. This isn't happening to me.

The door opened, and a woman marched in. I studied her warily. Her blonde hair was pulled tightly into a bun at the nape of her neck. She wore a white blouse and a pair of jeans. The plain wedding band on her left hand was the only jewelry she wore, and if I had to guess her age, I'd say thirty-something.

Wordlessly, she pulled out the seat across from me. The metal of the chair scraped against the cement floor, like nails on a chalkboard.

When she spoke, her accent was a faint European accent I couldn't place. "My name is Detective Christensen, and I work in tandem with the narcotics unit of the New York Police Department."

I didn't speak. I couldn't. Narcotics? Oh, this was bad. Very bad.

She picked up her pen. "Why don't we start with your name?"

I chewed on my lip, trying to remember what people said in the movies.

Her eyes narrowed. "Look. Don't get cute with me. We found enough cocaine in your purse to put you away, but I'm going to let you in on a secret. We don't care about a small time fish like you."

Not my cocaine. Not my drugs. I took a deep breath and remained silent.

"We need to know where you got the drugs and you can walk out of here with a sworn statement."

This was a nightmare.

She leaned back and crossed her arms over her chest. "We can do this one of two ways. You can cooperate and walk out of here in less than two hours, or we can arrest and process you. Then, we'll put you in a cell until your first of many court appearances. So, why don't you stop wasting my time and do this the easy way?"

My father was going to kill me.

"I'm going to exercise my right to remain silent. I want to speak to a lawyer," I blurted out.

She shook her head in disgust. "You want me to arrest you? Is that what you want me to do?"

I remained silent. My legs were practically shaking from fear, but I had to stick to my plan.

"Look." She leaned forward and softened her tone. "You really don't want to go that route. I get that you want to be a tough girl, but if you don't cooperate with us, you're leading yourself into a world of hurt."

"I'm going to remain silent." My voice wavered. "I know I get one phone call."

"A pretty young thing like you," her eyes flickered over me, "You have no clue what will happen to you in prison. When you're first led to your prison cell? All the inmates chant 'fresh meat, fresh meat.'"

That sounded worse than awful.

She paused. "You won't last a week in prison."

I was pretty sure she was right, but even if I wanted to talk, I didn't know what to say. When I had dropped my purse in the bathroom of the club, there hadn't been drugs in my purse. "I'm going to remain silent. Let me talk to my lawyer."

She shook her head but stood up. "Fine. Follow me." She led me down the hallway and stopped in front of a small room that held a phone on the wall. No chair. No furniture. "You can make your call here. This is a private line. Whatever you say during your call cannot be used against you in the court of law."

I stood there, unsure.

She rolled her eyes. "So...make your phone call."

I walked over to the phone and picked up the filthy, sticky receiver. I didn't have a lawyer. Without my cell phone, I only knew one phone number by heart. I took a deep breath and dialed. The phone rang five times as I eyed a piece of paper taped above the phone, noting the precinct number and address.

"Hello?" Emily sounded way too awake for the middle of the night.

"Emily?" My voice shook.

"Beth? What's wrong?"

I took a deep breath and glanced behind me. The detective stood outside the room, texting on her phone.

"I'm in trouble. I think I'm about to get arrested."

"Where are you? What's going on?"

"I'm so sorry. I didn't know who to call."

"Hang on a second." I could hear her talking to Jackson.

His voice came on, "Beth?"

"Hey, Jackson."

"Are you okay? Did they hurt you?"

"No."

"Do you know what they are going to charge you with?"

I squeezed my eyes shut, unable to process that this was actually happening to me. "Drug possession."

He was all business. "Do you know where you are?"

I read him the address and waited as he spoke with Emily.

"Beth, we're going to make some calls, okay? Emily has a great lawyer she's already on the phone with."

"Thanks." My voice wobbled.

"I'm sorry we can't be there right now, but I'm going to take care of this for you."

"Okay." I swallowed. "I'm really, really sorry."

"Don't say a word. Hang tight, and we'll get you out of there."

I stood there for a long moment after he hung up. I turned around and walked back to the detective.

She eyeballed me. "Let me guess. You've been instructed not to speak or do anything."

I gave her a small, apologetic look.

She shook her head. "Okay. Let's get you back to interrogation." She led me back down the hall, into the same room from earlier. "Wait here." She placed her palm on my shoulder and shoved me into the room before shutting the door behind me.

I sat back down. My left arm throbbed with pain. I wanted to drop my face in my hands and weep, but I wasn't sure who was watching through the mirror, so I crossed my legs and schooled my expression to nothing.

This was a nightmare of epic proportions. I really didn't want to think about how bad this was. I was starting to sober up, and the soberer I became, the more I realized how truly fucked I was.

My father was running for mayor.

If they found out who I was, if they actually arrested me, I would singlehandedly ruin everything for my father.

CHAPTER 5

THE CLOCK TICKED off almost another hour before the door opened. The detective stood by while a huge man, dressed in a grey tee and faded jeans, stepped into the room. My breath hitched in my throat as his eyes slowly took me in. His expression was impassive as his gaze moved casually down my body.

He looked familiar, but I couldn't place him. Who was he? Another detective? The 'bad cop'? He turned and gave the sour-faced detective a look that clearly said, 'fuck off,' which had her slamming the door behind her.

Now it was only the two of us. He crossed his muscular arms over his chest and leaned against the wall, dropping his eyes to the black military watch on his wrist. His messy dark-blonde hair stuck out wildly beneath his baseball cap, his sculpted face and hard jawline gave him a rough edge, and his wide sexy mouth was currently tight with annoyance.

If I wasn't in the middle of the biggest shit storm of my life, I might have appreciated that this guy was a solid ten on the scale of hotness, but right now I felt too freaked to care. I wanted to go home. The sooner, the better.

"Are you a cop?" I hated how stupid and hesitant I sounded.

"You don't recognize me?"

My jaw dropped. I'd recognize that voice forty years from now. The emotionless robot—sans the godawful *Duck Dynasty* beard. This was Theo's godfather?

"You look different." Totally smoking hot kind of different.

"I'm not the only one." His eyes traveled over my legs.

I crossed my arms over my chest, trying to hide my discomfort. The dress Janet had insisted I wear was ridiculous. Skin tight, short, low cut and white. I looked like a street corner regular, and I knew it.

He walked across the room, pulled the chair out and sat down across from me. I rubbed at a headache that was starting to throb in my temples. The hangover had officially begun.

"Am I going to be arrested?"

"No."

"How do you know that?"

"I talked to your lawyer. She suspects they don't have a solid chain of custody on your purse. It was dropped, found by a cop, and then you claimed it?"

"Yes."

He shook his head. "That's why you won't be arrested."

I breathed out a sigh of relief. "Thank fuck."

He leaned back in his chair. Again, he crossed his arms over his muscular chest. "What happened tonight?"

I swallowed. "My friend, Janet, wanted to go to a club."

My God, that stare. Just penetrating me.

I tried to look away from his eyes. "I don't typically party like this."

Those damn grey eyes gazed back, judging me.

I ground my teeth, feeling compelled to explain myself. "We started out in a normal club, but she wanted to try out a new club. It was a dive. I was in the washroom when all Hell broke loose. People were screaming and panicking, I lost my purse, and we got rounded up and searched. They carried out my purse and asked who it belonged to. Next thing I knew, I was in cuffs."

"Are the drugs yours?"

I flushed. Hard. "No." Again with that assessment. Embarrassment coursed through my veins. "I don't do drugs." I sounded terse and way too defensive.

"I didn't say you did."

"Your look did."

"What look is that?"

Dammit. Those eyes.

"Why are you here anyway?" I asked in exasperation.

"Jackson called me."

"Why?"

"To provide moral support."

"Well, you're stressing me out."

He laughed. Like full on, looked at the ceiling and laughed. I had a feeling this was the Porter that Emily had been trying to set me up with. What was the word she had used? Breathtaking? I couldn't even reconcile him with the bearded mute from a few months ago.

"You're different," I said slowly.

"I'm drunk."

"Oh." I blinked. "Is that why you're talking?"

Another look.

"Don't slip back into your selective mutism on my account."

"Maybe I didn't have anything to say to someone like you."

"Like me?" I bristled. "I'm fucking fantastic, you know. You'd be lucky to get someone like me."

He thought about that for a moment. "Yeah. Because bailing your ass out of jail for possession is on the top of my list for chicks I want to date."

I huffed. "Oh, what important thing did I pull you away from tonight? Drinking by yourself in a bar while cruising for easy chicks?"

"Trust me, the easy chick I could have picked up tonight would be too prim to put on the dress you're wearing."

I mentally had a flash of him pining some hot chick against the wall. For some reason, I didn't like that image. "You were with a woman when Jackson called you?"

He shrugged. "It was nothing."

How far had he gotten with his one-night stand? What exactly were they doing when Jackson called him? An image of him naked and kissing some chick in her bed came to my mind.

My face flushed. "How badly were you interrupted?"

"It didn't get that far."

"Does she have a name?"

Back to that look.

Slowly, it dawned on me that his one-night stand had honestly been that. For some reason, that shocked me. "I bet you don't even know her name."

"You're judging me?"

"Just trying to get you off your self-righteous throne."

"You should talk."

I took a deep breath. "I'm sorry Jackson called you tonight. He wasted your time."

"Doesn't matter."

"It does because you got dragged down here for no reason. I don't need you here."

That was a tiny lie. It was actually kind of nice that he was here. More than nice, if I was honest with myself. Even if he was utterly infuriating.

"I didn't do it for you. I did it for Jackson."

That made me pause. "Well, I appreciate the effort, but once I get out of here, you can go back to whatever—or whomever—you were doing before you got this call."

"I will."

"That's great."

"It is."

"I think I liked you better when you didn't talk."

He responded with a smile that was so sexy, it made my toes curl.

I had to work to keep the smile off my face. It was official. I'd gone insane. I was in a police precinct, and former *Duck Dynasty* wannabe had me fighting a smile. Maybe I was still drunk.

The door opened, and the detective entered with my purse in her outstretched hand. She glared at me. "You're free to go."

Porter unfolded himself from the chair and stood up. I stood up beside him.

"I don't know who the fuck you are," the detective started.

"None of your business," he interrupted. He held out his hand, and she reluctantly handed him my purse, which he handed off to me.

"I'm going to find out," she promised. "I'm sick as shit of people like you walking free."

"Back off," he growled.

She glared at Porter as she held the door open. He walked out first, and the tightness of my skirt and the length of my stilettos made it challenging to keep up with his long strides, but I did my best. In the lobby, I skidded to a stop at the sight of Yates, standing at the front desk.

"Beth." He scanned me up and down, his baby blue eyes wide.

"What are you doing here?" I refrained from pulling my skirt down.

"Janet called me. I came to get you out of jail." He appeared as confused as I felt as he took in my outfit, Porter, and my wild hair.

"Well, I'm out of jail."

"I'll take you home." His voiced reeked of the civil authority I'd learned to hate. "I have a car waiting."

I shook my head and stepped a fraction closer to Porter. "No, thank you."

Yates scrutinized Porter up. "Who the fuck are you?"

"This," I wrapped my arm around Porter's thick forearm, "is Porter."

"Beth." Yates' sounded exasperated. "The party is over. Now, let's go."

I hated how he reminded me of my parents. Blame the tequila, but I squished my body closer to Porter's and said, "Porter's my boyfriend." I could feel Porter looking down at me, but I couldn't force myself to look up into those knowing grey eyes.

I'd never seen Yates more stunned. "Since when are you dating anyone?"

I stroked Porter's arm up and down like I would a large dog. "We're very serious. The feelings we have for each other are very strong, aren't they, sweetie?"

Porter cleared his throat. "The feelings I have for you, I shouldn't say out loud."

I gave his arm a biting squeeze. "Because you feel so strongly for me...right?"

"To the point of almost being violent."

"Trust me, he means that," I assured Yates. I was sure he would call me on this farce, but he seemed too flummoxed.

He glanced between Porter and me. "How did you two meet?"

I sighed. "We met at Emily's baby christening. Our connection was instantaneous." I glanced up at Porter.

He stared at Yates with a straight face. "She made me speechless."

I sounded strangled. "The emotional support I get from Porter... it's like nothing I've experienced before."

Yates stood there, looking between us. "Janet never told me."

I patted Porter's arm. Repeatedly. "Some relationships you want to keep a secret for as long as possible."

"Or forever," Porter added, completely deadpan.

"Well, honey," I hung onto Porter's arm, "should we go?"

"Have a good night," Porter said formally to Yates.

Without looking at Yates, I walked out of the station, holding onto Porter's arm. To his credit, he didn't say a word. He hailed a cab, held the door open for me like the gentleman I didn't think he was and climbed in after me.

"Where to?" I tried my best to look innocent.

"You owe me for that. So, I'm crashing at your place."

"The hell you are!"

"I'd be happily asleep right now in some chick's bed if it wasn't for you."

"Right. The chick with no name. Fine. But you get the couch, and at the crack of dawn, you get out."

The cab driver waited patiently. I gave him my address when Porter reached over and yanked me to his side.

"What the hell?" I was a second away from shoving his ass out of the cab.

"Your little boyfriend is watching," he said, his lips against my forehead. "So play nice."

I peered out the grimy window. Yates stood on the top steps of the police station, hands in his pockets, watching as our cab pulled away. Sucking in my pride, I leaned into Porter's touch, too damn aware of the feel of his lips on my head.

This was a disaster.

CHAPTER 6

MY TERRIBLE DREAM involved my mom. She was lecturing me. What else was new?

I groaned and opened my eyes, blinking at the streaming sunlight hitting my face. God, my head. Throbbing pain made me wince. Mom's shrill voice filled the room. I shot up in bed.

What the hell?

Mom was in my apartment. And who was she talking to? The previous night came crashing back.

Getting arrested.

Porter.

Yates.

Porter. Oh, geez. Porter was out there. Alone. With my mom. And from the sounds of it, he was getting a hell of a lecture. I scrambled out of bed, wrapping my short robe around my body. I yanked open the bedroom door and sprinted towards the kitchen.

"I'm not sure what your intentions are with my daughter, but let me assure you—you're only a passing fling for her. She's destined to marry Yates. The sooner you understand that and move on, the better off my daughter will be." Mom's voice was so high, it could split glass.

I stood there, taking in the living nightmare in my apartment. Porter was fully dressed, leaning against the counter, casually sipping a cup of coffee. The bedding I'd given him was out of sight. Mom stood in the middle of the room, pointing her finger at Porter.

"Mom!"

She whirled around and looked at me, defiance pasted on her face. "Why didn't you tell us?"

"Tell you what?!" I crossed my arms, aware that my semi-translucent robe was about as revealing as the dress I wore last night.

"Why did I have to hear from Yates that you're dating someone?"

I swallowed, and my eyes shifted to Porter. Crap. This was so freaking awkward. "Mom."

"I told you to tell your parents about us," Porter said dryly.

My mouth dropped open. "What?"

He shrugged. My mind raced. Was he actually going to keep up this charade?

I turned to Mom and crossed my arms. "Yates has no business running to you about my dating life. It's none of his freaking business."

She wasn't backing down. "Language, young lady."

"I'm not going to marry Yates, Mom. I'm not. You have to accept my choices."

Her shoulders slumped, and a part of me hated how crushed she looked. "Beth."

I almost felt sorry for her. No matter how misguided she was, I'd rather see her angry than defeated. "Mom, please. This wasn't going to stay a secret. I just wasn't ready to share."

She shook her head, her features too pretty for the sadness tainting them. "I want the best for you. You're not getting any younger, and Yates is willing to marry you!" My mom's frantic panic to marry me off to the first willing man stung. Her lack of belief in my ability to find love felt like a pinprick to my already deflated confidence.

I took a few deep breaths before I managed to say, "I know you want the best for me."

She squared her shoulders and looked at Porter. "I apologize for my rude behavior."

He gave her a mild look. "That's not an issue, ma'am. I respect that you love your daughter."

"Beth's father and I would like to get to know you better. Tonight, we'd like you both to join us for dinner at the club."

Oh, Hell no.

"Mom—"

"Beth." She leveled me with a look. "If you're dating someone new, we'd like to get to know him. We need to make sure he's worthy of you."

"Thank you for the invite." Porter's tone was respectful.

She turned and looked at me, anxiety filling her eyes. "I really hope to see you and Porter tonight."

I swallowed. I needed to tell her the truth. "Mom."

She lifted her hand. "You can text me later."

She gave Porter one last look before walking out of my apartment.

I stood there for a full minute, staring at the closed door. Holy smokes. Did that just happen?

I slowly turned around and met Porter's eyes. "I'm sorry."

He shrugged. "Coffee?"

I moved to the counter and watched as he poured me a mug and set it in front of me. "I need cream."

"You're one of those," he said, but he reached behind him and grabbed the creamer from the fridge door.

I doctored my coffee and lifted it to my lips. How was I going to swing this? I'd need to text my mom and tell her that we couldn't make it. There was no way I was having dinner with her, Dad, and Porter. Nope. Wasn't happening.

Porter watched me. "What?"

"Did you sleep okay?"

"I've slept on worse couches."

"I'm sorry about my mom."

"She's acting like a mom."

"How long have you been up?"

"Awhile."

We drank our coffee in silence. I wanted to erase the last 24 hours from my memory. "Are you going to tell Jackson about last night?"

He shrugged. "Not much to tell."

I eyed him speculatively. He actually meant that. That humbled me. After everything I had put him through, he was still going to be a gentleman about it all. This man had given up sex to sit with me in jail, pretended to be my boyfriend to a jealous ex, and stood by while my mom reamed him out.

"Thank you for your help last night. I'm sorry I interrupted your evening with your lady friend."

"That's okay. I can come with you."

What the hell? Was he propositioning me? *I can come with you.* My mind went there. Him, naked and on top of me. Thrusting. His face wincing as he started to come. Would he be completely silent or would a harsh, manly sound rip out of his throat as he orgasmed? Christ, I wish I could control my thoughts. I could feel my heartbeat pounding in my stomach. The image turned me on.

"Excuse me?" I tried to sound scandalized, but I just sounded shocked.

"I can come with you. To meet your parents."

He wasn't talking about sex. He was talking about dining with my parents.

That's a hard no.

Mom would eat him alive. She was a ruthless snob, who looked down on everyone. And that was on a good day. If she saw Porter as a threat, it would be total annihilation.

"That's a terrible idea."

He took a sip of his coffee.

"I mean, I appreciate your SEAL friendship that you have going on with Jackson, and you've acted incredibly honorable, and Jackson will get rave reviews about you, but you're so off the hook on this, it isn't even funny. My mom is not someone you want to dine with."

"This isn't about Jackson."

I stopped short, coffee cup halfway to my lips. "It isn't?"

For the first time, he looked away from my gaze. "I need a favor."

"To do what?"

"It's a simple matter that needs taking care of."

"Is it illegal?"

"You're worried about illegal?" He checked his military watch. "A mere six hours after I picked you up from jail?"

I crossed my arms over the thin fabric of my housecoat. "I'm not sure we're at that point in our friendship that we're burying bodies for each other."

"What?"

"If Emily called me and she had some dead body in her kitchen, I'm her person. She'd call me, and I'd help her dispose."

"Of the body?"

"And the evidence."

"What does that even mean?"

"It's a measure of friendship. And no hard feelings, but I'm not ready to bury a body for you."

"There isn't a body."

"What is it?"

He rubbed the back of his neck and winced. "It's nothing illegal."

"So, you'd face the lion's den with me in exchange for a non-illegal act that you don't want to talk about?"

"I'm sure dinner won't be that bad."

"Ha! Well, right now, I want to shake on that deal, but I really don't think that's fair to you. You're turning out to be a decent guy, so it's only fair that you hear the disclaimer. You'd be safer swimming in a shark tank with twenty hungry sharks while wearing a raw meat suit."

He blinked.

"And," I continued, "you'd have to wear a suit and tie."

He shrugged. "Okay."

"I haven't even come close to warning you about all the perils you might face."

"Can you help me out or not?"

"What is it you want?"

"It's not a big deal."

"Why can't you tell me then?"

"I just..." He swallowed. "Do we have a deal or not?"

Even without knowing what he wanted me to do, I knew I was getting the better deal here. Sue me for being a ruthless business-woman. "We have a deal."

He held out his hand, and I placed mine in his. His hand was huge, big and warm, and his handshake was firm. A spark jolted up my arm, that had me tugging my hand out of his grip.

"We do."

"Fine."

"Good."

We stood there sipping our coffee in silence. Had he felt that spark too? His hand was as warm as I imagined it to be. Were we really going to meet my parents for dinner - as a fake couple?

It dawned on me that going forward, I could still pretend we were dating long after he was gone. I could tell everyone he was deployed overseas. Technically, I could keep Yates and Mom off my back for months by pretending I was dating Porter. It was almost too good to be true. I could enjoy months of freedom and peace from the relent-less pressure to get a husband and start producing heirs.

"How would you do it?" Porter's question cut through my thoughts.

"Do what?"

"Get rid of the body?"

I thought for a moment. "We'd wash the body in bleach in the tub, to get rid of all DNA and evidence. And then I'd drive the body in his or her car to some really remote location, and I'd burn the entire thing to the ground."

"You've really thought this through."

I shrugged. "I've watched all 12 season of *Bones*. But you should know, if we got caught, I'd take the fall."

"Honorable. Why?"

"Emily wouldn't survive in prison, and she has Theo to think of."

"And you would fare well behind bars?"

I thought about that for a moment, remembering what the detective said about prison. "I think it'd be a dark time in my life."

His lips twitched slightly.

Would my parents buy that we were even dating? I barely knew anything about Porter. Maybe we needed to talk about this. Share some details. "So. Now what? Do we do the whole green card, cue card thing, like Andy McDowell and Gerard Depardieu?"

"I have no idea what you just said."

"*The Green Card*. It's a movie. This guy from France wants a green card, so he strikes a deal with some chick to marry him. But the government comes after them, so they lock themselves in her apartment for the weekend and study cue cards about each other to beat the test."

"What happens?"

They fall in love.

"Nothing. That was a stupid example."

"Did he get a green card?"

"No. He got deported."

I deserved the slow blink he gave me.

I shrugged. "We'll be fine. We can wing it."

"I need to go get my truck."

A long beat passed between us. He stood there looking at me. *Oh.* Did he want me to drive him to his truck?

"I can drive you."

"You took your time on that one."

"You're finding your sarcasm. I applaud that."

"There's something about you that inspires it in me."

"I have no idea what you're talking about."

We both smiled into our coffee mugs. I didn't know what this was, but it felt right.

CHAPTER 7

AFTER THE FASTEST shower of my life, I drove Porter to his truck. The second he got out of my vehicle, I called Emily on speaker.

"Beth! Are you okay?"

Weird. Last night felt like a hundred years ago.

"Emily, I'm so sorry about last night."

"Don't worry about it. Are you okay?"

"I'm fine. The charges got dropped."

"Yeah, Porter texted us last night and told us that."

It burned me that he had thought to do that and I hadn't.

"I promised to text you!"

"Don't even worry about that. You're okay, and that's what matters."

"It gets worse."

"What!"

I confessed everything. From pretending with Porter in front of Yates to Mom's surprise dinner invitation. When I finished, there was nothing but silence on the end of the line. "Say something," I begged.

She didn't hold back her laughter. "I'm not sure what to say."

"Well, you and Jackson have been nothing but kind to me, and you sent me your friend to help me, and if he attends dinner with my parents, he won't come out of that as the same person he was going in. I'm about to break your friend."

She was full-blown laughing now. "Beth."

"I shouldn't let him do it. It's too cruel, even for me. And I've done some cruel things in my life."

"You haven't."

"Have so."

"Like what?"

"Remember when Cindy Morrison's locker had a garter snake in it? And she fainted?"

"Yes."

"That was me."

"Beth!"

"She was such a bitch to you. And I might or might not have catfished her with a certain quarterback."

"That was you?"

"I told you I was cruel."

Emily laughed until she snorted. "She blamed me."

"I know. I felt awful about that."

"I didn't. It was worth it."

"I don't want to break Porter. He's your friend, and he seems like a decent guy. No one deserves to go up against my mother."

"Porter can handle himself."

"Remember when I started dating Yates? Mom hated him for the first year, and he was the golden boy."

"What's the favor you have to do for Porter?"

I paused. "I don't know. He's very secretive about it. What's his story anyway?"

Silence.

Which meant only one thing. There was something big there. "Emily, tell me."

"There's nothing to tell." Her voice was prim.

"You're holding out on me?"

"It's not my story to tell, otherwise you know I'd tell you."

"But you're admitting there's a story."

Emily floundered like only she could. "I really like Porter. He's a very good person."

"What else?"

"I'm glad he's helping you."

"That's what you're going with?"

"Yeah."

"If tonight is a massacre, his blood is going to be on your hands too. Last chance for me to bail out of this dinner."

"I think it'll be good."

I snorted. "For who?"

"For your mom."

Huh. I hadn't expected her to say that.

———

"Stop freaking."

I perused Porter. He was wearing a black suit and, this time, a white shirt that actually fit around his neck. He looked really handsome.

"I'm not," I lied, as my racing heart flutter in my chest.

"You haven't stopped jiggling your foot since we started driving."

I worked to calm my leg. Tonight was going to be a nightmare. I was used to Mom. Few people knew how to manage her. I needed to be the strong one tonight. "I'm totally fine."

"Do your cue card thing."

"My what?"

"Give me some intel."

My mind swirled. Where to start? Mom was the biggest control freak I knew. She made it her life mission to make everyone in her world do her bidding. "About my mom?"

"Tell me about Yates."

My tone soured, "We dated for three years. He's part of my parents' world. Dad recently hired him as his campaign manager."

"What campaign?"

"Mayor of New York."

"You ended the relationship?"

A memory flashed through my mind of letting myself into our apartment. I'd moved into Yates' penthouse condo a year after we'd started dating. One afternoon, I had left work early due to a migraine.

When I entered the penthouse, the place was silent. I poured myself a glass of water in the kitchen, took my meds, and headed to our bedroom.

When I pushed open the door, Yates was vigorously fucking someone. My glass of water slipped out of my hand. I remember watching the glass bounce. Water splashed everywhere, but the glass didn't shatter. It bounced and then rolled away from my feet.

It's weird what you remember when life thrusts you into a life-changing moment.

And then Yates pulled out of the woman and stood with his hands held up in front of him, his hard, traitorous dick bobbing stupidly in the air. "I can explain."

Couldn't they always?

The shock had muted me. I didn't say a word when Traci, my boss, the woman who'd made my life a living hell for two entire years, sat up.

That was who he'd chosen to fuck.

Out of everyone he could have cheated on me with, he picked a woman that had routinely and systematically bullied me. He knew how she tortured me, stole my ideas and took credit for my projects. He held me when I cried over the way she treated me, yet he chose *her* to fuck.

That, even more than the cheating, had been the ultimate betrayal for me.

I had disappeared to a hotel for three days, devastated and broken, while everyone I knew tried to get in touch. The only person

I called was Emily. It took me another two weeks to find an apartment and get a job working at a temp agency.

Only then did I return to his apartment.

To end it and pack my stuff.

"I ended the relationship," I said to Porter, my voice cold.

"Why?"

"Because I deserved better."

"Remember that," he said, as he pulled his truck into the parking lot of Bayswater.

And for the first time in a long time, I remembered what healing felt like, and damn, if Porter didn't have a hand in that.

CHAPTER 8

"THIS WAS SUCH A MISTAKE," I whispered to Porter under my breath as we stood at the entrance of Bayswater's grand dining room.

My parents waited at their usual table. They were far away, but it wasn't nearly far enough.

He placed his hand on the small of my back and looked down at me. "It'll be fine."

"What's your last name?" An inordinate amount of panic surged through my body as we walked toward my parents.

"Lyons."

Porter Lyons. The name suited him.

Dad stood as we approached.

"Hi, Dad." I kissed him on the cheek and stepped back. "I'd like to introduce you to my boyfriend, Porter Lyons."

My father was a big man, but he was dwarfed by Porter's stature. They shook hands, and Dad's hands seemed so small in Porter's.

"Pleased to meet you, sir," Porter said.

"Call me Rich," my father said gruffly.

"Thank you." Porter nodded at Mom. "It's nice to see you again, Mrs. Stirling."

She sniffed, her expression borderline sullen as we sat.

"Well," Dad held the wine list towards Porter, "would you like to order us a bottle of wine?"

Dad had pulled this same shit on Yates, who had valiantly tried his best to order wine he thought my parents would like. The rest of the meal, Mom pulled a face every time she took a sip of her wine.

Porter shook his head. "I don't drink wine. You're better off ordering what you like."

Dad didn't know how to respond to that piece of honesty. He made a noise in his throat, and without looking at the menu, ordered a bottle of his favorite red. I ordered a double G&T, which I knew I'd need, and Porter stuck with water. After we ordered our meals, silence descended on the table.

"So, Porter, what kind of job do you have?"

"I'm in the Navy."

A huge smile broke over my father's face. "Really. That's fantastic."

What? No, wait. What?

Dad continued, "Everyone's so proud of the men and women that serve. Myself included."

"Did you go to college?" Mom asked.

"No, ma'am."

"Do you plan on attending college?"

"Mom," I tried to interrupt, but she was only getting warmed up.

Porter reached beneath the table and gave my hand a big squeeze. "Not at the moment."

Mom pinned Porter with another look. "Why not?"

"I'm very satisfied with my current line of work."

Dad regaled us with a long story about an old army buddy he used to know and what a great guy he was while Porter and I listened politely. Mom had that look on her face. The one where she looked like she wanted to kick Dad under the table. Our food arrived, and for a blessed minute, everyone was silent as they ate.

"So, Porter, where have you traveled?" Mom was the first to break the silence. At least she was trying.

"For work or for pleasure?"

"Either."

Porter looked over at me and laughed. "Well, I've been to Mexico for a vacation."

Dad nodded. "We love Mexico. We've been there a number of times."

"I'm sure your travel stories are more interesting."

"Where else have you been?" Mom pushed.

Porter paused, thinking. "I've been to Afghanistan, Iran, Iraq, Libya, Syria..."

OMG. I picked up my glass and drained it.

Mom couldn't keep the shock off her face. "I see. Any other places?"

"Those are the only places I can tell you about. The rest is classified."

Mom hated secrets unless she was in on them. "So, your work is dangerous."

Porter shrugged. "I guess. I don't really think of it in those terms."

"Lyons isn't a common name. Did you grow up in New York?"

"Montana."

"Oh." Her eyes widened. "That's unusual." As if a million people didn't live there.

I stole Dad's wine and took a long gulp.

"It's beautiful country out there."

"Do you own your own house, Porter?"

"No, ma'am."

"How long have you been dating Beth?"

"Sweetie, let the poor guy eat his steak. You can interrogate him over dessert." Dad gave us an apologetic smile.

"We've been dating since Emily's shower," I volunteered. "That's how we met."

My mom sniffed the air like it had a bad smell. "So, you're not too serious then."

Porter gave me a long look, and without taking his eyes off my face, he said, "I'm serious enough to make Beth's well-being my priority."

This guy deserved a freaking Oscar.

Our plates were cleared, and the finish line was in sight. Dad stood and placed his hand on Porter's shoulder. "Why don't we let the women enjoy their dessert while we retire to the billiards room for a drink," he suggested, in a tone that told me he was more than suggesting it.

I was thinking of any reason why we needed to leave when Porter stood up. "That sounds like a great idea," he said with an easy smile towards me.

Fear pricked my skin as I watched them walk towards the men's-only billiards room.

"I don't like him."

I glanced over at my mom. "Why not?"

"He's of questionable pedigree." This was Mom. This was how she saw the world.

"I think that's rude."

"It's the truth."

"Mom, Porter is a really great person," I barely knew Porter, but his actions to date warranted my defense.

"Yates comes from a better home, and his degree and MBA are Ivy League. He also knows how to dress and can work a room better than anyone."

"Yates is a liar and a cheat."

Astonishment rippled through her features. "When are you going to get over his indiscretions, Beth? Honestly, can't a guy make one mistake in his life?"

I leaned over the table and hissed, "He was sleeping with my boss. For months. It wasn't a drunken mistake after some bachelor party. He was having an affair with someone I knew."

Her eyes fluttered. "He said he was sorry."

"I know he's sorry, Mom. And I forgive him. I harbor no ill will towards him, but you need to realize I'm not interested in getting back together with Yates."

"For now."

"Mom!"

"You remember Lori McDavis?"

"What about her?"

"She was dating Mitch her junior year of college, and she broke up with him over one of his indiscretions."

"He was caught sleeping with her aunt."

"My point is, what is Mitch doing?"

I shrugged. "I have no idea."

"He works at a Fortune 500 company. His mom told me that not long ago, he bought a home in the Hamptons, and he bought his young, beautiful fiancé an Aston Martin."

"Good for him."

"What is Lori doing?"

"I have no idea."

She leaned forward. "Lori let herself get long in the tooth."

I laughed. "Does anyone even say that anymore? Long in the tooth?"

"My point is, Lori recently had her thirtieth birthday. She's still working, and I heard that she's dating a cop."

"Mom! That's perfectly respectable."

"Beth, there is nothing acceptable about dating a cop."

"Is this cop a nice guy? Does he care about Lori? Is he faithful to her? These are the important questions, Mom. You need to be worried about how big his heart is, not how big his bank account is."

"A man can have both," she argued.

"What's your point?"

"My point is, there's no room for someone like Porter in your future. He's a common soldier, who lives a military life."

"So?"

"Beth, be sensible."

This conversation was making me crazy. Every time Mom and I came together we had the exact same fight. Her view of the world was terrifyingly narrow. And it seemed the harder I fought to get out of her world, the harder she worked to pull me back. My path was unknown, and it scared her. Hell, it scared me. But the tug-pull between us promised to, one day, permanently ruin our relationship.

Sadness made my throat so tight. Why couldn't we just get along?

"Mom, I think I need some fresh air. Will you excuse me?"

CHAPTER 9

I STOOD outside on the balcony, breathing in huge lungfuls of air. I needed to cleanse myself from everything Bayswater. I should make it my mission to find Porter because who knows what kind of conversation he was having with Dad, but I couldn't seem to move my feet from that spot. I stood there rooted, breathing, trying to calm the erratic emotions that threatened to bubble out of me.

"Are you okay?" that damn smooth voice spoke from behind me.

I spun around. Porter stood there, his hand in one pocket, looking at me.

"I'm sorry."

His shoulder moved a fraction. "For what?"

I shook my head, ignoring his questions. "How were things with my dad?"

"Fine."

He moved over beside me, and together we examined the immaculate golf course. There wasn't a blade of grass out of place. Not a single leaf on the hedge had the balls to grow out of formation. It was complete overkill. I had no idea why people thought this represented beauty. For me, it represented control.

"What's your goal here, Beth?"

I swallowed. "What do you mean?"

"Why did you start all of this in the first place?" His lips moved to an almost smile. "Besides the fact that you're an obvious SD."

"What's an SD?"

"A shit disturber."

I paused and blinked at him. "Have you been talking to Emily?"

He smiled. "Nope. But I knew that about you the second I laid eyes on you." I wanted to ask him why he thought that, but he steered me back to the topic at hand. "What do you want, Beth? What is my role in all of this?"

"I'm sorry I mixed you up in all this. I just wanted some space to breathe. I never knew it would go this far."

"And you thought having a fake boyfriend would buy you that space."

"It was an impulsive move when I was drunk, but yes. In theory, I thought it would."

"You know what we call that in the military?"

"What?"

"A disruptive technique."

"Meaning?"

"Meaning, we disrupt the status quo of the enemy, and it shifts their energy to deal with that disruption, and their focus is pulled off the real issue at hand."

"You're my disruptive technique?"

He shrugged. "It's working, isn't it?"

My lips parted. "What do you mean?"

"If I wasn't here, what would you parents be talking about?"

"My lack of a career, and how they want me to move back home. Don't forget my lack of fashion sense, and when exactly do I plan on taking Yates back? God forbid I don't take back a cheater."

"And what are they focusing on tonight?"

"You."

He smiled. "It's working."

"But it sucks for you."

"I'm the fake boyfriend. It's doesn't matter what they think of me."

I blinked. Who even thought like that? "But doesn't it hurt your feelings?"

"Sweetheart, most days on my job, someone is trying to kill me. That's the kind of shit that gets me worked up, not whether or not your mom thinks I should go to college."

I debated his words. " People try to kill you?"

"They haven't succeeded yet."

I took a deep breath. "Why are you doing this?"

"I told you."

"Because you need my help."

"Yup."

I looked back into those amazing grey eyes. "And after you get my help?"

"If this works for you, it works for me."

"For how long?"

"When it stops working, it'll stop."

I took a deep breath. "Okay."

"Ready to go back inside?"

"Yeah. Let's say goodbye to my parents and get out of here." I paused. "What did my dad talk to you about?"

"Oh, not much," he dismissed. "All the usual stuff about wanting me to take care of his daughter."

"You don't have to take care of me."

"I know."

So why did it feel like he was?

———

When I walked out of my bedroom the next morning, Porter was stretched out on the couch and looking at his phone. He had folded up the bedding, and everything was back in its place. As far as house-guests, he was stellar.

I glanced down as I passed him. I saw a glimpse of a photo, but he placed his phone down too quickly for me to get a good look.

"How did you sleep?" I asked him.

He sat up. "Not bad."

How long had he been up? It was Sunday, sure, but I knew military-types got up early.

There was coffee on the kitchen counter. It was cool, so he'd probably been awake for some time. I poured myself a cup and took a sip, studying him. His attention was drawn back to his phone. Staring at an image that I couldn't quite see.

"So, is today the day I learn my fate?"

He glanced up at me. "About what?"

"The thing you need my help with."

He didn't answer.

I tried again. "I'm pretty sure after last night, you're favor could be illegal, and I wouldn't complain."

A ghost of a smile crossed his lips. "You'd help me deal with a body?"

I winced. "Not quite there yet, but maybe armed robbery."

He stood up. "Do you know how to shoot a gun?"

"No, but I could be the getaway driver."

"Do I have to share the loot?"

"Nope."

He put his hands in his pocket. "You don't need to help me."

I froze. "Why not?"

He didn't speak for a moment. "I'll get out of your hair."

"Where will you go?"

He shrugged and gave me a smile that didn't quite reach his eyes. Something was off.

I pressed again, "I want to help."

"You don't have to."

"I want to."

A long, suffering pause sidled between us. And then those grey eyes lifted up. "You sure?"

"Yes. Whatever it is, I'm in."

He studied me a bit longer. "I need to go pick up some boxes."

What? *That* was the favor?

"Will I need my flack jacket?"

The corners of his lips twitched upward. "Nope."

"Are we hitting the mob?"

"No."

"Breaking into a prison?"

Another smile. "No."

"Okay. I think I can handle it." I turned to put my coffee mug in the sink. "Are we leaving now?"

He was looking down at his phone again. "3 P.M."

"I'll clear my schedule."

"You have a schedule?"

I shrugged. "When you watch as much Netflix as I do, you need a schedule."

He was full-blown smiling now, and it felt victorious. "I'm going for a run."

"No problem."

I smiled as he left, but as soon as he closed the door, it wilted. Call it instinct, but I knew something was bothering my hot guest. And I needed to find out exactly what that was.

CHAPTER 10

THE SECOND he left my apartment, I called Emily. I needed intel.

"Hello?"

"Hey, Em."

"Beth," I could hear the smile in her voice, "How are you?"

"Good. What are you doing today?"

"Jackson is getting ready to ship out. He leaves tomorrow."

I paused. I knew that Porter was part of Jackson's unit, which meant he'd be gone, too. It felt weird knowing that Porter would be leaving soon. I wasn't sure how I felt about that.

"Porter didn't tell me that he's leaving."

She hesitated. "Porter is on a leave of absence."

"Oh."

Emily cleared her throat. "So, how's it going there?"

"Porter went for a run."

"And?"

"And he told me what the favor is."

"What is it?"

"We're going to pick up some boxes this afternoon."

She sucked in her breath. "Oh."

"Emily, you want to tell me what's going on?"

"I...you know."

"Please, Em." I wasn't above begging. "Porter was a rock star yesterday with my mom. He went way beyond the call of duty. Can you give me some hint of what's going on?"

I knew Emily. She wanted to tell me. She just needed more convincing.

I tried again. "Give me something to go on. So I can help him."

"It's his girlfriend."

My entire body ran cold. "He has a girlfriend?"

"He did. His ex. Her name's Felicia."

"And?"

"She moved with him to Virginia when he joined the team, and they seemed great."

I took a seat on the couch. My heart was pounding, and I didn't trust my legs to hold me up. "What happened?"

"When he came home from a deployment, she was gone."

"What do you mean, 'gone'?"

"She packed up their apartment and left."

"What?!"

"All the furniture. The dishes. Everything was gone when he got back. Jackson said that there wasn't a single thing left in that apartment. It was completely cleared out, except for his clothes. He said it was the loneliest thing he had ever seen."

I hated her.

Whoever she was, I. Hated. Her.

Empathy and emotion saturated Emily's voice. "He found out that she was in New York a couple days before Theo's christening."

Wow.

I shut my eyes, remembering how silent and emotionless he had been. He'd looked like a wild man with his beard and messy hair. And those eyes. Those silver eyes, just watching me.

I pressed my forehead against my palm, regret making its way through my body. "I thought he was an asshole."

"He wasn't himself that weekend. He hasn't been himself for months."

No kidding.

Emily continued, "She didn't leave a note or a message. She changed her phone number, too. But when he found out that she moved to New York, he applied for his leave of absence."

My mind raced. "She's here. Living in New York."

"Yeah."

"And today we're going to pick up some boxes."

"She took things that didn't belong to her. His medals of honor and his grandfather's watch. That kind of stuff."

"Why would she do that?"

"I think she wanted him to find her."

My mouth dropped open. "That's so mean."

"Porter asked for an L.O.A. to deal with his personal stuff. The second they got back from a turnaround, he headed to New York."

"When was that?"

"The night you got arrested."

I was the worst. It was official.

Emily kept talking, "I'm really surprised that he wants you to go with him."

No kidding.

I made a noise in my throat.

"What?"

I shook my head. "I'm an asshole. It's been all about me from the moment I met him."

"Beth, you've been great."

I sat there, thinking. "Has he seen her since then?"

"I don't think so."

"Have they talked?"

Emily let out a long breath. "I don't think so. Jackson said that Porter mentioned a text. But I don't think they've actually talked."

I thought about him lying on the couch, looking at a photo on his phone. Had he been looking at a picture of her? Thinking about her? Did he still love her?

"How long were they together?"

"Awhile."

"Which is how long?"

"I think maybe three or four years?"

"That's so long."

"I'm so glad you're there for him. Jackson's really worried about him. This is actually working out a lot better than we expected."

"How so?"

"We know where he is, for one."

I chewed on my lip. "Okay. Thanks. I understand why you didn't want to tell me that, but it's going to help me from making this worse."

"We really appreciate what you're doing."

I snorted. "I'm not 'doing' anything. Porter has been taking care of me more than I have of him."

"You'd be surprised."

"He's lucky to have you guys."

"How did last night go anyways?"

I laid back, resting my head on his folded bedding. I could smell him. Clean and masculine. "My mom didn't know how to deal, but Porter was a total gentleman. Really patient and sane."

"He's a good guy."

We both pondered that statement for a moment until I finally broke the silence. "Why did she do it? Why did she leave him?"

"We don't know. Porter said they were good right up until she left."

"What a mind fuck."

"Tell me about it. Text me and tell me how it went."

"I will."

"And Beth?"

"Yeah?"

"If you get a chance, teach that bitch a lesson."

I couldn't hold back my laugh. Maybe I would.

CHAPTER 11

SOMEONE ONCE SAID, 'It's strange how knowledge changes perception.' Learning about Porter and his past changed everything.

The drive to pick up boxes passed in complete silence. His silence held meaning now. What was he thinking? What could he possibly be feeling, knowing that he was about to face the woman who had up and left without saying goodbye?

I glanced over at him. He looked casual with his t-shirt and base-ball cap. His movements were calm and relaxed. No emotion marred his features. He didn't even look like he was deep in thought.

Was he feeling anything? Did this matter to him? Why had he asked me to come? For moral support? Or did he actually need me there to help carry his boxes?

We turned down a cute street that was lined with big, leafy trees and old brick apartments. He parked on the side of the road, killed the engine, then leaned forward and studied a building through the windshield.

I sat silently beside him. And we just sat there. He inspected the building, and I tried but failed not to look at him.

Moments ticked by.

He wasn't moving, but he was thinking. Those intelligent grey eyes took in everything about that building. But still, he didn't move.

The words blurted out of me before I could stop them. "What's her name?"

"What makes you think it's a woman?"

"It's always a woman."

He rubbed his face, then turned that intensity on me. But he didn't speak.

Those eyes. How did I ever think these eyes held no emotion? Right now, they were the color of a turbulent sea. Stormy grey.

"Do you want her back?" My question lingered in the cab. Like a faint perfume.

He dropped his gaze. "I don't know."

We sat there in silence, then he gave me a tight smile that was so full of regret and ambiguity, it made my heart ache.

"Do you want me to come in with you?"

He thought about that for a moment and slowly nodded. "Yeah."

"Okay."

He took a deep breath. "Okay."

I started to gather my purse.

He spoke again. "Can you do that thing?"

I froze. "What thing?"

He shrugged. "The thing."

My eyes were on his face. "Could you be a bit more specific?"

He opened the door. "The thing. Just do it."

I watched him walk around the front of the trunk before I scrambled after him. What the fuck was the *thing*? I had lots of things.

I caught up with him at the front of the building. He was buzzing an apartment.

A throaty voice filled the crisp air. "Hello?"

"Felicia. It's Porter." His voice was clipped. Cold.

"Come on up."

He held the door but didn't look at me. A staircase circled

around, but we stood and waited for the rickety elevator that was so old, you had to physically shut the door yourself.

I wanted to ask him about the thing, but I didn't. He was too focused. Too intense. It felt wrong to disturb him. The elevator creaked and groaned, carrying us up to the third floor.

He stepped out ahead of me. I heard that same voice.

"Porter, over here."

By the time I stepped out of the elevator, there was nothing but an empty hallway, but an apartment door at the end was open.

We walked towards the apartment. Porter pushed open the door, and we stood at the entrance, looking around. The apartment was warm. Cheerful. Homey. Artsy. I hadn't expected this.

Her voice sounded from the kitchen. "Port, when did you get into New York?"

Ballsy, how she acted like he was an old friend that she'd recently seen last week. She was so casual, so damned relaxed about this, it made me want to scream. This was not how you treated a significant other that you dumped without warning.

It felt disrespectful.

Four large boxes were stacked up against the wall. This was what she was giving back to him? A box for every year they were together. She got all the furniture, the bedding, the towels and the artwork, and he got his personal mementos back.

What a shit deal.

Movement caught my eye. A tall guy unfolded himself from the couch. He looked Bohemian with his man bun and beaded smock. I hate man buns. And hated them even more since this dude was wearing one.

"Hey, man." He sounded stoned, but maybe that was all part of his hippie persona.

It was all so cliché, I would have laughed had it not been at Porter's expense. Porter swallowed but didn't move a muscle.

"That's Marley." Felicia's voice drifted from the kitchen. "He's been an absolute lifesaver since I moved to New York."

Marley shrugged with a self-content expression. "I do what I can, right, babe?"

"You've been a fucking lifesaver," she answered back. "You've been fucking everything."

I hated her.

On behalf of Porter, I despised her with all my heart.

Porter and I made eye contact. I couldn't get a read off what he was feeling, but whatever it was, he was working to contain it. He was almost vibrating in his attempts to restrain his emotion.

Fucking fuck.

"I wished you had opted for the prison break in," I muttered under my breath.

His voice was so low, I barely heard him. "Roger that."

"Porter, when did you say you got to New York?" Her voice was so sexy. Alluring. Faintly husky.

"A few days ago." Porter's voice was flat. Emotionless. "Are these boxes for me?"

"Where are you staying?" She finally came out of the kitchen.

Felicia. Damn, she was hot.

Where did I even start?

Elegant bare feet. Cut off denim shorts that showed off extremely sexy legs. A ripped tank top that didn't entirely hide her smooth, feminine abdomen. Braless breasts that were the envy of every woman.

But her face. Petite, delicate features. Big, expressive blue eyes. Long black hair that hung down her back with that perfect, messy, just fucked look. Pillowy, pouty, pink lips. I needed to stop before I started to second-guess myself.

She stopped short, taking me in. She was shocked. "Who are you?" Her eyes drank in Porter, but they flicked back to me. Assessing me.

Well, I assessed her back. I could tell by the way she raked her eyes over him, she was still very much attracted to him. In fact, I would go as far as stating that she emotionally wanted him back.

So badly.

And suddenly, I knew what 'the thing' was. I knew what Porter was asking of me.

I was the fake girlfriend.

I tilted my head and held her in my gaze. Calmness washed over me. I knew what I needed to do. "I'm Beth."

Her eyes focused on my face. Weighing me. Measuring me. "Beth?"

She found me lacking. She took one look at me and dismissed me as a non-threat. I think when you're a petite version of a Victoria's Secret model, you can do that with pretty much every woman and be correct 99% of the time.

But there were two things she didn't know about me. For my entire childhood education, I had attended the most elite, all-girls prep school in New York. A place that taught us life skills to navigate the most atrocious social situations. And when our backs were against the wall, we learned how to go for the jugular. Secondly, if tested, I would score off the charts for being protective of friends and family. It was my thing.

I was a threat. She just didn't know it yet.

I leaned against Porter. He stood solid and strong. It was like connecting with a warm brick wall. "Porter is staying with me."

Porter continued to look at Marley like he wanted to throat punch him. I understood it, but it didn't add to my confidence.

She licked her bottom lip. This was not going the way she thought it would. "Port, you never told me you were dating someone."

"You never asked."

Delicate nostrils flared. "How long?"

I patted my hand on his flat stomach and beamed at her. "Long enough to know he's the catch of a lifetime."

Porter did the slow blink but didn't respond.

"My parents are absolutely in love with Porter." Smiling, I gave him a flirtatious glance. "Aren't they?"

That did make him look down at my face. I wasn't even sure he was still in his body. He was on automatic. He didn't speak.

I turned back to Felicia. "It's been lovely meeting you, Felicia."

Porter bent down and picked up three boxes, still not saying a word as he waited for me.

"Nice meeting you, Marley."

I picked up the fourth box. It was smaller than the rest, so I shifted it to one hand and placed my spare hand intimately in the back pocket of Porter's jeans. My heart pounded as we left a stunned Felicia in our wake, and the tight curve of Porter's ass burned my hand.

CHAPTER 12

THE SECOND we were out of sight, I retracted my hand, shifting the box, so I was holding it with both arms. In silence, we got back on the elevator. I pressed the floor-level button and dared to look at Porter's face.

His expression was flat. Some part of him had shut down.

"I did the thing." I sounded stupid stating the obvious.

Those eyes worked to focus on me.

I felt shaky. Like it had been my ex we had just seen. "She'll come after you."

"It's done."

"Not if you don't want it to be." I made a promise I couldn't keep, "Trust me on that."

"It's over."

The elevator ground to a halt. We carried the boxes across the lobby, and despite the fact that he had the most boxes, he held open the door with his foot for me.

"Porter," a voice sounded from behind me.

I glanced over my shoulder. Felicia raced down the stairs in bare feet, her long hair flying behind her. She sounded panicked.

"Told you," I said, as I stepped through the door.

"Wait!" she called in desperation.

Porter let the door shut, and he started down the steps. The door slammed open behind us.

"Please, Porter," she cried, running down the steps towards us. "Please. I need to talk to you. One minute."

Porter studied me.

I shrugged. "It doesn't hurt to listen."

With control, he set the boxes down on the ground.

"I'll go wait in the truck." I climbed into the car and tried not to look at them, but I couldn't help myself.

Next to Porter's big frame, Felicia seemed delicate and petite. She did all the talking, waving her arms around and continually pushing her hands into her hair to fluff it out.

Porter lifted his baseball cap off his head a couple times, but I didn't actually see his lips move.

My phone rang.

"Hey, Beth. It's Jackson."

"Is everything okay?"

He cleared his throat. "Emily caught me up."

"Yeah."

"I don't mess around with other people's lives, but I do look out for my friends."

"I know. What do you need?"

"Would you be willing to let Porter crash on your couch for a few more nights?"

"What? Of course."

Jackson hesitated, his voice pained. "He won't ask. You'll have to offer."

It should have dawned on me that he'd never ask. After watching this train wreck, I wanted to help. I needed to.

"I will. It's no problem."

What was the worst that could happen?

Porter picked up the boxes, and Felicia's movements got a bit more frantic. He said something to her, then he walked towards the truck. She stood there, biting her lip, looking like she wanted to cry.

Porter swung into the truck, beside me. He gunned the engine, hit reverse then somehow turned the truck around in the narrow street. Silence clung to us. I kept checking on him, but he seemed indifferent. Unaffected. Focused on driving.

Here went nothing. "So, are you going to hang around New York?"

Stone-faced, he rubbed the back of his neck. "Not sure."

"You know, you could always crash at my place. For as long as you want."

He glanced at me. "Why?"

"I don't understand your one worded question."

"Why would you offer that?"

Because Jackson asked me to.

Because I've done the three days in a lonely hotel after a breakup, and it sucks.

Because your friends are worried about you. Including me.

"Because I really like messy, non-talking, incommunicative, hard-to-read soldiers hanging out at my place, and I especially like helping them get their supermodel ex-girlfriends back. It's my go-to for when I need a pick-me-up."

He was silent for a moment. "I'm not messy."

"That's what you got from all of that?"

"I'm neater than you."

I focused on the ceiling of his truck and laughed. "Did you talk in your last relationship?"

"Why?"

"I don't know. The entire time you two were on the sidewalk, she did all the talking."

Nothing.

I valiantly continued, "I think you took your hat off a couple times. Is that some sort of code, because you should know that sign language is a lot more expressive."

"Sign language?"

"The official language of the deaf."

"I know what sign language is."

"Would you prefer morse code?"

I got a look for that, but I could feel him loosening up. He was starting to breathe. So, I took it one step further. I opened my phone and found an app that translated text into Morse code beeps.

I typed in the text: YOU'RE THE BEST LOOKING PRETEND BOYFRIEND I'VE EVER HAD. I pressed play, and a series of short and long beeps came out of my phone.

He listened, slowly blinking, his face tinged with amusement. It was enough to keep me going.

"How about this?" I typed in: I WANT TO HAVE PUBLIC SEX WITH YOU.

"Are you enjoying yourself?" he asked after I played that morse code message to him.

"You have no idea how much. Wait. One more."

IF YOU STAY WITH ME, I'LL DEMAND USE OF YOUR HOT COCK EVERY NIGHT.

He pretended to listen, and his lips twitched. "That sounds important. Are you going to translate?"

"Nope." At his silence, I relented, "Fine. The phone is going back in the purse. So, are you going to hang around in New York for a while?"

He cleared his throat. "You don't mind?"

"This morning, I offered to help you with an armed robbery. When you hit that level of friendship, couch surfing is a given."

"I appreciate it."

"Okay," I said in my most dramatic voice. "But just so we're clear, you can't go all frat boy on me."

His look demanded an explanation.

"You know, I don't want to be tripping over your dirty socks. You can't be messy."

"I'm not messy."

I smiled as I talked, "I equate frat food with fat food, and this ass can't handle pizza and beer every night, so if you eat that, don't offer it to me."

"Your ass looks fine."

"My ass looks more than fine. This ass is the result of hours of yoga and spin class, and because I don't feed it pizza."

I could tell he thought I was a bit crazy, but if it took his mind off things, I was okay with that. We drove in silence for a few moments, both lost in our own thoughts.

I had to know. "What did she say?"

He drove two blocks before he answered. "She wants to go out for dinner. To catch up. As friends."

"Translation: she wants you back."

"You don't know that."

"But I do." My breath hitched in my throat. "When are you getting together?"

"I didn't say I was."

"Wasn't that the point?"

"Of what?"

"Of me doing the thing."

"I don't know if I want to." Huh. Well, he did have the right to not want to see her. She had royally fucked him over.

"Well, where did you leave it?"

"I said I'd be in touch."

"Oh."

We drove the rest of the way home in silence. I helped him carry the boxes. He waited until the elevator door closed before he asked, "How do you know it's hot?"

"How do I know what is hot?"

"My cock."

What?

The elevator door opened. I rushed after him. "You know morse code?"

"Yup."

My face burned hot. What had I texted? Public sex. Demanding use of his hot cock. Every single night. Oh, God. "That's not fair."

His smile wasn't huge, but it was still a smile. "It was entertaining."

"I didn't mean it." I unlocked the door.

"I thought your messages were pretty clear. You didn't leave a lot of room for interpretation."

"Porter!"

He didn't laugh, but he did look amused. Under the circumstances, that was the best I was going to get. I watched as he set down his boxes in my front entrance.

My face was so hot. "I'm not hitting on you."

Grey eyes met mine.

"I mean, obviously! With your beautiful ex-girlfriend wanting you back and you driving home from seeing her. It would be completely inappropriate to proposition you at a time like that."

He let me marinate in awkward silence before he spoke. "It wasn't that inappropriate."

"It wasn't?"

"It was a good reminder for me."

Of what, I wasn't sure. Nor did I want to ask. "Oh."

He jingled his keys in his hand. "I'm going out for awhile."

"Okay."

"I'll try and be quiet when I come in."

"For sure."

And then he was gone, leaving me to wondering what exactly I was reminding him of.

CHAPTER 13

THE NEXT FIVE days passed like groundhog day. I'd get up early to go to my shit temp job. When I'd leave my room in the mornings, Porter was always gone already, his bedding neatly folded, not a dirty sock in sight. If it weren't for the coffee in the coffee maker and the lone cup in the sink, I wouldn't even know he'd slept over.

I'd spend the day working. And when I came home, there was usually some sort of delicious, healthy, home-cooked meal tucked in the fridge with a note telling me to enjoy. No pizza in sight. The kitchen was always immaculate. Fresh, expensive groceries would find their way into the fridge. But he was never around. As far as house guests, he was almost perfect.

Except I found myself hoping he'd show up.

Each night, I watched Netflix, waiting for him to come home, but he never did. Whatever he was doing, or whomever he was seeing, he did it late into the night.

I worried about him, which was silly because I didn't really know where he was. Perhaps he was spending every day with Felicia. Perhaps they were rekindling their relationship. I imagined lengthy discussions talking about what worked and what didn't. Maybe they were discussing how they could reconcile this situation. Could he forgive her? Did he want to?

Then again, he could be spending every single day sitting in some bar, then walking home over the highest bridge he could find, so what did I know?

Regardless, I worried.

And I didn't like how that felt.

Friday afternoon, after the shittiest day at work at my underpaid, overqualified temp job, I made my way home. All I wanted was a glass of wine and something really unhealthy to eat. I got the mail, kicking off my shoes as I walked in the door.

I dumped my purse and checked my phone. I had two messages. Maybe one of them was from my elusive roommate. I played my messages on speaker, cranked the cork out of the wine bottle I'd opened last night, found the biggest wine glass I owned, and poured until the bottle was empty.

The first message was from Mom. "Hi, Beth, this is your mother. I wanted to remind you that next Saturday, we have the gala, in which your father is announcing his candidacy. It's critical that you attend. I wanted you to see Donna for this event, but it's too late now for her to buy you anything, so I think you should wear the crushed, black silk Chanel."

I lifted my head, startled to see Porter standing in the doorway. How long he had been standing there?

Mom droned on. "I really don't know why you're so stubborn. Your father has worked so hard to provide you with a beautiful home, and you don't want to live in it, but so be it."

"Did I see split ends? I made an appointment for you to see Jimmy. He may not have time to give you proper highlights, but he'll make time to give you a trim. Honestly, your hair looks like you've got a $50 haircut. It's embarrassing."

"One more thing. Please, ensure your male friend stays at home. Let's face it. This gala is a black tie affair, and we both know this isn't his thing. That man probably doesn't even own a tuxedo. So, do us all a favor and leave him at home. We'll be sending a car so you won't be late. And please, don't disappoint us."

Thanks, Mom, for the nice mind fuck.

I averted my eyes from Porter and took a long sip of my wine before hitting the delete button.

The next message started to play. "Hello, Beth. This is Andrea Lowen from Marketing Now. We wanted to thank you for coming in for an interview. Though you interviewed exceedingly well, we went with another candidate. Best of luck in finding a new job."

I stood there for a long moment. I needed to think, but I was too sad to even process that. I would deal later with the fact that I seemed destined to work as a temp for the rest of my life.

Porter walked towards me. "Are you okay?"

"I was going to ask you the same thing."

"I'm good."

"Me too," I lied, taking another sip of my wine. "Just peachy."

"You sure?"

I picked up a large padded envelope that had no return address. "I feel some anxiety right now, but it has nothing to do with you and everything to do with my phone messages."

"Roger that."

I ripped open the envelope and pulled out a piece of paper. At first, my brain couldn't process what was happening. There were beetles. Big, black beetles. The size of freaking Chihuahuas. Most of them were dead, but one was still a tiny bit alive. It half dragged itself across the counter.

I screamed, then covered my mouth, backing away from that fucking nightmare. Porter reached over and scooped all the beetles back into the envelope and rolled it shut.

"Throw that out." I was hysterical, but I didn't care.

"What does the note say, Beth?" How was his voice so calm?!

"What note?"

"You pulled a note out. What does it say?"

My eyes dropped to my hands. I was holding a note. I shook my head and tossed it on the counter. Porter, using the edge of the envelope, flipped open the folded sheet.

In black marker, a message was scrawled: "IT'S IN YOUR BEST INTEREST TO CONVINCE YOUR FATHER TO STICK WITH WHAT HE KNOWS. YOU'VE BEEN WARNED."

What. The. Fuck.

I felt sick to my stomach. I couldn't even process what was happening.

Porter appraised me, so much concern on his face. "Do you know who sent this to you?"

"Just another fan letter from one of my fans."

I will not cry. I will not freaking cry.

The look he gave me—those grey eyes filled with such intense worry—tipped me over the edge. Tears spill onto my cheeks. "I need a minute."

Numb, I walked blindly into my bedroom and laid spread-eagle on my bed. Then, the tears came. Big, sobbing tears. Stupid, but I tend to cry under pressure.

And intense fear.

I didn't know how long I laid there—long enough to lament how much my life sucked. This fucking gala. Yates. My stalled career. That letter. I tried to push it out of my mind. I couldn't deal with it. Not right now. I was too emotional to start coping with it. It could wait. I should get up. I should start acting like an adult, but it was easier to just stare at the ceiling.

There was a tap on the open door. Too despondent to lift my head, I said, "Come in."

"I'm breaking a rule here, but I thought it might help."

I lifted my head. Porter stood there with a glass of wine and a pizza box.

I swallowed and sat up. "You brought frat food."

He lifted up the box. "I personally think your ass can handle at least one pizza, but say the word, and I'll remove this from your place."

I held out my arms and wiggled my fingers. "Want."

He walked across the room and handed me the wine. I scooted over and patted the bed beside me.

He evaluated me. "Do you want to eat here?"

"That depends." I picked up the remote. "Will you let me watch whatever tear-jerking chick show I want to watch?"

"Obviously."

"Then, yes. I want us to eat pizza in bed."

He placed the box on the nightstand. "I'll be right back."

He reappeared with plates, napkins and a beer. He settled on the bed beside me and handed me a plated piece of pizza at the exact moment I lifted up the remote. My hand hit the plate, and my pizza slid towards the bed.

He juggled the plate and saved my pizza but lost hold of his beer in the process. It dumped all over his shirt.

"Sorry," I cried.

"No worries," he stood up, set the foaming beer on the nightstand and peered down at his wet shirt.

He crossed his arms and pulled his t-shirt over his head. My mouth went dry as I took in his muscular core and broad pecs.

As he inspected his shirt, he seemed completely indifferent to the fact that I couldn't tear my eyes away from all those rippling muscles.

Work out much?

"I'm going to grab a dry shirt."

"Sure," I felt flushed as my entire body reacted to that manly vision that belonged on the cover of a men's health magazine.

Calm down, Beth. Just calm the fuck down.

But some things can't be unseen, and Porter's body was one of those things.

CHAPTER 14

WITHOUT COMPLAINT, Porter watched three episodes of *Grey's Anatomy* on Netflix. By the third episode, I could tell that he was actually getting into it.

"Who's that chick?"

"Addison. She used to be married to McDreamy, but their marriage broke up when she had an affair with McSteamy."

"Which one is steamy?"

"The big blond. He used to be friends with McDreamy, but the cheating pissed McDreamy off."

"And who's McDreamy with?"

"Well, he's supposed to be with Meredith, but they aren't together. Because she's pissed about him not telling her about Addison."

"He should have tried morse code."

I laughed. "It's a fail-safe in all relationships."

"Want more wine?"

"Hell, yeah."

He reached down to the floor and produced the bottle. I held my glass while he poured.

"You need a beer fridge in here."

"I might never get out of bed."

"It happens." I watched him crack another beer, and side-by-side, we sipped our drinks.

"Tough week?"

"Maybe. But maybe not as tough as yours?"

He shrugged and took another sip. "I've had better."

"Have you talked to her?"

"Nope."

Oh. Well, that was interesting.

"Are you going to?"

"Not sure."

I wanted to ask him what he did all day and night if he wasn't with Felicia, but perhaps I didn't want to know. Maybe he was whoring it up. This moment was nice. I didn't want to muddy this time by confirming he was having sex with someone else.

He cut into my thoughts. "Want to talk?"

"About?"

"That note."

"Not really."

He examined his beer can. "Okay. How about the gala?"

It shocked me how much I wanted to ask him to come with me, but knowing what the guy was going through, it didn't seem fair. "I hate those events. But I'll do my part. If I had something as important as that happening in my life, I'd want my parents there no matter how much we're at odds."

"Why do you parents want you back with Yates so much?"

"He has good pedigree. Ivy League schools. The right parents. All the connections. In their eyes, he's of elevated status."

"What about what you want?"

"They don't believe I know what I want. They think he'll make me happy."

Grey eyes peered at me. "You're all right, you know that?"

"You're not so bad yourself."

He set his beer can aside and leaned back on the pillow with his head behind his hand. "Can I make a request?"

"Always."

"You won't hold it against me?"

"I doubt it."

"You have to promise not to tell anyone."

"I'm the vault. People actually tell me that they call me the vault behind my back."

He caught his lower lip in his teeth, debating. "Can we watch another episode of *Grey's*?"

"Oh, my God." I burst out laughing. "You're joking."

"Hey."

I rose to my knees, lifting my wine glass in victory. "Yes, folks. Another closet fan is born."

He grabbed my hand, but he had a massive smile on his face. "You're blowing this out of proportion. I'm not a fan. But they left us with a cliffhanger."

I pushed his hand back, so it was pinned by his head. "Admit it. You took your first hit, and now you're begging for more."

He laughed. "You said you wouldn't hold it against me."

I was making him laugh. Why did that feel so damn good?

I drained my glass and reached over him to set it on the nightstand. "Think of what this would do to their ratings if they knew a decorated Navy SEAL was their latest fan."

One minute, I was leaning over him, and the next minute, he had me flipped over on my back until he was kneeling over me, his hands pinning my hands above my head.

"You promised me you wouldn't tell anyone," he growled, playfully.

My stomach tingled, but my brain told my stomach that he was only playing the role of a big brother. "Some secrets are too big to keep."

"You know, I'm skilled in various torture techniques."

My inner flirt raised her head. "If you're trying to turn me on, it's working."

Those grey eyes, so dark they were almost charcoal, dropped to my mouth. We were both breathing hard. Too much booze and temptation. I could see him internally debating.

It would be a total mistake, but didn't we deserve this? Hadn't we both been burned? Shouldn't we snatch our moments of happiness where we could?

He started towards me.

Thank fuck.

Eyes wide open, I watched as he lowered his face to mine. Our eyes locked, neither of us breaking eye contact. His lips were mere centimeters away from mine.

I'd never wanted to kiss anyone more in my life.

"This is probably a really bad idea." His breath whispered across my lips.

I breathed it in. "The worst."

"You want to stop?"

"Not particularly."

"Good answer."

A tinny version of Ozzy Osbourne's *Crazy Train* interrupted us. We both froze, eyes locked. He pushed himself up but didn't look at his phone.

It was her.

I knew it was.

"Do you have to get that?"

He shook his head.

"Do you need to go?"

"No."

He was still kneeling over me. Staring down at me. I knew he was thinking of her now, but he was sitting on *me*. He looked trapped. He was actually debating continuing messing around with me, even though his head was no longer in the game. Probably because he was so damn polite.

Sometimes, the kindest thing we can do for people is to save them from themselves.

So, I swatted his hard stomach, careful to keep my movements light. "Well, if you're not going to kiss me, can you do something useful and get me some more wine?"

He didn't move.

I gave him a playful shove. "Come on. If this is my cheat day, I want to drink myself into oblivion."

He stood up. Taking a deep breath, he ran his hands through his hair. I pretended not to notice, but who could miss the spectacularly impressive hard bulge in his jeans?

Jesus. I was walking on a fine line here. One that wasn't going to end well for either of us.

CHAPTER 15

I FELT SAFE AND WARM. As my brain slowly woke, my entire body froze.

I was draped over Porter like a lap dog. My legs were tangle between his, the left one bent and pressed between his legs, snuggled warmly against his package. My face rested on his hard chest, my arm slung around his muscular waist, and his arm wrapped around my back, holding me tightly against him.

I tried to keep my breath even while I thought. I was not a cuddly person. I'd been in my fair share of relationships to know that I liked my side of the bed, and I didn't like to touch my partner while I slept, no matter how much I loved them. So, why was I stuck on him like white on rice?

"Someone's in your apartment," he whispered, his morning voice raspy.

"What?" I lifted my head in shock.

"Whoever it is has a key."

The only person who had a key was Mom. And my landlord. Why would either of them be in my apartment?

"How long have they been here?" I kept my voice low.

"About five seconds."

A blood-curdling scream pierced the air. I froze, watching as Porter rolled off the bed and moved to the door with impressive speed. I scrambled after him, following him into my living room.

I almost ran into his back when he stopped short. I stepped around him. Mom was standing in the living room, her face a mask of disgust. Dead beetles laid scattered on the floor. She clutched the note in her hand.

"Mom? What are you doing here?"

She swallowed hard. "I'm here to drop off a clutch for you. For the gala."

"Why didn't you call?"

"Why would I call when I have a key?"

She never seemed to understand that the key was for emergencies only. That was a conversation for a later date. Right now, I was too busy looking at the dead beetles.

Shifting my gaze, I asked the obvious. "Were you reading my mail?"

She lifted her chin a fraction. "The envelope was lying on the counter. Want to tell me what that's all about?"

I glanced at Porter. Sometime in the middle of the night, he had taken off his t-shirt. Now, he stood there, wearing only a pair of jeans that hung low on his muscular hips.

I enjoyed my second viewing of his massive shoulders and muscular chest. Don't even get me started on his abs. He had a six-pack that showed off every single muscle, including the V that lead down to—.

I sensed his attention and forced myself to meet his eyes. Those piercing grey irises inspected me with a mixture of frustration and bewilderment.

I know. Mom can be a little much at times.

I debated how to approach this. "I got that letter last night."

"What did you do to make someone send you this?"

Patience. I took a deep breath. *Be patient.*

"I don't know." The dead beetles were as gross as I remembered. I shuddered. "I'm going to take it to the police and file a report."

"No. You will not be going to the police over this...this *hoax*."

Porter shifted beside me. I refrained from looking at him again because I knew a mere glance at his naked torso wouldn't suffice. A body like that needed to be lingered over.

I forced myself to keep my eyes trained on my mom. "Mom." I kept my voice calm because the last thing I needed right now was another fight with her. "I think the police need to know about this. At the very least, they need to have something on file."

Porter crouched down and shoved the dead bugs back into the envelope lying on the floor. I got a tiny bit distracted as I took in his broad back. Strong muscles flexed as he stretched to pick them up. What would it feel like to trace my fingers down that back while he moved on top of—

Mom's voice yanked me out of my inappropriate meanderings. "Your father doesn't need any type of police investigation going on during his campaign. That would be grossly unfair of you to do that to him. He doesn't need any bad publicity."

"I wouldn't be doing it to him," I protested. "Besides, no one's going to find out. I only want to file a report."

"No. I forbid it."

Porter stood, his body moving with panther-like grace, and held his hand out to Mom. She stared at it for several awkward moments, then with extreme reluctance, handed him the note.

"Beth needs to take this to the police." His voice was gravelly from sleep, but there was no mistaking his don't-fuck-around tone.

"Don't be silly. There's no need to involve the police."

"This note is not only hostile, but it's also threatening. Beth could be in danger."

"Well, you assured me you're doing your best care for Beth. Are you telling me your best isn't good enough?"

"Mom," I hissed, mortified.

"I'll do everything in my power to ensure her safety, but I'm not with Beth 24 hours a day."

"Well, it's not like the police are going to be following her around either. All they'd do is file a report. A report that would do nothing to ensure her safety but could do reprehensible damage to my husband's campaign."

"There should be a record of this harassment."

"Harassment?" She scoffed. "I hardly qualify that note as harassment. It's merely someone playing a prank on Beth. A bad one, but it's only a prank."

"You're willing to bet Beth's safety on that?"

Mom stiffened. "Are you suggesting I'm not concerned about Beth's safety?"

"Yes." If looks could harm, Porter would be a smoking pile of ash at this point.

Without another word, Mom picked up her purse, seared me with an accusing glare, and swung her jacket over her shoulder. "You won't help your father in his campaign because you're so busy in your life." Her eyes flickered over Porter. "At the very least, try and refrain from outright sabotaging your father's career."

"Mom," I tried. "Come on. Don't go."

"I'm going home. You can call me when you come to your senses." With another glare at Porter, she turned and walked out.

I stared at the door, waiting for her to come back but knowing she wouldn't. I hated fighting with Mom. Why couldn't we get along? It seemed like no matter what I did or didn't do, she was always disappointed in me. Perhaps she was right. Maybe the letter *was* a sick joke. Maybe Yates was trying to fuck with me.

Porter ran his hands through his hair, making it stick up in all directions. "What are you going to do?"

I took in his unbelievable body. Felicia was out of her mind to give him up.

"I'm going to talk to Yates. I need to ask him about the letter."

Porter didn't look impressed. "Will you take the letter to the police?"

"I'll think about it."

He studied me for a moment. "Do. I respect your mom, but she's way off on this one."

I couldn't face the idea that someone was actually trying to hurt me. "I will." I waited until Porter was in the shower before I dialed Yates' number.

"Hey, Beth."

"Yates." I tried to keep the coldness out of my voice. "I was hoping we could talk."

"Let's go for coffee."

Had he always been so high-handed?

"This can be handled on the phone."

"Meet me at our old place at 11?"

"No—"

The dial tone cut me off.

"Damn it!"

The last thing I wanted to do was see Yates.

CHAPTER 16

I SAT in the coffee shop, awaiting Yates' arrival. Yates thought the world should wait for him. He ran late for every meeting and appointment, whereas I was always early. It was one of many ways we were incompatible.

Finally, his blond head appeared at the door. He waved before making his way to the table. Bending over me for a kiss, he deliberately missed my cheek and stole a kiss from my lips. His expensive cologne lingered in the air.

I eyed the door, cursing myself for not choosing a closer table.

He sat down and stared at me. "I missed that."

I ignored his suggestive tone. "So, I hear you're my father's new campaign manager."

He smiled. "I am, and because of that fact, he's going to win."

I didn't come here to talk about Yates or the campaign. I pulled the offending beetle letter out of my purse, which I had sealed in a plastic bag, and slid it over the table to Yates.

"What's this?" He looked down at it.

"Hate mail. Be careful when you open it."

He gave me a questioning look, then opened the envelope. A look of disgust crossed his face as he peered at the beetles. He pulled the note from the envelope and read it. "Who's this from?"

"I was going to ask you."

Surprise, then incredulity, crossed his face. "You think I had something to do with this?"

I tilted my head, scrutinizing his expression. He seemed genuine. Then again, I had no clue he was cheating on me until I saw him balls deep in my boss. So, maybe I wasn't the best judge of deception.

I shrugged. "Did you?"

He sealed the letter and handed it back to me. "Beth, why would you think I'd send you something like this?"

"So, you didn't have anything to do with that?"

"Why would I send you hate mail? I want us to get back together." He leaned forward. "I want to marry you."

And I had wanted to marry Yates before I realized how selfish he was.

He leaned forward, his gaze lingered on my mouth. "I've talked to your parents."

I used to feel so much anger towards Yates, but somehow, in the last little while, I no longer felt anything towards him, except maybe mild annoyance.

"About what?"

"I've asked your dad for your hand in marriage." He gave me a tender smile.

I take that back. I worked to place my trembling cup back in its saucer as intense emotions flowed through me. I felt so much, it took me a few moments to even recognize what I was feeling.

Anger.

So much anger. I don't know if it is was the audacity of his high-handed behavior, or if it was because he actually thought I was so pathetic, I'd come crawling back to him and accept his leftovers.

"Why would you do that?" My voice was cold. The rest of my body, on the other hand, was flushed so hot, I was surprised I hadn't burst into flames.

"Beth." His exasperation was obvious. "Why are you fighting this? You know we're supposed to be together. When are you going to dump your military monkey? Your father thinks an engagement will boost his campaign numbers."

Military monkey?

How dare he criticize Porter?

"He's twice the man you'll ever be," I hissed. "And for your information, we happen to be engaged."

"Excuse me?" Incredulity spread across his face in an instant.

Oh, crap.

Did I really just say that out loud?

I licked my lips, trying not to show the panic squeezing my chest. "We haven't talked to my parents yet, so I'd appreciate it if you'd let me discuss this with them first."

He shook his head. "You're engaged. To that solider? What the fuck is going on?"

"I love him," I blurted out, piling lies. "He's the love of my life."

"You barely know him."

My fake smile twisted to a grimace. "When you know, you know."

Yates glared. "This isn't how it's supposed to go."

"Well, I'm sorry if I'm not living my life according to the plan you and my parents made for me." I gathered my things and stood to leave.

He reached across the table and grabbed my wrist. Hard. "Don't do it."

I yanked on my arm. "Goodbye, Yates. I'll see you tonight at the gala."

"How did it go?" a voice spoke from behind me in the apartment lobby.

I stifled a scream and turned to see Porter, who looked like he'd been running. Moisture slicked the edges of his hair, and he wiped his face with his sleeve. There was something about athletic men that was so attractive, I decided as I studied him. Athletic men were healthier, stronger, better.

"What?" He watched me watch him.

I averted my eyes. "Nothing."

In the elevator, a saxophone rendition of *Lady In Red* played over the speakers.

"How did your coffee go with Yates?"

"Oh..." I stalled and shifted my body to hide my wrist, which still had faint hand marks from when Yates had grabbed it. "Yates showed up late."

"Is he responsible for sending that letter?"

"I don't think so."

"Do you know that for sure?"

"He looked pretty horrified when I showed him the note."

It could have been an act. Yates was good at hiding things, and I was bad at finding them. Maybe I should have invited Porter. He would have seen through the bullshit. Didn't they train SEALs for that?

Porter met my eyes. "What did he say?"

"He asked me why he would sabotage my life when he wants to, uh, marry me."

Porter raised an eyebrow at me. "He asked you to marry him?"

"Not exactly." I blushed. "Yates insulted you, and in the same breath, he told me he asked my parents permission to marry me. Like it was up to them."

Porter looked interested. "What was the insult?"

I shook my head.

The corner of his mouth lifted. "What did he call me?"

My entire face was on fire. "He called you a 'military monkey.'"

Porter's eyebrows went up. "That's a new one."

"I told him you're twice the man he'll ever be... then, the words slipped out." I was pretty sure my face was an unhealthy shade of fire engine red.

He was smiling now. "What did you say back?"

I fidgeted with the collar of my dress, tugging at the neckline that suddenly felt so suffocating.

"Beth?"

"I told him I was already engaged... to you."

His smile slipped.

CHAPTER 17

WE STOOD there in complete silence. I worked to steady my breath. I think I'd shocked him or broken him or *something*.

"Say something, please." I was near begging.

But he didn't speak.

I didn't think I could handle it if Porter was pissed at me. For some reason, it was imperative to me that he didn't hate me for my latest transgression. Or any transgression, really.

We stepped off the elevator and walked to my apartment in silence. Inwardly, I freaked out. Would Porter leave? Had he had enough of the games I was playing with my family?

I could fix this. I'd just call Yates and tell him that I'd lied. It'd be an easy fix, and maybe I could convince Porter to stay, although, I didn't really want to examine why that was so important to me.

In the living room, Porter turned around and inspected me. For longer than was comfortable.

"What...are you thinking?"

"I think we should talk strategy if I'm going to be your fake fiancé."

My breath caught in my throat.

Shocked, "You're going to pretend to be my fiancé?"

He shrugged and eyed me speculatively.

"Why would you do that?"

"Not sure."

"Okay..." I felt uncertain about how to proceed. "What kind of strategy were you thinking?"

"Do you think Yates will tell anyone?"

I shook my head. "I don't think so."

"So, we keep up the pretense with only him."

"Okay."

"And we keep this to ourselves."

My breath rushed out of my throat. "Agreed."

"We'll remain friends. Our secret."

Translation: no more kissing.

Just two friends. One helping the other one out. I couldn't help but feel a bit disappointed about that, but I wasn't surprised either.

"Agreed."

He ran his fingers through his hair, making it stick up in all directions. "And before it goes too far, when you've got your situation with Yates sorted out, we'll quietly end this."

"Good plan." I nodded vigorously. Those were good terms. Terms I could live with. "Yes."

We stood there, staring at each other. I wasn't sure how I was even meeting his eyes.

"So, do I need a tux for tonight?"

The gala.

The *fucking* gala.

It was my turn to do the slow blink as I processed what he was telling me. "You want to come tonight?"

"Might as well."

"Okay. Yes." I searched for my phone. "I know a really great tailor that can have you fitted with a rental. It might cost extra for the rush, but they're the best."

I pulled out my phone and found the address. I wrote it on a piece of paper and handed it to him. "I'll call there. They'll be expecting you."

Hard-to-read grey eyes met mine. "Thanks."

"Thank you," I breathed. I had no idea why he was helping me out like this, but I was unbelievably grateful.

"I'll shower and then head out."

"Okay."

I called the tailor and gave him my credit card after Porter left. I flopped back on my bed. I debated calling Emily, but I had too much to say and doubted I could articulate any of it. This situation was getting complicated, but if it meant Yates would get off my back, it would all be worth it.

How had things gotten to this point? Porter had stood up for me, to my mom of all people. He would make an awesome boyfriend. Why would Felicia leave him? What could possibly have happened between them that she would leave without even saying goodbye?

I'd been living with him for a short time, and so far, I hadn't seen anything wrong with him. He was tidy, generous, and thoughtful. He also rocked a hot-as-sin body, and judging by the bulge I had seen last night, there were no size issues in 'that' department.

Maybe he was bad in bed?

I thought about the near kiss between Porter and me and immediately dismissed the thought. There was *no way* he could be bad in bed. Last night, he had effortlessly flipped me around in bed, indicating that he knew what he was doing.

I wanted to find out for myself.

Which was my dumbest idea yet. Porter had made it clear that we'd remain just friends. He was helping me out with this bizarre favor. And we shared a mutual friendship with Jackson and Emily. So, I needed to tuck my libido out of sight. I needed to control myself. I would not get drunk and throw myself at Porter. And I would refrain myself from embarrassing him and myself.

Desperate times called for desperate measures. The best way to ensure I didn't throw myself at anyone was to take care of business myself. I reached into my nightstand and pulled out my trusty vibrator. Porter wouldn't be home for at least another hour. I had time.

I kicked off my panties and climbed under my covers. I shut my eyes, trying to conjure my favorite fantasy.

Public sex.

I'd never done it, but I loved the idea of it. I pictured myself at the mall. Shopping in a skirt and extremely high heels. My faceless lover would come up behind me, grab my hand and pull me to some deserted back hallway. No one was around. I groaned, imagining as he spun me around, pushing me so I faced the wall. I could feel Porter's hand slide slowly up my thigh.

My eyes sprung open.

What was Porter doing in my fantasy?

I shut my eyes and willed him away, replacing him with my face-less lover. His hand slid slowly up my thigh, before reaching my pussy. He loved to fuck me fast and hard, exactly the way I loved it.

I turned on my vibrator and slowly worked it between my legs.

Oh, God. *Yes.*

He flipped my skirt up and whispered filthy things into my ear, his breath hot against my neck. The sound of his zipper, and then, he'd push himself into me.

I moaned. He took me rough and fast, hitting me perfectly with each thrust. I was so close. Porter's hot, thick cock pounded into me from behind. *Porter again!* Oh God, it might be wrong to fantasize about him, but at this point, I didn't care.

I moaned against his hand covering my mouth, trying to quiet my loud moans. I loved the feel of him thrusting into me, the sensation of being taken. I loved how he filled me. I was so close. I was going to come.

The door flung open, and I gasped, lifting my head. Porter stood in the doorway, looking around.

Is that a gun—a fucking gun—in his hand?

Violence filled his every feature, as he assessed the room before his eyes landed on me. "Are you alone?" his voice remained low, straight to the point.

I nodded, unable to speak. *Holy fuck.* I worked to even my breath, desperately trying to look like I was waking up from a nap—and not like I had six inches of a vibrating dildo inside me.

Porter lowered his gun and shook his head. "Sorry, I heard a cry. Like you were being tortured. Are you okay?"

"Fine." I all but choked out.

He stopped, his eyes narrowed. I could tell he was listening. The faint hum of my vibrator sounded from under the covers, which barely covered my waist. The vibrator was doing it's very best to get me off with its relentless movements inside me. I clenched my thighs together, hoping it would dull the noise.

It did, but that was almost my undoing. I fought my orgasm with clenched teeth.

Grey eyes met mine. Understanding dawned on them. "Oh, shit." He exhaled, but he didn't move.

Too late. I didn't know if it was the sight of him—his rippling muscles covered in a plain tee, holding a big gun like he was ready to defend me to his death—or the fact that I'd already been on the verge, but my body said, *fuck it.* My thighs clenched around the spinning, vibrating dildo, and I needed to come.

My head fell back on the pillow, my neck and back arched as sensations rolled through my body. Wondrous, fabulous, intense sensations. A moan escaped me. As sick as it was, it was hotter with Porter standing there, watching.

A cry escaped my throat as my hips and back arched toward the ceiling. My whole body trembled and jerked as I tried to control the orgasm washing over me.

When I came down from the pleasure, realization sunk in. Heavy breathing and buzzing filled the air. I needed to make it stop. I reached down and awkwardly, so awkwardly, managed to turn my vibrator off.

Silence echoed between us. Mortification didn't come close to describing how I felt. If a hole the size of Texas opened up and sucked me into the ground, it wouldn't be big enough.

Porter stood stock-still. His intensity shocked me. Hot lust burned in his eyes as he took in the thin tank top covering my heaving chest and hard nipples. His skin flushed red, and he breathed hard enough that I could see his ribcage rise and fall.

My little show had turned him on.

"Porter." My voice was hoarse and raspy, like rough sex personified, but I couldn't stop it. I couldn't control myself. I should say something. Smooth this over. Crack a joke. Ease the tension. But words eluded me, and I couldn't say anything but his name.

He swallowed. Hard. He was visibly fighting himself. Fighting *this*. Us. What would I do if he whipped off his shirt and approached me?

You'd welcome him with open arms, Beth.

Our gaze held. His resolve visibly wavering. If I made a move towards him, he'd lose this fight. Instead, I stayed silent. I didn't know what held him back, but I didn't want to get him in a moment of weakness. I wanted him to make that decision with his brain, not his dick.

He swore softly under his breath, turned, and walked out, shutting the door firmly behind him. I groaned, plopping my head onto my down feather pillow.

See that, Beth? Neither his brain nor his dick wants you.

CHAPTER 18

I TOOK a page out of my mom's book, who is the master of burying her head in the sand, and I pretended that Porter hadn't just seen me in the most compromising of situations. I showered, styled my hair into a high chignon, and applied flawless makeup that made my blue eyes pop, and my lips look pillowy soft.

The Chanel dress I wore brushed the floor, the square line and nipped waist flattering my figure. The back dipped so low, I didn't bother with underwear. The diamond drop earrings my grandparents have given me for my 16th birthday adorned each ear, and the strappy black heels caressing my toes were the highest I owned.

Porter was in the kitchen. I could hear him, and the last thing I wanted to do was face him. Did he still want to come to the gala or did he have his bags packed? I couldn't blame him if he was done with this charade. This was supposed to be his safe haven, but so far, it had been nothing but a whole lot of drama and angst.

Time to face the music.

Walking into the living room, I focused on the black Chanel clutch, making sure I had everything I needed. The truth was, I needed a few more seconds before I had to make eye contact.

I lifted my head and froze. Porter took my breath away. Hand in one pocket, he looked fabulous in his bespoke tux. Mouthwateringly hot. I wasn't usually at a loss for words, but my mind went blank.

"You look beautiful."

I shivered as his eyes took me in. "You look beautiful, too....in a very manly, masculine sort of way."

A long, wavering silence hovered between us. His jaw was tight as he stared back at my face. On edge. Maybe I should say something. About before. I wanted to, I mean, I really wanted to, but the words stuck in my throat, and I was barely getting air into my lungs as it was.

My phone buzzed.

"The car's here." I turned in relief.

We didn't speak as we made our way down to the car. The driver held the door open for me. I took a deep breath as Porter made his way to the other side. I really needed to break the ice. This tension between us was practically vibrating the air. No pun intended.

The vehicle moved.

Porter spoke from beside me. "I apologize for coming into your room unannounced."

Coming.

He didn't mean it like that, but good God, that word would never be the same.

Too embarrassed to look at him, I focused out the window. "I'm sorry, too. I didn't intentionally mean to...uh...."

"Show me the grand finale?"

The grand finale, is that what he called it when I orgasmed in front of him?

Yeah. That.

"Yes."

"That's what made it so damn hot."

My head whipped around, noting that the heat had returned to his eyes. "I'd have thought that was a bit high on the kink factor for you."

Grey eyes held mine. "It turned me on, but as far as my kink meter goes, it didn't even register."

Oh, wow.

"Are you trying to tell me you're kinky?"

"For some women, I'm out of their comfort zone."

"Now you have my attention."

It was his turn to look out the window. "I'm not for everyone."

"You'd be hard-pressed to find one woman who agrees with that statement."

He met my eyes again. "Felicia and I weren't compatible."

The idea was ludicrous. They were both so beautiful in their own right.

I bit my lip. "How could you two not be compatible?"

"She preferred things a bit... tamer."

I worked to keep my mouth from dropping. Felicia looked like her calling in life was to have wild sex. How could she possibly be tamer than him? Porter was the all-American guy, with his healthy, athletic glow and blue jeans and tees. He drove a pickup truck for crying out loud! He looked like he invented the missionary position. I was supposed to believe *he* was the kinky one?

"Exactly how kinky are you?"

"The women I've met prefer to be in control in all aspects of their lives. And most of them have trouble relinquishing that control in bed."

I worked to keep my breath even. "And you?"

His pause killed me. "I get off being completely in control when I have sex."

My stomach whooshed like I was racing down a roller coaster. I had a vision of him holding my arms above my head. Perhaps tying them to the bedpost. Doing every dirty thing he wanted to my body while I lay there, restrained, only able to take.

Heat traveled over my body. This conversation was turning me on. I was clenching my thighs together, and I had to work to relax them. My throat dried as I spoke. "So, do you have some sort of red room, like *Fifty Shades of Grey?*"

His eyes dropped to my mouth. "I don't need toys or for my partner to call me 'sir'. I like to be in charge."

Something hot and electric crackled between us. I tried to deny it, but I couldn't ignore the way I worked to breathe like a normal person. "And that's a problem?"

His eyes darkened. "For some."

If I was an addict, this conversation was my drug of choice. I couldn't get enough. "What else?"

He weighed me. Measured me. "I like a good dose of dirty talk."

Oh, my. Did they teach Navy SEALs to read minds? This was my fantasy. "What's wrong with that?"

"Most women aren't really into that."

I wanted to raise my hand and shout, "Pick me!" Instead, I cleared my throat and said, "They don't know what they're missing."

The moment was broken when the car halted, and the driver rounded the car to open my door.

We had arrived.

My entire body trembled as I stepped out of the car. It should have been from nerves, from my fear of fucking this up for Dad. But it wasn't. It was Porter.

Always Porter.

CHAPTER 19

BAYSWATER'S BALLROOM had been transformed for the gala. In the foyer outside the ballroom, my parents held a reception line that would make the queen envious.

"Beth." Mom scrutinized me. "You're flushed. Is everything okay?" The woman had an amazing ability to pinpoint exactly what I tried to hide.

I glanced at Porter. His lips twitched.

I changed the subject. "Mom. You remember Porter."

Her expression cooled as she shifted her gaze to him. "Of course."

"Good evening, ma'am."

"Porter," Dad's voice boomed, his smile huge. "So nice you could make it."

"Thank you, sir." Porter's manners were the only genuine thing in a mile radius.

"I was just telling some of my colleagues that my daughter is dating a military man. Everyone here respects and appreciates your service." Dad's eyes shone. "I'd love to introduce you around later."

Oh, boy.

Dad was in full-blown campaign mode.

"I'd be happy to, sir."

"Fantastic." Dad beamed at Porter, barely sparing me a glance. "That's fantastic."

"We're going to find something to drink." I nodded my head toward the ballroom.

Mom frowned at me. "Aren't you going to join the reception line?"

No chance in hell.

"We'll come back," I lied, as I slipped my hand into Porter's hand and tugged him away.

We stood on the sidelines of the ballroom. It was a monstrosity of a room, with a dozen chandeliers and elaborate pillars. French doors opened to the huge stone balcony. The room was filled with New York's elite. Some people I recognized from the front of the society pages, other people I had grown up with.

A waiter handed us flutes of champagne as we assessed the party, trying to take it all in.

"So, what's our endgame here?" Porter spoke into my ear.

I worked to not shudder at the feeling of his hot breath on my ear. "Our goal is to survive this night while keeping a low profile."

Which wouldn't be an easy task considering this was my father's big night.

"Anything I should know?"

I paused, thinking. "Don't commit to anything. If someone invites you out, politely deflect but don't commit."

He snorted. "Okay."

We stood and silently watched as people milled around. I couldn't get Porter's words out of my head. He admitted that he loved to take control during sex. My kink was I loved to give up control. When I was between the sheets, I wanted to be bossed around.

I peered at Porter through my eyelashes. I needed to remember why it would be a bad idea to sleep with him. He was my houseguest, and he was nursing a broken heart.

He was best friends with Jackson and Emily, which meant I'd

probably see him at family events until the end of time. And he didn't seem interested in anything but a friendship with me. Plus, he was helping me out with the whole fake-fiancé thing.

Sleeping with this man would be a stupid move on so many levels, but that didn't stop this intense physical longing I felt for him.

"What are you thinking about?" His low voice broke through my thoughts.

"Is that why you two broke up?" I couldn't bring myself to say her name.

Grey eyes widened at my intrusive question. He knew exactly what I was asking. He took his time answering. "Those are my preferences, but by no means are they mandatory. Once I figured out that she wasn't into that, I was fine with slow, meaningful sex and cuddles." His tone held so much dry sarcasm, I almost choked on my champagne.

"Are you telling me you reined back all your kink?"

"It wasn't that bad."

I thought about my own past. It wasn't like I had been super honest with Yates about my preferences between the sheets. "I get it."

"You do?"

I nodded. "Oh yeah."

Porter looked like he wanted to say something but the dinner gong sounded.

———

"You deserve a treat for putting up with this night." I stared up at Porter's face.

I'd downed more than my fair share of wine as I feigned interest in painful conversation with table mates I barely knew. The speeches were worse, and I was grateful when the tables were cleared.

Porter cocked a brow, interest brimming in his eyes. "Like what?"

"Maybe another episode of *Grey's Anatomy*?"

"How soon can we leave?" A smile teased his lips.

"Soon."

A woman in a pale blue dress caught my eye. She reminded me of Traci, but it couldn't be. What would my former boss be doing at this gala? I strained my neck, struggling to see if it was her. I caught a glimpse of her profile. I was almost certain that was Traci, and if she was here, I wanted to know why.

I shifted my gaze to Porter. "Will you excuse me a moment?"

"Of course."

I took off across the room, weaving around couples, catching and losing sight of the woman. She disappeared around the corner. I only caught a glimpse, but I swore that it was her.

I managed to weave my way through the crowd and reached the corner when a strong arm grabbed mine, spinning me around.

"Where are you rushing off to?" Yates' voice drawled.

I tried to yank my arm from his. "Yates, let me go. This isn't funny."

"I need to talk to you." His voice was serious, but I didn't care. He stopped being my problem when he cheated on me.

Speaking of, I needed to find Traci.

"Later." I managed to yank my arm from his. "I'm in the middle of something."

He stepped in front of me, blocking my path. "What are you doing?"

I peered around him. "Did you see Traci walk past here?"

Yates glanced over his shoulder. "Are you serious?"

"I saw her. She was wearing a light blue dress. Her hair was pinned up."

A smug expression crossed his face. "When are you going to admit to yourself that you're not over me?"

"What?" Displeasure wrapped itself around my vocal chords, seeping into my tone.

"You're obsessed with Traci. You keep bringing her up. Now you're seeing her like someone would see a ghost? You know this has nothing to do with her and everything to do with me."

"Excuse me?"

He lowered his voice. "The fact that you can't let her go tells me that you're still stuck on me and what happened."

"Don't be an ass."

"It's true," he insisted. "Even this whole charade with your military man. That's your elaborate ruse to get me back."

"You're insane."

"He's all wrong for you."

"At least he's faithful to me."

Two spots of color stained Yates' cheekbones. "I'm not going to move on. You and I are destined to be together."

"No."

"Quit screwing up my life."

"How am I screwing up your life? You have nothing to do with this."

"I have everything to do with this." The guy wasn't making any sense.

I stepped back. "Good night, Yates."

"Your father is going to put a stop to this nonsense."

I froze. "Excuse me?"

He leaned down and hissed in my face. "Should have seen his face when I told him. You think he's going to let you marry some common soldier? Think again." Holy shit. Yates told my father I was engaged to Porter?

I glared up at him, infuriated beyond belief. "You told him? How dare you!"

He shrugged and put one hand in his pocket, already bored with this conversation. "You think I'm going to let you marry that guy?"

"Screw you, asshole."

I turned and walked away, holding my head high, but I was rattled inside. Dad knew? And he hadn't said anything? This fiancé ruse was supposed to be exclusive to Yates, but now that Dad knew, I felt the tethers between Porter and me tightened.

And I dreaded telling him.

CHAPTER 20

I FOUND PORTER OUTSIDE, leaning against the huge stone railing of the balcony. He looked like a model in an expensive ad. He fit into this world better than I did.

"Find what you were looking for?"

"Porter..." I paused, trying to find the words.

"What is it?"

A voice spoke over the loudspeakers. *"May I have everyone's attention, please?"*

Dad was about to announce his candidacy. We could listen to the announcement, then leave. I'd tell Porter that Dad knew about our fake engagement on the way home, but first, we needed to get through the speech.

I gave Porter an apologetic smile and promised, "Just one more event. Dad's going to announce his candidacy, they'll have their first dance, then we can go."

Porter offered me his arm. I slid my hand onto it, and we entered the ballroom. Everyone had stopped talking and stared at my parents on the stage.

Dad looked out into the audience, spotted me, and said into the microphone, "Beth? Will you and Porter please join me on stage?"

Oh, boy.

Porter and I shared a glance. I felt like I was walking to a guillotine as the crowd parted for Porter and me to approach the stage.

"What's this about?" he asked quietly against my hair.

"No idea," I spoke through my fake smile.

Dad talked to the crowd about leadership and his background in business before he announced his plans to run for mayor. The clapping sounded like thunder.

He raised his hand, silencing the obedient group. "I have one more announcement. I wasn't going to say anything, but I'm so damn proud, you'll have to forgive me." He glanced over at me and held my gaze. "Porter Lyons, my daughter's boyfriend, is an esteemed member of the military. We all love the men and women that dedicate their lives to the service of this great country, so it's with both pride and joy that I announce that wedding bells are in the near future for this happy couple."

What. Just. Happened?

Flashes of cameras temporarily blinded me, but not before I saw the shock cross Porter's face.

"Come here, my darling daughter." Dad opened his arms, inviting me in for a hug.

With robotic legs, I moved to hug him while the crowd cheered and yelled.

He kissed both my cheeks. "I couldn't be more happy for you, Beth."

I moved to hug my mom, aware that Porter was shaking Dad's hand.

Tears welled up in Mom's eyes. "He's not my first choice," she whispered. "But this is going to be excellent for your father's campaign. And I'm going to put my differences aside and plan the wedding of the century for you."

Speechless. No words came out of me.

Dad approached the mic. "I invite you all to join us in our celebrations."

On cue, the band started. I watched, numb, as Dad led Mom down to the dance floor. Porter moved to stand beside me, his expression carefully blank.

"I don't know what to say," I said through my pained smile.

He grabbed my hand and tugged me off the stage. I didn't ask where we were going when he pulled me past the crowd that circled the dance floor. He led me out of the ballroom and searched for an empty room. I tripped behind him, terrified of what he would say. Whatever it was, I deserved it.

He opened the door to a smaller banquet room and ushered me in. The room was dark, lit only by the streaming moonlight shining through glass windows. He walked away from me. And for a long, terrible moment, we didn't speak.

He turned and looked at me. Like, really looked at me.

"I'm sorry," I started.

"For what?"

"For all that."

"Did you tell your dad?"

"No!"

"So, don't apologize."

Okay, then. More silence. This game had escalated beyond either of our expectations. Would he walk? My heart beat faster.

"So much for keeping this to ourselves."

"Are you mad?"

"No."

I looked around the room. If he wasn't going to lecture me, what were we doing here?

"What do you want to do?" his voice was quiet but calm.

"What do you mean?"

That grey stare held my gaze. "This is your life, Beth. I'm only an actor in all of this. Eventually, I'm going to go back to my life, and this won't impact me, but you're going to have to deal with a wedding that doesn't happen."

The thought was sobering. I hadn't considered that. As far as I'd been concerned, this was all about keeping Yates at arm's length. Now that this was public, it was an entirely different matter. Mom had just promised she was going to plan the wedding of the century. Telling my parents that this was just a joke on Yates was a conversation I didn't want to have.

I swallowed. "You're worried about me?"

"A little bit."

"Mom is already planning the wedding. Dad announced this to the entire world." I tried but failed to keep the panic out of my voice. "Why would Yates tell my dad about this?"

"Maybe he thought he'd put a stop to it?"

"If that was the case, it backfired."

"Why don't we get out of here? We don't need to make any decisions tonight."

"Yeah, good idea. I'll quickly say goodnight to my parents."

We found Dad at the bar, getting a drink. What could I say to him? This was his night. His moment.

He glanced at Porter before saying, "Sorry for springing that on you both. I wasn't going to say anything, but I looked over at you, and I was so proud of my little girl."

Tears blurred my eyes. I couldn't remember the last time he'd said he was proud of me. The fact that he was proud of me over a lie, just made it worse. "It's okay."

He reached forward and warmly shook Porter's hand. "Son, welcome to the family."

"Thank you, Sir."

"Are you two lovebirds heading out?"

I nodded because no words would escape. I was completely blank. At a total loss as to how to handle the magnitude of this lie. He winked broadly at Porter.

"Good night, Dad," I managed, before turning to walk. It took half of the length of the ballroom to realize Porter wasn't behind me.

He was shaking hands with Dad again. I should end this charade. Immediately. Tomorrow. I would deal with the entire mess tomorrow. I waited for Porter in the lobby, then he ushered me to the car.

We were halfway home, both silent. Lost in our own thoughts.

I turned to him. "What did my dad say to you on the way out?"

Porter sighed and reached into his jacket pocket. "He wanted me to give you this."

It was a ring box. With trembling fingers, I lifted the lid. Grandma's engagement ring. "He gave you this?"

Porter's expression was hard to read. "He said this ring had always been your dream ring."

Oh no.

I stared down at the jaw-dropping, five-carat, perfectly round diamond set in a platinum band, encrusted with smaller diamonds. As a child, I'd always grabbed Granny's hand to stare at it.

Even in the dim light of the car, the diamond caught the light and sparkled.

"What did you say?" My voice shook a bit.

"I told him I'd buy you my own damn ring, but he said this ring was part of your grandma's will, and she wanted you to have it."

I told him that I'd buy you my own damn ring.

I looked over at Porter. He was staring silently out the window, wearing a killer tux, looking like he had lived in this world his entire life.

"Are you upset?"

He gave me a wry smile. "Mildly affronted because I'd never let my fiancée wear a ring her father gave me."

My fiancée.

I swallowed. "Sorry about that."

"I guess it doesn't matter, since this is a charade and everyone is going to expect a ring, and there's no way I'd ever be able to afford a ring like that."

It was easily worth six figures. When I was a girl, I had childish romantic dreams about this ring. I daydreamed about a handsome prince, sweeping me off my feet with a romantic proposal. Now I had the handsome prince, but he was only pretending to be mine, and there was no romantic proposal in sight.

It dawned on me that, in my haste to lie my way out of an uncomfortable situation, I was ruining future moments. If I ever had a real fiancé, would we still want to use this ring? If we did, would I think of Porter and this moment every time I glanced at my ring finger? The whole thing saddened me.

"I think I'm in over my head."

Finally, a truth, but it didn't make anything better.

CHAPTER 21

I STOOD, waiting for my Americano when I noted someone sitting at a table. Actually, it was the newspaper they were reading that I noticed.

There, on the front of the paper, was a photo of my parents, myself and Porter. We were on the stage from last night, and we were smiling. It was the headline that made my heart pound.

STIRLING HEIRESS SAYS, "YES!"

No, no, no! I grabbed my coffee and rushed to the corner store. I found four more major newspapers that announced my impending nuptials on the front page. I bought them all, and with my head bowed, headed back to my apartment.

I was dreading seeing Porter's face. He'd already gone to the gym when I'd woken up, and I'd immediately dipped out for a coffee. There were hundreds of newspaper stands in my area. Oh, God. Had he seen the headlines?

This was bad. My lie was publicly announced to eight million strangers. How the hell was I going to tell Mom that this relationship was a sham? There was no way. At this point, the best I could do was plan a fake break-up. Right?

I almost ran into someone heading into my building. "Sorry." My apologetic smile slipped almost instantly.

Felicia.

She stared at me with red eyes. Blotched red painted her cute nose, and she'd obviously been crying. Extensively.

"Felicia."

"I need to talk to you." Her voice was so much smaller than the last time I'd heard it.

"Of course." I opened building door.

We rode the elevator in silence. I prayed that Porter was home because this was one conversation I didn't want to have on my own. I unlocked my front door and ushered her in. We were alone.

She evaluated my apartment. Disbelief filled her features. "This is where you live?"

"How did you find me?"

"I called your dad's campaign manager, Yates. His name was in the newspaper. He gave me your address."

Fucking Yates.

"Okay," I said slowly, shoving the newspapers on the island. "Would you like some tea?"

"No, what I want is for you to get the fuck away from my man." She radiated with emotion, and despite the fact that she was makeup-free and had been crying, she was still one of the most beautiful women I had ever seen.

"I don't really know what to say," I said carefully.

"Porter is mine. He's always been mine, and he always will be," her voice hitched. "I don't know how the fuck you got him to ask you to marry him, but this wedding isn't going to happen."

If only she knew.

The irony almost killed me. "I think this is a conversation that you should have with Porter."

She crossed her arms over her full breasts. "How can I talk to him when he refuses to talk to me? He won't answer my texts, and he won't return my phone calls. I've left him dozens of messages."

"I don't know what to say about that."

"You stole him." She pierced me with her blue gaze. "I finally got him to New York. I finally got him to care enough to come after me, and suddenly, there you are. But you should know there's no way you can compete with what he and I share. He loves me."

I stared helplessly at her.

"He loves me," she repeated with force.

I believed her. And it struck me that this engagement was not only wholly screwing up my life, but it was screwing up Porter's future, too.

"Why did you leave him?" I asked, truly baffled. I felt angry at her, too, for hurting him. No matter how good he was at hiding his wounds, I could still see them. "You had everything with him, but you left. Why?"

"You have no idea what you've gotten yourself into, do you?" She scoffed. "Porter doesn't allow himself to be happy."

I stood completely still. What did that mean?

She gave me a sad smile. "He hasn't told you, has he?"

"Told me what?"

"He hasn't forgiven himself. His entire life is about self-retribution. I stupidly thought that if he felt a loss big enough, then maybe he would feel enough in his heart to fight for us."

"That's why you left?"

Her eyes filled with tears. "He came for me. He found me, but you ruined everything. You can never make him happy, you know that?"

I knew that, but I couldn't exactly tell her that.

"I want you to break off your engagement. If you have a sliver of love in your heart for him, you need to set him free," her voice wavered. "He was close with me. He was so close to being happy with me." She silently turned and walked out.

What a fucking mess. She loved him. That, I believed. He had come after her. And I had somehow gotten in between them. I had lit a fuse for a massive bomb that was set to blow up my life, but it hadn't dawned on me that Porter's life would be collateral damage. And according to her, he was already damaged, punishing himself for something that was none of my damn business.

I needed to make this right. And somehow, I needed to get Porter back on track. The guy had been nothing but good to me, but it wasn't acceptable that his charity should cost him his future happiness.

I grabbed my purse. This engagement needed to end. No matter what. I would tell my parents the truth and let the chips fall. And then I would do my best to steer Porter back to Felicia.

CHAPTER 22

I RODE the elevator down to the garage. When the door opened, there stood Porter. His hair was damp, and he wore a faded grey t-shirt that stretched across his fantastic chest.

We gazed at each other.

"Going somewhere?" His tone was relaxed.

"I'm going to fix this mess I got you into." I stepped past him.

He grabbed my arm gently. "What do you mean?"

"Felicia dropped by."

Those gorgeous grey eyes widened. "Where is she?"

"She left."

He winced and rubbed the side of his jaw. "What did she say?"

Was it true? Did he really not allow himself happiness? Why would she say that?

I needed to ask some hard questions, but I wasn't sure I'd like the answers. "Why are you so agreeable about this fake relationship?"

He shrugged. "It's no big deal."

"What about you?"

Wariness seeped into his posture. "What about me?"

"Why did you come to New York?"

"What do you mean?"

"You came here to get back more than a few boxes, didn't you?"

Something crossed his face, but he didn't answer.

"Fine." I took a step back. "If you want to screw up your life, that's your business, but I'm not going to help you fuck up your happiness." I stepped around him and walked past parked cars, the sound of my footsteps echoing off the cement walls. I reached my car and was about to open the door when a strong hand grabbed me and spun me around.

He was towering over me. "You're not fucking up my happiness." His voice was calm, but his intense expression penetrated.

"That's not what Felicia told me."

"I don't know what she said, but I can make my own decisions."

"She loves you."

"She left me," he practically yelled in my face.

We stood too close.

"This is such a colossal mess," I yelled back, pushing against his hard chest.

He didn't budge. "I know."

My chest rose and fell with the weight of my emotion. "Our faces are plastered on the front of every newspaper. Announcing our fake engagement."

"I know."

"I'm freaking out. I've resigned myself to the fact that, when this entire thing blows up, I'm going to have to move out of the country and change my name, but I can't be responsible for messing up your life, too."

"My life was messed up long before you even met me."

"It can be fixed. Felicia said she's been calling you. She said you don't call her back."

"I can't." His voice was low, his gaze troubled.

"Why not?"

He struggled to find the right words. "I can't deal with her right now."

It was my turn to be bewildered. "You don't want her back?"

He pushed his hands into his hair. "I don't know what I want."

I spoke slowly, "Is that why you've been so unbelievably agreeable about all of this? Because you wanted to prevent yourself from taking her back?"

Conflicted emotion flashed across his face. "I don't know. Maybe."

I don't know why that one word hurt so much, but it did. There it was. He loved her, but for whatever reason, he couldn't deal with her right now. I suspected I knew how he felt, but hearing it made me feel alone.

I tried to put my feelings into words. "My entire life I've been on the wrong side of everything. Yates was always taking my parents' side. I know that you're not real, but for a moment I actually thought you were on my side."

"I *am* on your side."

"No. You're using this situation to deal, or not deal, with the woman you love. You've always had your own agenda."

"I'm trying to help you. If it helped me, too, why is that an issue?"

Because at the end of this, he still had someone who loved him and wanted him back. At the end of this, I would need a witness protection plan to protect me from this disaster. Porter had felt like my partner-in-crime, but that, like everything else in this situation, was a delusion.

"Just once, I want someone to have my back," my voice cracked. "I need one person in my corner. And I unfairly imposed that role on you. So I apologize. I'll fix this. I promise." I turned to unlocked my car door, but before I could open the door, two strong arms planted on either side of me, holding the door shut.

"What makes you think I'm not in your corner?" His lips were against my ear. His hot breath made me shiver.

I dropped my head as a wild tremor zipped up my spine. "You don't have to do this."

"Do what?"

"This," my voice cracked.

"Are you talking about the fake engagement?" His lips traced along the side of my neck. "Or are you talking about this?"

"What do you think?" I evaded the question, as my head arched to expose more skin.

"I think we both want the same thing."

He wasn't talking about our engagement, that much was clear. Oh, my. I knew what he was implying. God help me, but I wanted what he was offering.

"We do?"

His body moved against me, pushing me, so the cold glass and metal of my car pressed against me. "I think we do."

A moan escaped me when his big hand wrapped around my throat. He was gentle, but the message was clear—he was in charge. It turned me on so much it made my knees fucking weak.

"What about our rule?"

"I won't tell anyone if you don't."

I whimpered as hot lust rushed through my body.

And then that smooth voice growled low in my ear, "Are you going to tell anyone?"

My entire body trembled. This. This was precisely what I wanted. "No."

"Are you sure?" His teeth grazed the skin of my neck.

I squirmed, loving how his huge body had me pinned. "Yes."

He moved his hand from my throat to my hair, tugging my head back. I gasped into his mouth as it covered mine. It should have been an awkward kiss, but his mouth somehow managed to slant perfectly over mine.

My lips parted and his tongue dominated. My neck arched back further as I submitted to his kiss. Oh geez, his mouth. It was perfect. He tasted minty and smooth. Hot with so much lust, I moaned.

The shrill sound of my phone jarred my living fantasy. He lifted his head from mine, both of us breathing hard.

"You should answer your phone."

"I don't want to," I whispered.

"If we break this rule," his rough voice affirmed his desire, "everything will change."

"It will?"

"It will. Is this something you want?"

CHAPTER 23

HE STEPPED AWAY FROM ME. My whole body trembled as I clung to the side of my car. I listened to his footsteps retreat, and I wanted to yell after him that his hot body was exactly what I wanted, but I didn't turn around.

Now what? I tried to think, but my brain was muddled with white-hot lust. I got into my car, even though I knew I wouldn't be heading to my parents. I would willingly enter social exile if it meant I could have sex with that man.

I leaned my head against the steering wheel. That had been the most erotic, most intense sexual moment of my life to date. The desire I felt was so intense, it almost scared me.

Now what?

My phone pinged. Distracted, I pulled out the phone and replayed my message.

"Hey, Beth, this is Emily." She was silent so long, I was sure she'd hung up. "So, I was reading the newspaper, and it says you and Porter are engaged? Um. Do you have time to call me?"

An hour later, I sat on a park bench, my phone pressed to my ear. I had spilled my guts to my best friend, excluding some of the more salacious details, and now, silence screamed down the line between us.

"Say something," I urged Emily.

"Are you going to sleep with him?" she sounded both fascinated and scandalized at the same time.

"I don't know."

"I think you should," she encouraged me.

"What? You're supposed to be my voice of reason."

"I've always thought Porter was super hot."

"Emily."

She laughed. "It's his stare. It reminds me of Jackson. He's all intense and bossy."

"Yes, that."

And that kiss. The way his muscular body had pinned me. He'd been gentle but entirely in control. I'd felt safe, cared for and completely dominated. How was that even possible? Every time I recalled the feeling, my stomach felt shaky.

"What about Kirk?" she pressed.

"Who?"

"Kirk Browning. The love of your life?"

"Oh, you mean the father of my future children."

"Kirk has been your measuring stick for all men. And now Porter makes you forget who Kirk Browning is? I think you like him," she accused. "You like Porter."

I dropped my face into my hands. Damn. Leave it to Emily to point out those uncomfortable feelings I worked to avoid. "He's a friend."

She snorted. "Did he use his tongue when he kissed you?"

That tongue. It had felt like magic when he'd kissed me.

"Yes."

"Then, he's not a friend. Do you think he wants to date you?"

"Definitely not. He's using this situation to avoid Felicia, the woman his loves."

"That doesn't mean anything."

Leave it to Emily to be the amusing yet unrealistic romantic.

"I'm pretty sure this situation doesn't mean anything to him."

"Would it just be sex?"

"Friends with benefits?" I tried.

She paused so long it made me question everything decision I had made in the last five years. "Are you okay with that?"

I could still feel his big hand around my neck while he held me against my car. I shuddered at the memory. "Maybe this is something we both need."

The smile came through her voice. "I get that."

"You don't have to sound so smug."

"You never know where these things lead."

"Em, you need to brace yourself. This isn't going to have some fairy tale ending. With my fake engagement being spread across all of New York, this reads more like a tragedy."

"How long are you two going to pretend to be engaged?"

"I don't know," I answered honestly. "It's such a mess. Mom promised to plan the wedding of the century."

"She will, too."

"All of this because I was pissed at Yates. Because I wanted to wipe that perma-smug look off his face. I need to learn some self-control."

"I heard something about Yates."

"What?"

"Kimmy said she heard a rumor that his father is having some financial trouble."

"What? What kind of trouble?"

"I don't know all the details, but apparently, it's significant."

"How significant?"

Her voice was serious. "Extremely significant." She was holding something back.

"What else?"

"Kimmy doesn't know everything."

Okay. That meant that it was something big, and it was probably about me. "Spill it. Under the fourth agreement of the best friendship act, you're obligated to tell me."

"Don't be mad."

"Em, I won't be mad."

"Because that's part of the fourth agreement, too. You can't get mad."

"Come on, tell me."

"Kimmy said that's why Yates is pursuing you again."

"Why?" I was lost.

"Because."

"Emily. Help me connect the dots."

"Your money. Or you family's money."

White-hot rage blinded me for a moment. Suddenly, it all made sense. Yates' family was in crisis. What did a wealthy family do when they were going bankrupt? Anything in their power to reverse the process.

What had Yates said to me at the gala? Quit screwing up his life. Ha! One of the reasons why I'd loved dating Yates was that money had never been an issue between us. We both came from wealthy families. He had his own inheritance. I never had to worry that he was dating me for mine.

He didn't actually want me back. My face burned hot. All of this, this sham, was a stupid ploy to get to my father's money. None of this even had anything to do with me.

"Say something," Emily whispered in my ear. "I can tell you're mad."

"I'm not mad," I said between clenched teeth.

"You are. I shouldn't have said anything."

I took three even, deep breaths. "I'm not mad at you, Em."

"I think there's a part of Yates that still loves you," she said in a tiny voice. She was the one person who was always rooting for me. No matter what.

Tears stung my eyes. "I miss you."

"I miss you, too."

"When this shit storm passes, you mind if I head down there and spend a week hanging with you?"

"I'd love that. So would Theo."

"I'm over my head here, Em."

"You can do it."

"I need to figure out what I'm doing."

"You will."

"Should I sleep with Porter?

"Yes!"

We both laughed.

"Okay."

"Are you mad about Yates?"

"Livid."

"Yeah, I thought so."

"Any parting advice?"

"Yes. Don't wait until your wedding day to break off your engagement. Sending all those gifts back was a real bitch."

CHAPTER 24

THE MORE I thought of Yates, the more the pieces fell into place. His family needed money, so he sought the nearest cash source. I may not take any money from Dad, but I was his sole heir.

Mom came from significant money, but Dad was in a different league. He'd taken his inherited fortune and worked his entire life to multiply that amount over and over again.

Yates knew my biggest weakness was my relationship with my parents, which was probably why he'd become Dad's campaign manager. If he had my parents' support, he could increase the pressure on me to take him back.

He must have been desperate. I gave a short laugh. My fake engagement with Porter must be messing with his plans. It was stupid, but that made me feel a tiny bit better.

A sleek black town car, like the one Mom and Dad used, rolled to a stop across the street. The driver exited and opened the back door. A man in a black suit and sunglasses unfolded himself from the back seat.

He straightened his lapels and walked towards me. I squinted at him. He looked familiar, but I couldn't place him. Was he a friend of my father? Where did I know him from?

He sat down on the bench beside me. It was probably in my best interest to leave, but it was broad daylight, and there were enough people around that I wasn't too worried about my safety. I was, however, really curious about what he would say.

"Good afternoon, Beth."

I turned my head towards him. "Do I know you?"

His eyes were hidden beneath his aviator sunglasses. "Michael Renner."

The current mayor of New York?

I shifted to get a better look at him. "What do you want?"

He didn't spare me a glance. "You're father announced his candidacy."

"So?"

"It might be in your best interest if you convince him otherwise."

"Excuse me? What are you trying to say?"

He stood and peered down at me. "Your father doesn't know what he's gotten himself into."

Disbelief coursed through my veins. "What makes you think I have any power over him?"

He smiled benignly. "No one has more power over a man than his daughter."

I swallowed hard. "You seek me out and make vague, underwhelming threats. My father must be a big threat to you."

His smile never slipped. "Don't test me."

"Don't threaten me," I shot back.

His hand reached out, roughly grabbed my chin, and forced me to lift my face upwards towards him. "Feisty. You must know that's my weakness."

"Fuck you." I knocked his hand away.

Again with the creepy smile. "In a different time, I'd take great pleasure in taming you."

"In a different time, I'd take great pleasure kicking your balls back into your body."

He reached out and lightly tapped my cheek with the flat of his hand. "Maybe when you're father gets crushed in the elections, you'll allow me to take you to dinner. There's a lot I'd like to teach you."

I glared. "You disgust me."

He stood there for a long moment. "I look forward to the day when you beg me for forgiveness for speaking to me like this."

The man scared me. Before I could reply, he was moving across the street. He entered his car, and it slowly pulled away.

What the fuck was that?

I looked up and down the street. The mayor of New York had verbally threatened me, and no one had noticed.

Suddenly, I didn't feel that safe.

After driving aimlessly around the city for a few hours, I still had no answers. I was avoiding Porter and my apartment. I didn't want to see him until I had this sorted out.

I should set the guy free so that he could move forward and figure his life out. I should be honest with my parents and jump off this runaway train before my lies took us all down.

If I came forward with my secrets, would Porter still want to sleep with me? Would he move out? I wouldn't lie—I had a serious case of lust for that guy. Call me selfish, but for once in my life, I wanted to experience mind-blowing sex.

God knew, despite my best efforts, I was well on the path of everyone around me. Marrying some guy, who'd give me 2.5 kids and a home in the Hamptons. Another Yates, hopefully without the cheating. Was it wrong to want to experience something amazing? I was under no illusion that Porter and I had a future, but damn, I wanted a taste of what he offered.

I had no answers. Not for Porter. Not for myself. Tired of

driving, I made my way home. Porter's truck wasn't in any of the visi-
tors' stalls, so I let myself into the apartment with ease.

It was dark and completely silent. I dropped my bag and kicked
off my shoes, before turning on some lights. Seeing Porter's boxes still
stacked against the wall made me breathe a sigh of relief.

I wandered over to the island, where he'd left another note:

Went to grab some takeout for us. Hope you're hungry.

For a fake-boyfriend, he set the bar high for all future relationships.

I changed into yoga pants and a soft t-shirt, opened a bottle of
wine, and tasted my first glorious sip when he walked in the door. He
paused when he saw me. Our eyes met over the wine glass.

"Hope you like Thai food." He carried two white paper bags
to me.

"Thai Heaven is one of my favorite places to eat." I grabbed
plates.

In silence, we opened containers and filled our plates. He had
pinned me against my car while kissing me! I wracked my brain for a
thousand things to say, but he was the one person capable of making
me tongue-tied. So, we ate in silence.

"How's your food?" he finally broke the ice.

"Delicious. Especially the awkward silence."

He smiled into his beer can. "Want to talk?"

"Depends on what the topic of conversation is."

"Did you talk to your parents?"

"No."

"So, we're still engaged."

"For now."

He looked down at my granny's ring that sparkled on my finger.
"Are you going to wear that ring?"

"A girl needs some perks for taking a wrecking ball to her own
life."

"What did you do this afternoon?"

"I talked to Emily."

Amusement twinkled in his eyes. "Oh."

"What's that look for?"

"Trying to imagine that conversation."

I took my time answering. "I might have told her some things."

"And?"

"And," I played with my chopsticks, "she approves of all things Porter."

"Does she?"

"She does."

"Tell me something else." He held my gaze.

"I saw the mayor today."

"Of New York?"

"The one and only."

"What happened?"

"I was sitting on a bench, and his car rolled up. He came and sat beside me. He knew my name."

"What did he say?"

"He told me it was in my best interest to convince my father not to run for mayor." I could feel the shift in Porter.

He'd been relaxed, but now, alertness filled his every crevice. "What did you say?"

"I'm paraphrasing a bit, but I told him I wanted to kick him in the nuts."

"What else?"

I glanced down at my plate. "He grabbed my face."

"Motherfucker." Porter's eyes were like grey ice.

"And he said something about taming me and looking forward to making me beg for forgiveness."

"You're telling me that Michael Renner threatened you, touched you, then threatened you again?"

I shrugged. "It's not a big deal."

"I beg to differ."

We stared at each other.

He lifted his hand and gently pushed a strand of hair off my face. "Are you okay?"

For reasons I couldn't even begin to explain, that gesture made me want to burst into tears.

I am Beth Stirling. I don't cry.

I gave him my best wry smile. "I'm fine."

"Did he hurt you?" Damn those grey eyes and the way they seemed to see all the messy parts of me.

"He scared me a bit."

"I'm going to kill that motherfucker," Porter promised as he stood.

I grabbed his hand. "No, it's fine."

"No, it's not."

"Please. This is my father's stuff. This is typical political intimidation."

"You're father will want to know about this."

"No," I urged. "Absolutely not. He'd have the same reaction, only worse."

"Good. One of us needs to take care of this. So, it's either your dad or me, Beth."

"No." I shook my head. "Renner isn't going to do anything more than a few idle threats. But he wants to trip up my dad. And this is exactly how he'd do it."

He picked up our plates, stood there for a moment, and with complete frustration, carelessly tossed them in the sink with a loud clatter, food and all. He turned and focused on me, his hands fisted at his side. He was about to speak, and I was pretty sure I didn't want to hear what he had to say.

I beat him to the punch. "Promise me you won't do anything."

He leaned over the counter at me. "Why'd you tell me if you didn't want me to take care of this?"

Because if my body ends up in some river, I want one person to know.

"Just wanted to tell a friend."

He went completely still. He stared at me while frustration rolled off him. And then he was moving, taking his keys and wallet with him.

"Where are you going?"

"Out."

The door slammed behind him.

CHAPTER 25

IT WAS after midnight and Porter still hadn't come home. I'd cleaned the kitchen, paced, drank wine, paced, checked my phone about a hundred times, paced, bathed until the water turned cold, and paced some more.

Porter was unpredictable, and I had no idea if he'd respect my wishes and leave this alone or take matters into his own hands—maybe even tell my father? I honestly couldn't take the tension anymore. I needed to chill out.

I pulled on a tank top and a pair of panties before I climbed into bed, begging sleep to take me.

⸻

I startled awake. A dim light crept into my room from the hallway, and I followed it into the living room. The stove's exhaust light cast long shadows around the room.

Porter sat, fully dressed, on the couch. In the dim light, his expression was hard to read.

I hovered by the hallway. "You're home."

"I am," he said flatly.

I wrapped my arms around my waist, feeling too exposed near him. "Did you go talk to my dad?"

"No."

"How about anyone else?"

"I respected your wishes, Beth." His gravel tone sounded unimpressed.

"Thank you." Unsure, I stood silently, taking in his face and body. "Where did you go?"

"A bar."

Oh.

"Are you drunk?"

"I drank."

I felt like I should have said something, but words failed me.

He turned his face away from me. "I don't have a lot of self-control right now, Beth. You should go back to bed."

I shivered in anticipation at his low tone. "Are you telling me you're in a bossy mood?"

He met my eyes, piercing me with their intensity. "You don't know the half of it."

I hesitated, wanting to find out exactly how bossy this man could get, and partly fearing where that would lead us. "That sounds like a warning."

"That's exactly what that was." His eyes trailed down my body with such heat, it staggered me.

I couldn't remember the last time a man had looked at me like that.

"Come here," he instructed.

I took a few steps closer.

"Closer."

I moved up to stand between his open legs. He reached up and grabbed my wrist, tugging me down, so I straddled his lap. I wanted more than anything to touch him, but instead, I sat on his muscular thighs and appraised him.

"You pissed me off at dinner tonight." He brushed my hair back off my shoulder.

"I know."

"You think I can't protect you?"

"I know you can. I'm just not sure it's your job."

"I'm a SEAL. It's my job to defend and protect."

I chewed on my bottom lip. "I meant, I'm not sure if it's your job to protect *me*."

"Don't see anyone else fighting for the position."

"Well," I swallowed, "these days, that's the plight of a single Manhattan woman."

He traced one long finger over my tank top, down my sternum, between my breasts and down to my belly button. Our eyes met.

His voice vibrated low, "If we cross the line here, I don't care what we're calling this, it'll become my responsibility to protect you."

"Why?"

"Because I don't let anyone fuck with what's mine."

Oh.

My mouth parted in shock. Lust. Desire. But mostly shock.

His thumb slipped under my shirt, brushing against my bare stomach. He cocked his head slightly. "You got a problem with that?"

"With me becoming yours or you protecting me?"

"Either."

"No problem," I breathed.

Who the fuck was this guy? I examined his face, willing his gorgeous features to reveal the mystery I called Porter. With one smooth movement, he stood and flipped me around until I sat on the couch and he knelt between my legs.

I gasped when he yanked me down, so my ass was on the edge of the couch. The way he smiled should've scared me, but it thrilled me to my core.

"Lift up your hips," he instructed.

My feet went on tippy toes on the floor, and my breath caught in my throat when he yanked my panties down my legs. He tossed the offending fabric over his shoulder and pushed my legs apart, spreading them wide, exposing me to him completely.

Holy fuck.

Eyes wide, I clutched the couch and watched, mesmerized, as his big hands pushed beneath my tank top until it bunched up, exposing my chest. He grabbed my hands and placed them on my breasts.

"That's where your hands belong. Playing with those gorgeous nipples."

I laid there, not moving. Not playing.

"Show me," his rough voice encouraged me.

With shaking fingers, I plucked at my sensitive nipples, toying with the hard, pebbled buds. He watched me for a few moments, hunger devouring his gaze. Satisfied, he lowered his face between my legs. His lips nibbled on the soft inner skin of my thigh, grazing his teeth against the skin. Our eyes met.

His tongue licked up the length of me, sending me back onto my tippy toes. "You taste amazing."

I whimpered when his hands pressed on my thighs, pushing them further open. His tongue swirled and plundered. Sucked and invaded. His relentless explorations intoxicated me.

I loved the way his big hands pinned my hips down. I loved the feeling of his mouth on me. My head tossed back and forth. I gasped and bucked while my fingers pinched and tugged my nipples.

I trembled. My entire body shook. Time slowed down. Time sped up. The man had skills, serious skills, skyrocketing me towards my grand finale without mercy. He made a noise, rumbling with plea-sure, and it vibrated against my core. I was coming. Hard, fast. My body arched against his mouth as a scream escaped my throat.

His mouth worked over me until my shuddering body collapsed. He lifted his head, studying me. I laid sprawled open to him in a wanton and drugged state. Porter had exceeded my expectations, and I could barely think.

I didn't understand when he gathered me in his arms and easily lifted me up. He carried me into my bedroom and laid me down on my bed. It took me a moment after he straightened to his full height to realize he was putting me to bed.

"You're leaving?"

He pulled the covers over my naked body, his voice matter of fact, "If I stay, I'm going to fuck you senseless."

"I'm okay with that."

"I'm drunk, and when I take you, I want to be completely sober."

Not *if*, but *when*.

"Will you lay with me?" The words spilled out of me before I could stop them. "Just until I fall asleep?"

"You really like to tempt fate," he growled, but he whipped his t-shirt off his muscular chest and pulled the covers back. "Move over."

I rolled onto my side and swallowed a sigh when he wrapped a big hand around my waist and dragged me back, so I was snug against his body. "I thought you didn't do cuddles," I mumbled against my pillow, loving how safe and warm I felt.

"I don't." He buried his face into my neck. "Now go the fuck to sleep."

"I feel safe," My post-orgasm coma made it difficult to speak.

"It's not only a feeling."

"What do you mean?"

"What did you give me tonight?"

"I didn't give you anything. You gave me an orgasm."

"But what did you give me?"

My tired brain worked to answer that one. "My body."

"You gave me your body," he patiently explained.

"I don't understand."

"We crossed the line, Beth."

"I'm yours?"

"To protect."

I thought about that. "And to fuck."

"Do we even have to say that? That's a given."

"How did we get here?"

"I carried you."

"I mean, this conversation."

"You said you feel safe. I'm telling you it's not only a feeling, but you're actually safe. You're sleeping with a SEAL."

"Are you sober yet?"

"Want to fuck?"

"Hell yeah."

"You're so tired, you can barely speak."

"Give me a minute."

"I'm going to give you a lot more than a minute, Beth. You just don't realize it yet."

I could barely form words, "I want to ask what that means, but I'm too tired."

"You can ask me in the morning."

My last thought before sleep claimed me was *how much time would he give me?*

CHAPTER 26

IF WE CROSS THAT LINE, everything changes.

I couldn't get Porter's words out of my head. Everything had changed, but not in any tangible, measurable way. I *felt* different. When Porter had said that things would change, he meant we'd no longer be just friends. But I hadn't realized that *I'd* change.

And I couldn't even process the fact that he'd accepted me as his responsibility. I considered myself a strong, independent feminist of my generation, so why did my heart race and my breath catch when he'd said being with him meant I belonged to him. It was so caveman, it was ridiculous... but also hot as fuck.

What was even crazier was that I didn't think this was just in-the-moment dirty talk. He actually believed it. This was part of the ancient male code Porter lived by.

I liked the feeling. Way too much. But these were the kinds of feelings that led to dangerous thoughts and daydreams. And when you were faking an engagement to your parents and eight million other strangers, the last thing you wanted to do was start believing your own lie.

Which was why I was hiding out at the corner coffee shop, watching the rain pour onto the pavement on the other side of the window. My phone startled me. I groaned when Mom's face showed up on the screen.

"Hello?"

"Darling, where are you?"

"What do you mean? Did we have an appointment?"

"No, but I'm at your place right now with your betrothed and our wedding planner, and the blushing bride is nowhere in sight."

What the living fuck.

And "my betrothed"? Who spoke like that?

"Don't move." I stood up, grabbing my bag. "I'll be home in five minutes."

Her voice sounded satisfied. "We'll wait."

<hr />

I burst into the apartment and gawked at the intimate scene. On the couch, Mom and a petite Asian guy, who wore a lime green vest and matching bowtie, sandwiched Porter. A five-inch binder rested on Porter's lap, and Mom and Bowtie leaned over his big arms as they all read together.

"Beth!" Mom didn't hide her shock. "You look like a drowned rat."

I didn't doubt that. In New York, flagging a cab on a rainy day, was about as probable as winning the lottery. In my panic, I'd opted to jog through the rain. Now, my soggy ponytail stuck to the side of my neck, and I didn't even want to see what my makeup looked like.

Porter evaluated me with interest. I couldn't meet his gaze.

"What are y'all doing?" I tossed my jacket over a chair and stalked to the kitchen. I grabbed a clean tea towel to blot my face.

The three of them remained sitting and watched as I returned and stood in front of the couch.

"Darling, this is Roo, our wedding planner." Mom patted his arm.

Roo offered me the top of his hand as if he wanted me to bend down and kiss it.

"Hey, Roo." I awkwardly shook his limp hand. My eyes skidded over to Porter.

He looked miserable. Despite myself, laughter threatened to bubble out of me. I worked to remain composed. I needed to get this situation under control.

"Your fiancé is divine." Roo grabbed my hand and studied the ring. "So is that ring."

"Thank you." I raised my eyebrows at Mom. "Would you mind coming and talking to me while I change?"

In the bedroom, I whipped off my wet shirt and dug through my dresser for something dry. "What are you doing here?"

"What do you think we're doing?"

"Mom, a wedding planner?"

"Do you really think that either of us can plan a wedding of this scale by ourselves?"

"This scale?"

"Darling, I've thrown some magnificent parties in my day, but a wedding of this magnitude is beyond even my capabilities. Roo is the best. He was part of the team that helped with the royal wedding. We're lucky to get him at such short notice."

I pulled a dry t-shirt over my head. "Royal wedding? Mom, come on. Porter and I are trying to get used to the idea of getting married. We want to take our time with this." A long time. The longer I could delay setting the wedding date, the better off we'd all be.

"Beth," her scandalized voice following me as I stepped into the bathroom. I winced at the mascara that smeared down my cheeks like sad clown make-up. "We don't have time. Even Roo said he'd be challenged to plan a wedding of this size in twelve weeks."

I pulled the towel down from my freshly washed face and stuck my head out the bathroom door. "Twelve weeks?"

She had disappeared.

I stalked back to the living room. "Twelve weeks?" I put my hand on my hips. "Really?"

"It's going to be perfect." Mom looked at Roo, who nodded vigorously. "Plus that's the only time we can book St. Basilla's church. We lucked out due to a cancellation. That church is typically booked out two years."

"Why do we need that particular church?"

"That's the only traditional church that can accommodate eight hundred guests. Everything else is five hundred or less," Roo explained.

"Eight hundred guests?" I turned to Mom. "Please tell me you're joking."

"Sweetheart, you've no idea how much stress Roo and I have had over the guest list. We were up all night. We culled over four hundred people from our original list, and it was agony."

Eight hundred wedding guests.

"Porter and I want to have an extended engagement," I said firmly.

"Porter already said we could proceed with that date, and Roo has already booked the church," Mom pushed. "Now, sit down beside Porter. We have so many decisions we have to make."

I cleared my throat and scorched my fake-betrothed with a look. "Sweetheart. Would you mind talking to me in the bedroom for a second?"

He unfolded himself from the couch quicker than I thought possible, handing Roo the binder. "Sure."

The second the bedroom door shut, I turned to him and hissed, "Twelve weeks? Are you kidding?"

He put his hands on his hips and leaned towards me, equally emotional, "Have you met your mother? I'd rather negotiate with a Taliban terrorist than her. And don't even get me started on Roo. The guy is like a dictator prince."

"But twelve weeks?"

He ran both hands through his hair. "You can change the date."

"I tried, but you already agreed. You heard them. Roo already booked the church."

"They ambushed me. I was in the shower when they came in. Not into your apartment either. Roo burst into the bathroom and started talking. What was I supposed to do?"

"You were supposed to hold the front."

We glowered at each other. Why did he have to look so hot with his big shoulders and that sexy mouth? I remember what that mouth had done to me last night.

Fuck it.

I launched myself at him. He spun me around, pinning me against the door. I groaned as his lips captured mine.

"Sorry," I moaned into his mouth, arching my back as his hands pushed up the back of my t-shirt.

"God, you taste as good as you look." His hot mouth trailed down my neck. "Like rain and sex."

"What are we going to do?" My fingers twisted into his thick, soft hair, and his hands reached under my butt, lifting me, so my legs were wrapped around his waist.

"We can fix this." A big hand covered my breast, pinching my nipple through my bra.

"How?"

He ground me into the door. "I'll tell your mom that we're going to elope."

I lifted my head. "You'd stand up to Mom for me?"

"Right now, you could get me to do pretty much anything."

I laughed against his mouth. "Tell me you're sober."

"Oh, I'm sober."

Knock. Knock.

"Beth? Are you two finished talking in there? We have so much to get through," Mom's voice sounded on the other side of the door.

We froze

"Coming, Mom." I slid out of his arms. "Are you ready?"

He winced and looked at the ceiling. "Give me a minute."

I brushed my hair from my face. "Let's go."

He grabbed my hand and placed it on his monster hard-on that bulged in his jeans. "I don't want to scare your mom."

CHAPTER 27

FIVE MINUTES LATER, we reappeared in the living room. Judging by the disapproving sniff from Mom and the smirk on Roo's face, they knew we'd been doing more than talking.

"Porter wants to say something," I announced, completely throwing him under the bus.

Mom inspected him over her reading glasses. "Yes?"

"Beth and I are going to elope," he said, his tone was one hundred percent don't-fuck-with me and as edgy and intense as I've ever heard it.

She stared at him for a long moment, then waved her hand dismissively. "Nonsense. Now, Beth, sit down. We absolutely must go over who'll be in your bridal party."

I implored him with a look.

He shrugged and mouthed, "I tried."

"Try harder," I mouthed back.

He focused on Mom for a long moment.

She raised her head and stared him down like a four-star general. "Anything else, Porter?"

He debated and then slowly shook his head. "Nope. I'm on my way out. Take care of my bride for me."

I shot hate-daggers at him and mouthed, "Traitor."

He laughed out loud, which caused Roo and Mom to look up from the binder.

"Sorry." He reached for the door. "Leaving now."

———

Five hours later, I laid exhausted on the couch. The front door open, and Porter stuck his head in.

"They're gone," my voice was tart.

He swung open the door and stepped in.

I sat up. "You bailed on me."

"Sorry."

"You fed me to the wolves. What happened to standing up to my mom for me?"

He walked into the kitchen and opened the fridge to pull out a beer. "I was taught that sometimes retreating is the best defense."

"You're a SEAL. It's one socialite," I chastised.

He pointed his beer at the door. "Your mom is not a job for a single SEAL. I'm not sure an entire army could stop her."

Amused, I slumped back on the couch. "I know."

"So, what did I miss?"

I exhaled. "We're having six attendees each. You don't know five of your best men, but after a near temper tantrum, I managed to secure the coveted roles of the matron of honor and best man for Emily and Jackson. Our engagement party is next Friday. And I fought a long and hard battle over not having smaragdine as our theme color."

He looked interested. "What color did you pick?"

"I wanted pink. A soft, petal pink, like a dahlia."

"That sounds nice."

"I lost that battle."

"What color is smaragdine?"

"Emerald green. I hate emerald green."

Our eyes met. His regretful expression said, 'I am sorry you feel like shit, but I'm way over my head on this chick stuff.'

"This is completely out of control," I moaned into a pillow.

"I hear you."

"We need a plan." I reached one arm up to him, my tone dramatic. "Please help me."

He laughed. "Come on. Get your shoes on."

"Where are we going?"

"I'm taking you out for dinner. We'll talk strategy."

⸺

We sat in a booth at a cute fresh food bistro.

"How are you holding up?"

I pushed my hair off my face. "I've had it wrong my entire life. I thought my dad was the bossy one, who needed to be in control, but I think he might be the puppet for my mother, the puppet master."

Porter laughed. "Now I know where you get your spine of steel from."

I snorted. "Hardly."

"You're tougher than you look."

"I lost every battle I fought today. Which is stupid to even be fighting in the first place, since it's over a wedding that's never going to take place."

He studied me with soft cashmere grey eyes. "How do you want to do this?"

"You mean our break up?"

"Yeah."

"You could allegedly cheat on me."

He winced. "Try again."

"We could fight over money."

"I don't give a shit about money. You could be the one to cheat on me."

I shuddered. "Never."

"You could stand me up at the altar?"

"You mean a runaway bride?"

"Yeah."

"My mom would never forgive me."

We shared another look.

I slowly spoke, "You could leave me at the altar."

He held my gaze. "Seriously?"

"Do you have any better ideas?"

"Any idea would be better than that one."

"Like what?"

He reached out and grabbed my hand. "Maybe we can stage a break up right before the wedding."

My brain went there - that plan would maximize our sex time.

It might have been the worst reason in the world to delay ending this charade, but I couldn't be held responsible for my train of thought. "That could work."

"And we would have some time to come up with a plan on how to do that."

"I like it."

We both shared a look, more heat that humor. I dropped my eyes and played with my fork. Who was Porter? What had his childhood been like? Did he have a family?

"What's Montana like?"

"Not like New York."

"Well, what's your family like?"

Those grey eyes questioned my interest. "I'm the youngest of six boys."

That surprised me. "Is your family still there?"

"Yup, they all live there. All of my brothers are ranchers."

"And your parents?"

"Still ranching." This man fascinated me.

MY FAKE FIANCÉ   173

"Did you ever want to stay in Montana and become a rancher?"

"That's exactly what I wanted."

"So how did you end up in the military?"

Something passed across those grey eyes. "I left home the day I turned 18 to join the military."

His eyes shifted away, letting me know that he didn't want to talk about this. The waitress interrupted us with the bill. Porter reached out and took the billfold.

"Let me help," I tried.

"Got it covered."

"Well, thanks for dinner."

"My pleasure."

I excused myself to wash my hands and put on fresh lip gloss. I stared at my blond reflection. I wanted this man. That kiss against the bedroom door had held so much promise.

We were both sober, which meant one thing. A ripple of excitement coursed through me. I tossed my lip gloss back into my purse and turned to leave. A thick masculine arm wrapped around my neck, pulling me into a choke hold from behind.

Oh my God!

I frantically clawed at the arm, as my perpetrator half dragged, half propelled me to one of the stalls. The nauseating smell of stale cigarettes and alcohol burned my nose.

So much air cut off from my throat that my scream sounded like a wheeze. He pushed my face against the cold metal wall of the stall. His big, bulky body pressed against mine. Terror blinded me.

"Please," I rasped. "Don't hurt me."

Something cold pressed against my throat. I felt a pinch and then something warm, oozed down my neck. My own blood. It took my brain a few seconds to process that the tip of a knife was pressed against the skin of my throat. Cutting me.

"Tell daddy dearest to drop out, or someone is going to get hurt," he snarled.

I nodded frantically. Terrified. The metal of the knife dug deeper, and I immediately stopped nodding.

"Are you going to tell him that?"

"Yes!"

"Don't turn around." He lowered the knife. "If you see my face, I'll kill you."

My eyes squeezed shut. A lone tear trickled down my cheek. "Okay."

He stepped away from my body, and I heard the sound of the heavy bathroom door swing open, then gently bump shut. I staggered to the mirror above the sink.

In shock, I stared at my reflection. A lone rivulet of blood trickled down my throat and created a red stain on my white blouse. With trembling hands, I pumped out a paper towel and tried to blot it.

My face was a white mask with dark and prominent eyes. I must have walked back to the table, but I didn't remember moving. Porter stood, grabbed my shoulders, and took in every detail.

"What the hell?"

"He's gone," I croaked. My throat closed so tight, I was surprised I could breathe.

Porter's nostrils flared in rage. His high cheekbones colored with emotion. He appraised the restaurant, suddenly a soldier, assessing all threats. "What did he look like?"

"I don't know."

"Did you see his face?"

"No."

"Color of his hair?"

"No. Nothing. He approached me from behind." I took a deep breath. "He's gone, Porter."

He turned like he was headed for the restroom.

Terrified of being left alone, I begged, "Please don't leave me."

He focused back on me. Two warm hands—so soothing, so safe—touched my neck. "I want to see your cut, okay?"

Eyes wide, I let him pull the paper towel away.

His eyes studied my wound. "Your cut isn't too deep." Grey eyes clashed with mine. "Did he touch you anywhere else?"

I shook my head, fighting tears.

I will not lose it here.

I will not cry.

"I'm going to call the cops."

"No," my voice came out strong. Stronger than I felt. "No police." Surrounding patrons watched us with interest. "Not here."

He put his hands up, cupping my face, his eyes filled with a flash of rage that would scare the average person. "I'm going to kill the fucker who did this, okay?" he promised.

I shook my head. I was going to lose all my composure if he kept this up. "Can you stop being so nice? It's going to make me cry."

He put a protective arm around me and then started to steer me out of the restaurant. "I'm taking you to the hospital. No arguments."

CHAPTER 28

I SAT on the bed in the Emergency room while Porter stood guard beside my bed. He looked lethal, eyeballing every nurse or doctor who dared approach me. Even though my wound had stopped bleeding, the doctor still thought it warranted one stitch. I also received a tetanus shot, and now we waited for the police to come and question me.

"I'm here for the stabbing," a female voice sounded.

"Bed three," a nurse answered.

I turned toward the voices and watched as Detective Christensen approached us. Out of every detective in the city, she had to show up? Seriously? Porter stiffened beside me.

She paused when she saw the two of us. "Well, isn't this interesting," she spoke slowly, a small smile on her face.

Porter made a noise in the back of his throat that sounded like a growl. I didn't speak. We both watched as she, with deliberate movements, pulled a pad of paper and a pencil out of her pocket.

"My name is Detective Christensen." She was enjoying this. "And your name is?"

"Beth Stirling."

"You look pretty good for being stabbed, Beth Stirling." She eyeballed me. "Where were you injured?"

I pointed at my neck.

She leaned in and took a closer look. "I've had paper cuts that were worse than that."

"Excuse me?"

"Never mind. Why don't you tell me what happened."

I explained everything I could, my voice wobbling dangerously at times, as I remembered the details of my attack.

She chewed on the end of her pencil and checked her notes. "So, you didn't see your perpetrator, and he didn't say anything other than to ask your father to drop out."

"He wasn't asking. He was threatening!"

"Drop out of what?"

"My father is running for mayor."

She raised her eyebrows. "So, do you have any enemies?"

"No."

"Any drug deals gone bad? Any angry dealers you owe money too?"

"I don't do drugs," I said tersely.

"Says the person who was caught with almost half a pound of cocaine in her purse a couple of weeks ago."

"Those charges were dropped."

"Of course. Anything else you'd like to add?"

I glanced up at Porter, who stood there with his legs wide and his arms crossed over his formidable chest. The look he gave Detective Christensen was unnerving.

"I received a threatening letter last week. The envelope was filled with big, dead beetles."

"Dead beetles?" Amusement laced her voice.

I glanced up at Porter. "This is bullshit."

"I agree."

Detective Christensen rolled her eyes. "Fine. Do you have this alleged letter still?"

"Yes."

With boredom, she handed me a card. "When you get the chance, bring it down to the station." I didn't speak. Suddenly, I felt completely exposed and helpless.

The police didn't believe I was in danger.

———

The drive home started out in silence. Porter reminded me of the emotionless robot I had first met at Theo's christening.

"You know, when I was in that washroom, I feared for my life."

His jaw tightened.

"I wasn't sure if he was going to slice my neck open or gut me like a fish. I didn't know if he was going to assault me." Tears blurred my eyes, but anger hardened my voice. "And I don't appreciate anyone insinuating that I was overreacting."

"You're not."

"You're the only one who's taking this seriously." I wiped a tear from my cheek. "Thank you for not making me feel stupid."

His hands tightened around the steering wheel. "I'm sorry I let that happen to you."

What? Why was he blaming himself for this situation?

"You didn't let anything happen to me."

"That should have never happened on my watch."

"Porter, this wasn't your fault."

"I should have walked you to the washroom."

"You're not my bodyguard."

Grey eyes flashed at me. "I'm supposed to fucking protect you, and I failed tonight."

"No." I shook my head. "Please."

"Things are going to change. We've been half-assing this, and going forward, things are going to be different."

What that meant, I had no idea, but I could tell by his tone that it would make no difference to argue. "Okay."

At the apartment, he made me stand at the front door while he walked through. When he was done, I headed straight for a long hot shower. All I wanted to do was crawl into bed, hopefully with Porter beside me.

When I finished, I found him in the kitchen, standing at the island, with a fierce if not frustrated, look on his face.

"How was your shower?"

"Good."

"You heading to bed?"

I wanted to ask him to come sleep with me. Sex was the last thing on my mind, but tonight I'd definitely appreciate having a SEAL sleeping beside me. I opened my mouth to ask him exactly that when his phone, which laid on the counter between us, vibrated.

A beautiful photo of Felicia flashed on the home screen. Felicia was calling Porter. Could my night get worse? It was stupid, but after the night I'd had, it felt like a betrayal.

While I felt all these stupid feelings for the man before me, he was getting calls from someone else. I had to remind myself that they'd been together for years before I came on the scene. I was the interloper. And Porter and I were only supposed to be friends.

I lifted my chin and gave him a steady look. "I'll give you some privacy."

"Beth."

That word held so much meaning, but I didn't know him well enough to be able to interpret. I walked into my bedroom and shut the door. I needed to remember that this man wasn't mine.

He felt like he was mine. He lived with me. He kissed me. We were fake engaged, and he made wild promises about protecting me, but the fact was he remained emotionally entangled with Felicia.

She was working overtime to get him back. Even though he seemed somewhat indifferent to her overtures, it didn't mean it was over between them. He may have been avoiding her, but he also wasn't exactly shutting her down.

I needed to remember he wasn't emotionally available. Which made him exactly the kind of guy I typically dated.

The kind of guy that broke my heart.

CHAPTER 29

"YOU'RE GOING to talk to your dad tonight?" Porter asked me again.

"Yes, I promise." I refrained from rolling my eyes.

We had gone to blows over this a few times in the last week. He wanted to hunt my father down and tell him about the beetle letter and the attack in the bathroom. I knew how Dad operated. You couldn't make him do anything. So, I left a few messages and now waited for him to call back. Despite my attempts to talk to him, Dad hadn't returned any of my calls.

Things between Porter and I had shifted. In the last week since my attack, Porter had taken it upon himself to become my personal bodyguard. He drove me to work, picked me up, and basically never left my side.

The funny guy that I liked to banter with had been replaced with a dangerous soldier, who acted like we were under attack. He guarded me like it was his mission, and not once did he let his guard down. It comforted me, but it also left me confused. I mourned the loss of chemistry and sexual tension between us. Ever since my attack, Porter had been a completely different guy.

There had been no more hot kisses, no more physical overtures.

I shifted the conversation away from me. "So, have you talked to Felicia?"

He glanced over at me. "No."

Of course not. He was too busy acting like my security detail to worry about his own life. I found myself constantly wondering what was happening between them. Did he still want to go back to her? Did he still have feelings for her?

I pushed for some sort of clue from him by feigning indifference. "You know, you don't have to worry about me. If you want to spend time with her, you can."

"I know."

Did he *want* to spend time with her?

"What does that mean?" the question blurted out of me.

His look held meaning. "I'm not a player."

"What does that mean?"

We pulled into the parking lot of Bayswater.

He turned off the engine, and his grey eyes rested on my face. "I'm a one-woman kind of guy."

He got out, leaving me reeling with that statement. I knew he was a one-woman kind of guy. But who was the woman - Felicia or me? Did he still want Felicia? Was he impatiently waiting for this nightmare to be over with so he could get back together with her?

▭

The hundred-person engagement party was in full swing when we walked in.

Mom rushed up to me. "You wore the pink Chanel," she admired me with approval. "That was my first choice."

Mom had left no less than three phone messages instructing me to wear this dress. I had been tempted to wear whatever the hell I wanted but decided it wasn't worth the fight. My usual rebellion against Mom didn't hold the same appeal it used to.

"Of course."

"Well, you look simply gorgeous." She tucked her arm into mine. "Come. There are so many people I want you to meet."

Meet. As in, be introduced for the first time. As in, I don't know anyone at my own engagement party. I sighed and glanced back at Porter. Our eyes met. His expression matched my feelings - he was dreading tonight as much as I was. I let myself be pulled around by Mom.

The party was a mind-numbing whirl of small talk and champagne. Mom laughed gaily with everyone, talked a hundred miles a minute, and always worked into the conversation a reminder of Dad's upcoming election.

"Where's Dad?" I asked her when we had a moment alone.

"His flight from Hong Kong was delayed, but he's going to come straight here."

I made eye contact with Porter from across the room. Three men stood around him, talking, but he seemed indifferent to the conversation. Instead, his gaze watched me with such intensity, a shiver wracked my body. Beneath Porter's exterior simmered a forcefulness, a ferocity that excited me. It awakened in me, a longing, a hunger, that I desperately wanted to explore.

"Where are all the waiters with the hors-d'oeuvres?" Mom fussed, pulling my attention away from Porter. "I'm going to go find Roo. He needs to be on top of that."

I stood back, grateful for the small reprive. My feet were killing me, and my cheeks hurt from smiling so much.

"I see you're still engaged," a voice spoke low in my ear.

My entire body stiffened. "Hello, Yates." I didn't bother hiding my sarcasm.

He moved to stand beside me. "You're making a big mistake."

I glanced across the room at Porter. He politely listened to an older man speak.

"No. Marrying a cheating philanderer would have been a big mistake."

"I hear you ran into some trouble last week. Someone trying to warn you off?"

I spun around and glowered at him. "How do you know that?"

He shrugged. "I know way more than you think."

"What does that mean?"

He downed the remained of the amber liquid in his glass. "Watch your back." He walked away.

Determined to find out what he knew, I started to follow him, but Roo appeared at my side, tugged on my arm, holding me back.

"Not now, Roo." I tried to shake him off.

"The cake is about to come out."

"Fine," I dismissed.

"There's someone in the kitchen who wants to speak to you. She's causing a scene."

I paused. "Who?"

"She's not on the guest list, and she's threatening to come out here and talk to you in front of all these guests unless you go and talk to her."

I hesitated. Was it Traci? Did she have some sort of information?

With one last frustrated look at Yates' back, already halfway across the room, I sighed. "Fine, show me the way."

Roo led me through the double swinging kitchen doors. "When we bring out the cake, the media will take photos of you and Porter, so be sure to smile with your teeth."

We stepped into the bustling kitchen. The bright florescent lights burned my retinas. Kitchen staff in white aprons loaded trays of pastries. A monstrous, tiered cake sat on a cart, ready to be rolled into the party.

"Where is she?" I searched the room for Traci.

"Right there." Roo pointed into the corner. "Who is she?"

Felicia.

CHAPTER 30

SHE WORE A PLUNGING red dress that effortlessly showed off her killer assets. Her perfectly-tossed black hair hung down her back. Her beauty literally took my breath away.

I didn't look away from her as I addressed Roo. "Leave us."

"But," Roo protested.

My eyes narrowed on Felicia. "Now."

He drifted away from me to admonish the guys who were about the wheel the cake out. Felicia gave me a cold smile as I walked towards her. How exactly should I handle this?

I graced her with a fake smile. "Hello, Felicia."

"You're still engaged."

"Last time I checked. What are you doing here?"

"I came to talk."

"To Porter? He's right outside."

"I came to talk to you."

"Okay." I lifted my hand up. "So talk."

"I told you to end your engagement with Porter."

This chick had a lot of nerve. Yes, my engagement was a charade, but she didn't know that. Did she?

"This is definitely a conversation you should be having with Porter, not me."

She stepped right up into my face. "He's supposed to be with me."

The day we went to pick up his boxes, she had been so horrible to Porter. It'd pissed me off then, and it pissed me off now. "If he wanted to be with you, he'd be with you."

Her smile widened. "He's too loyal. He doesn't want to abandon you."

I rose to the bait. "You talked to him?"

"I talk to him all the time."

Jealous burned my gut. I swallowed, at a loss for words. "If Porter wants this engagement to end, he'd end it."

Her eyes narrowed, "He's trapped. You've trapped him. He doesn't feel like he can leave you right now."

Heat washed over me. She could easily be speaking the truth. The past week, Porter had been all about keeping me safe. Any kind of sexual tension between us had all but evaporated. I could easily imagine him telling her how he felt trapped by me. Trapped by duty. Trapped by the lies I had spun around him.

He'd told me he wasn't a player. Claimed he was a one-woman kind of guy, but he had given me no reassurances that I was the woman of his affections. I also knew Porter was such a stand-up guy that he'd never willingly abandon me in my current predicament.

The thought made me nauseous. I needed to get his side of the story, but not here. Not with the media and all my parents' closest friends standing by.

I squared my shoulders and lifted my chin. "I'm at my engagement party. Leave the premises, or I will call security." I turned my back on her.

Ahead of me, two chefs opened the swinging doors while another one slowly wheeled the giant, tiered cake toward the party. Something soft hit me in the back of the head.

I blinked in disbelief at the soft cream puff lying on the floor. "Did you throw a pastry at me?"

She grabbed another one off the tray and fired it towards me, this time hitting me square in the chest.

I didn't think. I grabbed a mini lemon custard pie off the tray beside me and threw it at her. I hit her on the shoulder, and lemon custard splashed down her dress with a satisfying thump.

She inspected her stained dress and glared at me. With determination, she fired a strawberry tart at me, which I deflected with my forearm. Strawberry sauce ran down my arm like blood.

I picked up a cannoli, and with the precision of a baseball pitcher, hit her on the top of her forehead. Juicy cream splattered across her face, smearing in her hair.

An indignant noise escaped her. She tossed a peach tart. It skimmed my shoulder, spraying peach compote up my neck. Anger blinded me. I picked up two puffy, cream-filled pastries and stepped forward, dragging both down the front of her dress.

Disbelief coated her eyes. Venom flashing across her delicate features. "You bitch."

I scoffed. "I'm the bitch? I know exactly how you abandoned Porter."

She reached out two hands and shoved me. "I told you why I did that. I needed him to know how he felt about us."

I shoved her back. "If he wanted to be with you, he'd be with you."

Rage filled her eyes, and she barreled towards me, her entire weight pushing me backwards. For someone so tiny, she had a surprising amount of strength. She caught me off balance and propelled me backwards. To prevent hitting the ground, I stepped back, again and again, unable to catch my balance.

"Look out," someone said.

My ass hit something, giving me enough stability to grab her shoulders and twist. I flipped her around, and now she was the one flying back, not me. She held onto my shoulders with both hands, pulling me down with her.

In slow motion, we landed on the cake. Felicia was almost lying flat on top of it. Cake and icing spattered out on either side of her. I half fell on top of her, pushing her further down onto the cake.

I reached above her shoulder, trying to find something, anything, to give me enough support to lift myself off her. Instead, my arm sunk up to my elbow in soft cake.

"Get off me you bitch," she cried. Her hand smeared down my face, dragging the sweet cake and icing across my cheek and mouth.

Using every abdominal muscle I had, I managed to lift myself off her and stand.

"Beth," Mom cried out.

I froze and lifted my eyes.

We were in the middle of the party.

A hundred guests stood in a circle, looking at us with equal measures of shock and disbelief. Flashes of light blinded my eyes as photographers took multiple pictures of us.

Felicia rolled on her side, across the cake, and managed to stand up herself. Her long, dark hair was now white with frosting. I checked my own dress. Chunks of cake and icing fell in heavy plops at my feet.

Mom stood there with her hands over her mouth. Roo sat on a chair, his head between his legs, his breathing easily mistakable for hyperventilation. The silence deafened as a hundred pairs of eyes watched us.

I cleared my throat. "I apologize for ruining the cake. I know that all of you were looking forward to it."

Felicia pointed at me. "This woman is a man-stealer. Porter is my boyfriend, and she did everything in her power to break us up."

Everyone in the room gasped.

"Ex-boyfriend," I confirmed, my chest heaving with so much adrenaline, yet I still couldn't get enough oxygen into my lungs.

"I love him." She spoke to the entire room. "And she stole him from me."

More gasps came from everyone around the room. Two security guards came rushing into the room. They evaluated Felicia and me, not knowing who they needed to apprehend.

"Don't look at me," I warned them.

The two men slowly approached Felicia, flanking her on either side. "Miss, we're going to have to ask you to leave the premises."

"Porter!" She twisted around, looking wildly at the crowd. "Baby, come on. You know you love me. The only reason you're marrying her is for the money."

The crowd started to whisper and talk amongst themselves. I stood there and watched as they ushered Felicia out, too afraid to look at the expressions of everyone around me. Now I was the only cake-coated person in the room.

I had one option.

I hauled my purse up over my shoulder, and with more dignity than the queen herself, I walked through the parting crowd toward the doors. No one approached me as I made my way down the long hallway.

To my immense relief, a cab was waiting at the bottom of the front steps. Without giving the valet the chance to move, I opened the door of the cab and got in.

"Lady, you can't get in here with that mess," the driver barked at me.

"I was in a three-tiered cake fight. With my fiancé's ex. And she called me a man thief - so I don't care what you charge me as long as you get. Me. Out. Of. Here."

And then I burst into tears.

He started to drive.

CHAPTER 31

WITH STICKY HANDS, I paid the driver when my door wrenched open. Shocked, I glanced up to see Porter, standing beside the cab.

"Get out," he demanded.

"You okay?" the cab driver asked uneasily.

"I'm fine." I stepped out of the cab.

"Why did you leave like that?!" Porter towered over me. His eyes were a flinty cold grey as he rolled his shoulders, emotion interwoven with the tension in his body.

"What?"

His gaze was so angry and frustrated. "You left the party alone."

"So?"

"You're not supposed to be alone. I can't protect you if you take off like that."

I marched through the lobby of my building and punch the elevator button. "I don't even know why you're here."

"What are you talking about?"

"Felicia!" I yelled.

"What about her?"

I stepped into the elevator and punched my floor button, taking all my anger out on the button. "She told me all about your phone calls. How you want to be with her. How you feel trapped by me. That the only reason you're with me is that you feel guilty about leaving me."

Incredulity spread across his features. "And you believed her?"

I got off on my floor and stomped toward my apartment. "Look. I get it. I get how I've essentially dragged you into this mess, and now, with everything going on, you feel like it's your duty to protect me, but it was never supposed to go this far. You were never supposed to give up your happiness for me." My hands were shaking so hard, I struggled with the lock.

He took the keys from me and unlocked the door for me. His calmness infuriated me. "I told you. I haven't talked to Felicia."

I had believed him before. Exactly like I had believed the lies of my other two cheating ex-boyfriends. But no more. I knew better. If there was smoke, there was usually a fire. I strode into the apartment and headed straight to my bedroom. He followed behind me.

I didn't turn to look at him. "I've seen her call you."

"So what? She calls me. Have you ever seen me pick up the phone?"

"Like every other guy, you're smart enough not to pick up in front of me."

He stepped closer to me. "Is that what this is about?"

This felt like a real relationship and a real fight. Which made no sense, because all of this was supposed to just be pretend. But I couldn't seem to stop myself.

I was yelling. With real emotion in my voice. "Did you notice the major cake fight I was in with your girlfriend? You keep telling me that you're not interested in talking with her or being with her, yet she showed up at our party! And she's pretty convinced that you two are getting back together. Why would she think that if she wasn't getting some encouragement from you?"

"She's not my girlfriend, and I haven't talked to her since we picked up the boxes."

"I don't believe you." I know I sounded like a jealous, insecure girlfriend, but I couldn't seem to stop the words from pouring out of my mouth. "You're exactly like every other guy. You want your cake and to eat it too. Well, not with me. You can take your cheating ass and get out."

"I'm not a cheater." His nostrils flared. "I've never cheated at anything in my entire life."

"You're just like every other guy."

"Take that back."

"No," I flung at him. "I should've never trusted you." I stalked into the bathroom and turned on the shower.

Two strong hands wrapped around my waist and pushed me into the shower, spinning me around. The cold water poured over my head, making me gasp. His mouth covered mine, the contrasting temperatures making his lips feel like fire against mine.

His body pressed my back against the cool tiles of the shower, his hands cupping my face. I moaned into his kiss, loving the taste of him, gasping as his mouth moved down the side of my neck.

"You taste like cake," he growled.

"Porter," I managed.

He stepped back and feasted his eyes on me. He had removed his suit jacket, and now, warm water poured over his white dress shirt, showing off his sleek muscles through the wet fabric. "Why do you think I want Felicia?"

I shook my head, uncertain how to respond. He spun me around, so my face pressed against the cold tiles. His hands pulled my dress up over my hips. Breathing hard, a noise escaped me when his fingers pushed beneath my thong and slid along the length of me, teasing me.

"I told you—if we cross that line, you're mine," his voice was muffled against my neck. "I also told you I'm a one-woman man." His teeth grazed my sensitive skin. "Newsflash, Beth. We crossed that line, and now you're mine."

I couldn't respond. I was too busy focusing on his fingers that teased my entrance.

"Move your legs apart," he commanded.

I swallowed and stepped wider, opening myself further to his touch.

"Do you believe me?" He sucked on my neck while his fingers stroked my folds.

My head fell back when his fingertips grazed my clit. Did I believe him? Right now, at this moment, with those fingers touching me, I'd believe anything.

"Oh, yes." I pressed my hot forehead against the cool wall.

"Turn around." His fingers disappeared, and he stepped back.

I slowly spun around, so my back pressed against the shower wall. His hair was wet and slicked back off his face, making the angles of his face seem harsh and masculine. He was unbuttoning his dress shirt.

"Take off your dress," he demanded.

With shaking hands, I reached behind my back and unzipped my dress. I shrugged it off my shoulders, then peeled the wet fabric down my body until it dropped at my feet.

"Get naked," he instructed, his eyes dark.

I stepped out of my bra and thong and stood there while his grey eyes, full of lust, traveled down my body.

"The things I'm going to do to you..." he promised.

I couldn't wait.

CHAPTER 32

"GET ON YOUR KNEES."

I lowered myself to my knees, then looked up at him from the submissive position. He reached out a hand and pushed my wet hair off my face. I reached out, and with unsteady hands, undid the belt on his pants.

He was rock hard, his massive erection jutting against the fabric of his dress pants. I swallowed in anticipation and drew down the zipper of his pants. His huge cock strained against his boxers.

He put a hand under my chin and lifted it up, so I looked up at him. "You're so mouthy. You know what I want to do to you when you're so mouthy?"

"What?" I pushed his pants down over his hips. Pushing his boxers down felt like unwrapping a wedding gift.

His cock was a monster. Huge, with a girth that should have scared me. Instead, my stomach clenched in anticipation. I couldn't wait.

"I want to fill that sweet mouth of yours with my cock until you choke."

Yes. Me, too.

He kicked off his pants. I grabbed the base of him, my fingers not even coming close to wrapping around it. I pulled it down towards me and drew the tip of him into my mouth. Salty pre-cum leaked out of him, and I shut my eyes and moaned, sucking more of him into my mouth.

"Oh, yeah." His hand rested on the back of my head, his fingers gathering my wet hair into a makeshift ponytail. "Your mouth feels so fucking hot."

I worked him over like a professional. My hand pumped the base of his cock while my mouth sucked and my tongue swirled.

"That's it." He groaned. "You can take more of me into your sweet mouth. You know you can."

I strained my jaw, taking more and more of him in until I was almost choking. His strong hands held my head while his hips slowly pumped, pushing himself deeper down my throat.

I moaned, my eyes on his face. Loving this. Why did I love this so much? I wanted more. I wanted to swallow him up. I wanted all of him. I couldn't get enough.

My whole body trembled in lust. I squeezed the base of his cock harder, massaging his balls gently with my other hand, loving the feeling of his heavy, rigid length gliding against my tongue.

He tugged on my hair, pulling me back. My eyes remained on his face, as my mouth sucked harder, trying to keep him in my mouth, but he tugged himself free.

I eyeballed his cock as it bobbed tantalizingly in front of my face. I strained against his hold on my hair, trying to bring him back into my mouth.

"Stand up," he demanded.

I didn't move fast enough for him, and his hands shifted beneath my arms, easily lifting me to my feet. I was weak with lust. So drugged from need that I almost couldn't stand.

Two big hands pushed my wet hair off my face. "Beth."

"Yeah?" My eyes clung to his hot gaze.

He was breathing hard, but he easily lifted me up in his arms. My legs wrapped around his waist and my arms wrapped around his thick neck. I gasped when my back hit the cool shower wall. "Tell me you're on the pill."

"I am."

He put his hand between us, positioning himself at my entrance. "I owe you some foreplay."

I laughed and fisted his hair in my fingers. "Just fuck me already." My head went back, hitting the wall when he slowly began to push into me.

Yes, oh, yes.

Sensations sparkled up my spine as my body opened to accommodate his enormous length. Our foreheads met, both of us breathing hard when he pushed balls deep inside me.

"I've had a fucking hard on since the day I first saw you." His mouth moved against mine. I opened my mouth, and we kissed wildly. Sucking and tasting like our lives depended on it.

I lifted my head. "Since the christening?"

He grew even bigger inside me. "No, before that."

I froze. "Before?"

He stared into my eyes. "I saw you when I landed in New York. Jackson picked me up and dropped Theo's bag off to Emily. You were there." He kissed my neck, just below my ear. "So carefree, and so fucking hot." His rough hand gripped my thighs, running his nails against the sensitive skin. "All legs, begging me to spread them and claim your tight pussy as mine."

I couldn't process this, especially with his cock buried deep inside of me.

His teeth grazed my earlobe. "And the christening... the entire time the minister talked, I was doing math equations in my head, trying not to embarrass myself with a raging hard-on."

I pulled my head back, looking into his eyes. "Are you serious? Why?"

His fingers dug into my ass, lifting me up, and then he was

thrusting into me. *Yes! God, yes!* I clung to his shoulders, tightening my legs around his ass for more leverage.

"First it was your shoes. Those insanely high heels."

I moaned as he pumped deeper into me. Sensations shot up my back, as every nerve screamed with pleasure. "My shoes?"

"And then it was your scent. Enveloping me. All I could smell was your perfume. You smelled so good my dick was instantly hard."

His rhythm was perfect. Hard and fast. Driving his big cock into me with a perfect, relentless force that liquefied my insides.

I clung to him. "You barely spoke. And you were so cranky."

He gave a breathless laugh. "I didn't want to date you. I wanted to fuck you. Senseless."

"Faster," I begged. "But you only stared at me."

He began to pump harder. My back slammed against the slippery wall. I could feel my insides tighten around him, creating an almost unbearable friction.

"I was undressing you. Imagining putting my cock in your mouth. Pushing my tongue between your legs. Wondering if you tasted as sweet as you smelled."

My core quivered as my orgasm roared towards me. I tried to hold it off because I needed to hear this. "That's what you were thinking about?"

"I was thinking about how I wanted to drag you off to the nearest washroom, pull down your panties, shove up your skirt and put my hand over your mouth while I buried my cock deep inside of you."

"Oh, God." My eyes squeezed shut as a tingling started up the back of my legs. "You should have. Why didn't you?"

He laughed harshly. "You think you would have liked that? What would you have done if I had leaned you over the bathroom counter and fingered you until you came all over my hand? Would you have screamed? Gasped? Spread your legs wide open so I could properly fuck you?"

My orgasm jerked through my body. I felt my entire core clamp around him, and then I was convulsing. Thrashing in his arms as I came undone with the most intense orgasm of my life.

"That's it." He crushed me in his arms, not giving me any time to recover. He intensified his movements, pounding into me. I felt like a rag doll, impaled by his huge dick, being fucked senseless.

I squeezed him tighter, barely hanging onto my sanity when he shouted something indecipherable. He jerked up into me, again and again, streaming his release into my body.

I panted. I was completely spent. My head on his wet shoulder, I clung to him, digging my fingers into his biceps. I could feel his deep breaths against my cheek as his cock twitched and moved inside me.

I unfolding my legs, and he lifted me off him. I stood in front of him on unsteady legs. He cupped my face with his hands and kissed me hard on the lips.

Without saying a word, he gently shampooed the cake out of my hair. Eyes shut, I tried to process what had happened. I tried to think, but I couldn't. All I could do was feel.

I felt so damn good.

I moaned when he moved a soapy washcloth over my sensitive body. Then, he spent even more time, removing the shower head and rinsing my body off with tantalizing skill.

He led me out of the shower, wrapped me in a huge bath towel before swinging me into his arms. With utmost care, he laid me down on the bed.

My eyes begged him. "Don't leave."

"Sweetheart, that was the appetizer. I'm not going anywhere." He dropped, naked and still wet, on the bed beside me.

I rolled onto my side and studied this beautiful man through my eyelashes.

"I need a minute." His eyes shut. "And then we can get onto the main course."

I laid my hand on his hard chest. "Did you mean that?"

He cracked open one eye. "Mean what?"

"Did you really find me sexy at the christening?"

He smiled, his eyes drifting shut. "Yup."

"But I was such a royal bitch that day."

His smile grew wider. "That's what made you so damn hot."

CHAPTER 33

THE MAIN COURSE exceeded my wildest fantasies. Porter woke me up by flipping me over onto my stomach, dragging me back, so I was on my knees, my face against the bed.

While he held my hands behind my back, he knelt between my spread legs. His fingers pushed deep inside of me, grazing my g-spot. His body was sheer perfection, and his cock was a nymphomaniac's dream, but it was his dirty words that fueled the raging fire inside of me.

"You like that? When my fingers are deep inside of you, touching you?"

"Yes!"

"How about my cock? You want to suck on it? You want me to shove my hot cock down your throat?"

"Yes, oh, yes."

"You're such a good dirty girl, aren't you? You like it when I sink my cock deep into your sweet, hot pussy?"

"Yes, so much."

"Beg for me."

"Please. Please, fuck me."

He pushed his huge length deep inside of me, and my entire body clamped around him. "Like that?"

I squirmed. "Yes, just like that."

"You're so tight. You sure you can handle this? Being fucked without mercy?"

"Yes, please, yes."

He was bossy as fuck in bed. He pushed my body to come again and again until I was a trembling, shaking, quivering mess, sated and drunk on desire. He would bring me to the brink of orgasm but not quite, instead pushing my head down, making me suck on him, reaching around behind me, and fingering me until I screamed around his cock.

He flipped me around the bed. Rode me hard. Made me ride him. He loved to pin my arms, making me take his pleasure until I thought I'd lose my mind. He fucked me with his tongue, his fingers, his cock. Without mercy, he brought me to orgasm so many times, my voice became hoarse, and my limbs ceased to work.

Only then did he relent, allowing me to curl my back up against him while he wrapped his big arm around my waist. Big spoon and thoroughly fucked little spoon.

"Ready for dessert?" He nibbled on my neck.

I whimpered. He laughed.

"Are you always like this?" I managed to ask, my eyes glued shut, my body was one big, happy, throbbing sensation.

"I told you how I liked to fuck. With complete control and a lot of dirty talk."

"You should come with a warning label." I tried but failed to open my eyes.

"Too much?"

"No. I hate to inflate your ego, but that was the best sex of my life."

I felt his smile against my neck. "Go to sleep."

I woke up alone with a note on my pillow, telling me Porter had gone for a run. I rolled over and shut my eyes in ecstasy as I caught his scent on my pillow. How was it possible for another human being to smell that good?

I stretched my stiff limbs. Last night might have been the best night of my life, but now I was back to reality, and I needed to deal with Mom and try and explain last night. I wasn't looking forward to the task.

Once dressed, I dared glance at my phone. Only seven phone calls from her. Better than I expected. Before I could dial, my phone rang.

"Hey, Mom."

"Hi, darling, how are you this morning?"

What? "I'm fine."

"I'm so sorry your party was ruined by that dreadful woman, but don't worry. Roo and I handled the press."

"You did?"

"They all signed non-disclosure forms before the event, so their film was actually the property of Bayswater. And they all agreed to keep the cake incident out of the press."

"They did?"

"Yes. They weren't exactly happy about it, but they know the rules, and if they want an exclusive invite to your big day, they'll keep their mouths shut."

"What about the guests?"

"Oh, they loved the scandal. If anything, it made getting an invite to your wedding an even more sought-after commodity this summer. You know how they are."

I did know, which is why Mom's blasé response baffled me. "Uh-huh."

"Tonight, your father is throwing the first pitch from home plate at Citi Field. It's a charity fundraiser, and we need your and Porter's attendance." Was it weird that she wasn't asking me about how Porter and I were doing after last night?

"Okay."

"Great. I think your Tory Burch cropped white pants along with a loose blouse, preferably in the colors of your father's campaign, will do nicely."

Knowing I was getting off easy, I wasn't going to argue. "Okay."

"See you tonight. Roo will text you the details. Don't be late, okay?"

"Okay."

I set my phone down, baffled by Mom's reaction. I got scolded if I wore shoes from last year's collection, so this response was completely out of character. Maybe Roo was rubbing off on her.

I stood in the kitchen, thinking. Yates had insinuated that he knew who had attacked me. I hadn't had the chance to ask him about his ominous warning, but I planned on rectifying that today.

———

"Do you think he's home?" Porter pulled his truck in front of Yates' building.

After explaining what Yates had said to me last night, Porter had agreed that we needed more information. Without talking about the night before, he had merely showered and gotten ready to drive me here.

"He'll be home. Yates likes to sleep in."

"I'm coming in there with you." Porter turned off his truck.

Flashes of last night flooded my memory. The way Porter touched me. The way his big, hard body had thrust so deliciously into me. The feeling of that mouth, bringing me to a spine-cracking orgasm. The dirty words that had rolled off his tongue when his fingers had been deep inside of me.

"Are you okay?" he interrupted my thoughts.

I blinked, bringing myself back to the conversation. "Yates won't talk if you're there."

"I'll wait outside his door, but if you think you're going into that building alone, think again."

I knew this side of Porter. It was his non-flirty, non-negotiating, protective side. "That's fine."

The code to Yates' apartment building was the same. I hadn't called ahead of time. I figured the element of surprise would work best to my advantage. I knocked, and Yates took his time answering.

When he finally swung the door open, he wore only a pair of jeans and no shirt. His body looked thin and weak compared to my memory of Porter's body. "Beth, what are you doing here?"

Not waiting for an invite, I stepped into the apartment, leaving Porter in the hallway. I got straight to the point, "What do you know about the person that attacked me?"

Yates turned away from me. "I don't know what you're talking about."

"You knew someone had attacked me, and you knew they were warning me off. You also told me that you knew way more than I thought."

"Beth, I was drunk last night."

"You told me to watch my back. What do you know?" I crossed my arms.

"Nothing."

"Yates, the police are involved. You need to tell me what you know."

"I don't know anything."

"Your comments last night say otherwise."

He ran his hand over his mouth. "I heard some rumors. That's all."

"What kind of rumors?"

"That Renner plays dirty."

"The mayor? You think he's involved?"

"Maybe. I don't know."

"Well, what do you know?"

"Someone approached me the other day and asked me if I had any incriminating photos of you."

"Excuse me?"

"You know, like nudie shots or something like that."

"Yates!"

"I didn't give them anything. I don't even have any photos of you like that, and if I did, I certainly wouldn't sell them."

"Who was it?"

"I don't know."

"Was it the media?"

"I don't think so."

"You think it was someone connected to Michael Renner?"

"Look, Beth, there are rumors that Renner is knee-deep in corruption and the mafia. He needs to win the next election. The mafia needs him to win the next election. What none of them needs is someone like your dad to come in and clean the place up."

"You're his campaign manager."

"I'm not saying that I'm not on your dad's side, but I do know that his opposition is seriously threatened by how well your dad is doing in this race."

"And that is why they're coming after me."

"Yes."

"They think that if they come after me and threaten me, it might persuade my father to drop out."

"I think that's their goal, yes."

Son of a bitch.

"Well, the Stirling's aren't intimidated by a few threats."

Yates' concern was genuine. "That's where you're wrong. These guys play dirty, Beth. You need to watch your back."

"Thanks for the warning."

"Hey, you want to get a drink tonight?" he asked with way too much hope in his voice.

I flashed my ring. "Only if my fiancé's invited."

"Maybe another time."

CHAPTER 34

FROM THE VANTAGE point of the executive box, I studied the baseball field full of screaming fans. Behind me, Dad's influential friends mingled. Porter stood beside Dad and laughed at someone's joke. Despite the fact that he was surrounded by some of New York's wealthiest people, he seemed entirely at ease.

Mom came up beside me and followed my gaze. "You look like a woman in love."

In love? With Porter?

"I do?" my voice sounded feeble.

She laughed. "You know, I never thought I'd say this, but Porter's growing on me."

What rabbit hole have I been dropped into?

"He is?"

She took a sip of her wine. "He looks fabulous in a tux, he holds his own with everyone we know, and he seems absolutely besotted with you."

I couldn't keep the incredulity out of my voice. "He does?"

"Last night, when you left, he was frantic to go after you." She sounded heartfelt. "That's all I've ever wanted for you. Someone to love you."

I swallowed hard. It was getting more and more difficult to remember that this was one big, fat lie. Everything felt real. The engagement. My impending wedding. My relationship with Porter. I wanted it to be real, and that was a big issue for me.

"I'm truly sorry about last night, Mom."

She made a noise in her throat. "I'd have done more than push that hussy into a cake. How dare she sneak into Bayswater with her cheap shoes and cleavage to steal your man."

My man. I studied Porter. As if he could sense my gaze, he glanced at me. His penetrating gaze scorched me, making my stomach pitch like I was riding a rollercoaster.

I wanted him. Again. Last night should have satisfied me for a lifetime, but my need for him felt insatiable.

"The event photographer is coming to the box in fifteen minutes." Mom patted my arm. "So, touch up your lipstick and make sure you and Porter are touching in the photo. We want to dispel any nasty rumors, okay?"

"Thanks for all your help." I meant it. I couldn't remember the last time Mom had made such an effort. For the first time that I could remember, I was getting along with my parents. I wished it could be like this all the time.

She touched my face gently. "Darling, this wedding is my crowning achievement. I can't tell you how proud I am of you."

Too bad this was all a lie. How much would Mom hate me when the truth came out?

⸻

My parents, Porter and I grouped together for photos. As directed by Mom, Porter stood behind me with his arms loosely wrapped around my waist. My hand that showcased my ring rested lightly on his arm.

"Okay, just need to change the flash." The event photographer bent over his camera.

Porter leaned down, placing his mouth against my ear. "You know what I'm going to do to you tonight?"

I bite my lip and shook my head.

His low voice was for my ears only. "I'm going to do the filthiest things to you. I'm going to make you come until you can't breathe."

My response was a harsh intake of breath.

"You'd like that, wouldn't you? You're such a dirty girl. You can't wait until I bury my face between your legs and push my cock into that sweet, tight pussy of yours."

I nodded, working to keep a neutral expression on my face, but I could feel the heat climbing up my neck.

His lips grazed my ear. "I think tonight you're going to be my little slave. I think I want a little strip tease when we get home. What do you think about that?"

I imagined Porter lying on my bed, his big cock in his hand. His eyes dark as he watched me seductively peel off my clothes. Maybe he'd give me some instructions while I stripped. Perhaps he'd get extra bossy.

I sucked in a breath. "I'm completely on board."

"You think we should find a closet around here, so I can give you a preview of what's to come?"

I swear my entire body trembled, but my answer was firm. "Yes."

His laughter warmed my ear. "Let's see what we can find."

When the photos finished, someone called Porter away, and I saw an opportunity to speak to Dad.

"Hey, Dad." I walked up to him at the bar.

"Sweetheart." He smiled broadly. "Sorry I missed the big event last night."

"Did Mom tell you?"

"She mentioned some nonsense about an uninvited guest. I've already reamed out security at Bayswater."

"Oh." I rubbed my sweating palms against my pants. "Dad, I need to talk to you about something."

"My secretary mentioned you called a couple times. Sorry, my trip was packed with wall-to-wall meetings."

"That's okay, Dad, but I really need to discuss some things with you."

Dad smiled at someone behind me. "Hey, Collins. Did you see my pitch at the start of the game?" Collins said something back. Dad touched my arm. "Sweetheart, I'll try and call you this week, okay?"

"Dad, it's really important."

"Okay, sweetie." He patted my arm and moved behind me.

I sighed and downed my wine. Maybe I was overreacting. Perhaps all of this was getting blown out of proportion. It wasn't like Porter was going to let anything happen to me.

"What's wrong?" Porter approached me.

"I tried to talk to my dad, but he's not really interested in hearing anything I have to say."

We both looked over to where Dad laughed with four of his friends.

"I'll get his attention for you." Porter took a step towards him, but I grabbed his arm and pulled him back.

"Not here. He knows I want to talk to him."

Frustration creased his face.

I decided a little bit of distraction was in order. "What do you say we forgo the closet and head home for the main event?"

That got his attention. His eye darkened. "Right now?"

I stepped closer to him, "My inner stripper is begging to come out and play."

He groaned, "Let's go."

CHAPTER 35

PORTER'S CELLPHONE rang as the cab pulled up in front of my apartment. With his phone tucked against his ear, he fished money out of his pocket, while whoever he talked to, gave him an earful. He wasn't even getting a word in edgewise.

"Let me pay." I grabbed his arm.

He shook his head, shoved money at the driver and spoke into his phone, "I hear you. No, I get that, but I don't deserve any of that. I don't even think I should vote."

Porter walked a few feet away from me. One hand covered his ear while he listened with intense concentration. "I get that, Jordan, but I haven't been back there in years. I have no say in this decision. Nor should I." He paused so long, I thought he'd hung up. "Is that what Dad told you to tell me?"

There was a small grocery store right across the street. I could really go for some ice cream. I waved at Porter and pointed at the grocery store.

He lifted up his finger to say, "give me one minute."

"Jordan, I honestly have no say. I support whatever you guys decide." His voice indicated the seriousness of the conversation, and I didn't want to bother him.

Porter's back was to me as I dashed across the street. I glimpsed back at him. He didn't even know I was gone. I found some ice cream and a cheap bottle of wine. I paid for my purchases, and I got halfway across the street when I heard someone calling.

"Miss! Miss!"

I turned. "Are you talking to me?"

The clerk waved something at me. "You forgot your wallet in the store."

Porter and I briefly made eye contact.

"What the fuck," he mouthed.

I turned back to the store. A squeal of tires and the surge of an engine roared through the air. I froze as those headlights sped towards me.

"Beth!" Porter shouted.

I stepped back into the other lane, but the car veered into that lane. I stumbled forward, and it surged back towards me. This fucker was trying to hit me.

I started to run. It was too close.

Oh. Shit. *This is going to hurt.*

I hit the ground. Pain laced up my arms, and something cold and wet tricked against my hands. Miraculously, I was still breathing.

I heard the store clerk's voice. He sounded so far away. "Lady! Are you okay?"

I was being rolled over, and suddenly, Porter's face was mere inches from mine.

"Shit." He touched my arms, my face, my neck. "I'm so sorry. Beth. Say something."

"Something is leaking. Am I bleeding?" I asked in a daze.

He shook his head. "You're wine bottle broke."

"My ice cream," I said lamely.

"We'll get you some more."

Everything hurt. Were my wrists broken? It felt like my kneecaps had been removed, like my hips had been jarred so hard, they had popped out of their sockets.

"Did the car hit me? I think the car hit me."

"That wasn't the car." He shone his phone flashlight into my eyes exactly like a doctor would.

"Something hit me. I'm pretty sure it was the car."

Remorse crossed his face as he studied my wrists. "That was me. I tackled you."

Our eyes met.

"You tackled me?"

He put his hand beneath my neck and gently pulled me into a sitting position. "I don't think anything is broken, but you're pretty banged up. I'm taking you to the hospital."

In shock, I glanced down at my hands. My palms were skinned to a pulpy mess. The knees of my pants were ripped, but there was no blood. And every single bone in my body hurt.

Queasiness rolled over me. "I feel weird."

He lifted me up into his arms. "You might have a concussion."

I stared up at his face while he carried me. "You saved me."

"I hit you with all my weight and drove you into a cement sidewalk. I'm not sure if that qualifies as saving you."

"My hands are stinging."

He flinched. "Fuck, I'm so sorry, Beth."

"It's not your fault. I wanted to get some ice cream. You were right there," I babbled in shock.

"I was distracted. I was on the phone."

"Why would someone try and run me over?"

He opened the truck door and put me down on the seat with so much gentleness and care, it made me want to weep. Didn't he know by now that kindness was my undoing?

He secured my seatbelt over my hips. "We'll get to the bottom of this okay?"

I wanted that, sure, but I was startled when I realized I wanted Porter—this, being cared for—more.

Two hours later, I waved my bandaged hands at Porter, who sat on the edge of my bed in the ER.

"Sexy, hey?" I rolled my eyes.

He lifted one of my hands and kissed my fingertips. "You've got sexy covered."

Our eyes met. The weird thing was I knew he meant it. I really liked this guy. Not only as a friend. I had feelings for him. Big feelings. I didn't know how to process that, but the need to let him know was growing stronger.

I hated that I was fake-engaged to him. I wanted everything with him to be real. "Porter, there's something we need to talk about."

"De ja vu," a familiar voice interrupted my confession.

I sighed and turned to take in the blond woman that had appeared beside my bed. "Detective Christensen."

She flipped through my medical report. "It says you were involved in a hit and run?"

"An attempted hit and run."

"Trouble sure seems to like to find you."

"Do you get sent out to mock all victims of crimes or is that something you reserve for only me?"

"What can you tell me?"

Porter cut in. "It was a black Oldsmobile Cutlass Supreme with a soft white top. It went from approximately six miles per hour to thirty-five miles per hour in the span of one block. Beth tried to dodge it, but the vehicle deliberately tried to hit her."

"What else?"

"The driver was a white male, 40-50 years of age. He had no facial hair, and he wore a hat and dark-rimmed glasses. Aviators."

"Did you get a license plate number?"

"GAN 4563. New York plates."

She raised her eyebrows at me. "So did the car actually hit you?"

I shook my head.

"How did you get hurt?"

"I knocked her down to avoid her being clipped by the vehicle," Porter answered for me.

"And where exactly did this take place?"

I cited my address to her.

She tucked her stubby pencil back into her pocket. "Okay. Let me run those plates and see what we can see on the street cameras. Lots of streets don't have cameras, but if they do, and if what you are saying is true, then this would be considered attempted murder."

I gasped.

She gave me a grim smile. "Along with mocking our victims, we also consider attempted murder a pretty serious crime."

"What happens now?"

"I'm going to run those plates, and I'll get back to you."

—

Another hour passed before I was released from the ER. Porter wanted to carry me to the truck, but I insisted on walking. I hobbled beside him and tried not to groan. Every single step hurt like a son of a bitch until Porter took pity on me and literally swept me off my feet.

I was about to protest out of stupid pride, but my phone rang.

"Beth? This is Detective Christensen, I'm going to need you to come down to the station."

CHAPTER 36

"WHAT IS THIS?" I asked as she urgently ushered Porter and me to a small, windowless brick room with a laptop.

"There were cameras on the street. We caught the whole thing. I want you to watch this and tell me if you remember anything else."

She hit play. There I was, grainy and grey on the screen, crossing the street. The store clerk came out and called to me. I turned around, and the car pulled out from the curb and began to speed towards me.

Exactly like a deer in the headlights, I wasted valuable seconds trying to decide which way to run. When I started to run, I was agonizingly slow. My fate seemed inevitable.

Out of nowhere, with the speed of a greyhound, Porter raced towards me. He moved so fast, but the car was dangerously close. Like a professional football player, making the tackle of his life, he flew through the air.

He landed on top of me, knocking me forward. The car swerved hard, trying to hit us, before speeding off. Porter made a noise in the back of his throat and turned his back to us.

"You saved her life." Detective Christensen spoke. "She might be a bit banged up, but if you hadn't done that, it would've been much worse."

He paused when she spoke, but without looking back, he walked out. Detective Christensen and I shared a look.

I bit my lip. "He feels guilty."

"That man deserves a medal. He risked his life saving yours."

"I know."

"We have a hit on the car. Plates and car were both stolen."

"So, you can't find this guy?"

She shut the laptop. "We found him. An hour ago, his body was found in this car, under a bridge, not ten blocks from your place."

"What?" I put my bandaged hand to my forehead in shock. "What happened?"

"Two bullets to the back of his head."

Panic laced my voice. "I don't understand what is happening. This doesn't make sense."

"I don't know what to tell you, but we'll be doing everything we can to investigate exactly what's happening and who this guy is."

"What should I do?"

Her concern was real. "Stay vigilant about your safety until we can get to the bottom of this. And keep that big guy close. He looks like he's doing a good job keeping you safe so far."

I pulled my stiff body up from the chair. "Can I go?"

"You're free to go."

Shouting sounded from outside of the room.

"What the hot hell?" Detective Christensen flung open the door. "Oh, shit." She disappeared.

I limped to the door and took in the chaos. Yates stood in the middle of the room, screaming while blood spurted out of his nose. Two officers pinned Porter against the wall as they handcuffed him.

One officer bled from his lip, the other bled from his nose. A table was flipped, three chairs laid on their sides, and another officer leaned against the counter, holding the side of his head.

"What the hell is going on here?" Detective Christensen strode into the middle of the mess.

Porter turned, his eyes finding me. He had no expression on his face.

"This guy jumped that guy over there." One officer jerked the cuffs on Porter, making him wince. "When we tried to pull him off, he resisted arrest."

"For fuck's sake." Detective Christensen pushed the officer out of the way. She took keys out of her pocket and removed the handcuffs from Porter. "This is my victim's fiancé."

Porter turned and eyeballed Yates, reminding me of a predator debating how best to launch his next attack.

The detective pushed her finger up in Porter's face. "You're going to calmly walk this shit off, right?"

He rubbed his wrists and, with a dark glance my way, gave a short nod.

She turned to Yates. "Who the fuck are you?"

"Beth is the love of my life," his bloody hand muffled his voice, "and that barbarian attacked me in cold blood."

She assessed Porter. "I assume you have a good reason for attacking this man?"

"He's following Beth. I wanted to know how he knew she was here."

Her head volleyed back to Yates. "That's a good question. How did you know Beth was here?"

Yates winced. "I want a lawyer."

She pointed at Yates. "Put this guy in room three. And let him call his lawyer."

The officer glared at Porter, but he led Yates out.

Yates yelled over his shoulder. "You're arresting the wrong man. He's an animal. Did you see what he did to my face?"

She jutted her chin at the other two officers. "Go clean up."

They both shot daggers at Porter but obediently left the room.

She crossed her arms and gave Porter a pointed look. "You think this Yates is part of this?"

I relayed my conversation with Yates, told her about our history and how he was now my father's campaign manager.

"Do you think he's following you?"

"How did he know she would be here?" Porter butt in.

She shook her head. "No clue, but I plan on finding out."

Porter gave a sharp nod.

She crossed her arms. "Do me a favor and don't take out half my team next time?"

He remained expressionless.

She sighed. "Go home. Get some rest. I'll be in touch."

CHAPTER 37

BACK AT THE APARTMENT, I did my best to hide how much my body hurt.

Porter walked to the bathroom. "I'm going to run you a bath. You'll feel better after you soak."

I held up my bandages and followed him in.

He ran my bath, then turned to me. "I've got you covered." He carefully undressed me and lifted me into the tub. "Keep your hands on the edge of the tub."

I should have felt self-conscious about my naked state, but the warm water felt too damn good. I laid back and observed Porter with half-shut eyes. He sat beside the tub, and his hand rested on my stomach. He appeared lost in thought.

"Does this mean our hot night where I'm the sex slave is canceled?"

His tone remained dry, "Oh, I think I've done enough damage to your body tonight."

"Porter," my voice went soft.

His eyes lifted to mine. "I shouldn't have taken that call."

"I shouldn't have gone to the store by myself."

"I was distracted."

"You're not to blame. You saved me."

"I also hurt you."

His evident guilt told me I needed to change the conversation. So I asked a question I wasn't sure he'd answer. "Who's Jordan?"

His jaw tightened. "My brother."

Ahhh. "Okay."

"My dad's retiring from ranching."

I waited, hoping that he'd share something of himself without me asking.

Don't make me pry. Please, don't make me pry.

"My dad owns one of the biggest ranches in Montana. As each of my brothers grew up, he parceled off exactly one-sixth of his land to each of them."

"Okay."

He swirled his fingertips over my stomach. "He ran his family like a democracy. Each time he did that, all of us had a vote. He said this was our future, and we all had a say. Everyone had to vote, and everyone had to vote yes for it to happen."

"Oh, wow."

His eyes lifted to mine. "The remaining sixth piece of land, he's been ranching. He's parceled everything else off to my brothers, and now he wants us all to vote on giving the last piece to me."

My mouth parted as I remembered his side of the conversation.

I hear you. No, I get that, but I don't deserve any of that. I don't even think I should vote...

I get that, Jordan, but I haven't been back there in years. I have no say in this decision. Nor should I...

Jordan, I honestly have no say. I support whatever you guys decide.

"You don't think you deserve that," my voice was soft. I had no idea of the history of his family, but I knew that he felt he didn't deserve his piece of land.

"I know I don't." Sadness seeped from his eyes.

I lifted a bandaged hand and touched his face. He turned towards it and kissed my hand. Our eyes met again.

"I think you deserve the world." I meant it.

He studied me for a long moment. "Why?"

"I just do. I think you're incredible."

"Beth."

I had no idea why, but tears spurted out of my eyes. I clumsily wiped them away with the back of my bandages. "Sorry. I never cry."

"Talk to me."

I hated that I was screwing all of this up. I hated that I made Porter pretend to be something fake because he was the most authentic person I knew. Right now, he was the only thing that made sense in my life.

But how could I tell him that? How could I say to him that I felt real feelings for him? I was shocked that the guy was still here. A teary, emotional confession was exactly what this man didn't need.

"I'm screwing this all up."

He reached forward and wiped one of my tears off my cheek. "Hey, come on."

I squeezed my eyes shut. "I just...you're just...I think you deserve it all. All the happiness *and* your piece of land."

His smile was bemused. "That's why you're crying?"

My bottom lip trembled hard. "Pretty much."

His teeth flashed as his smile grew. "You're really cute when you cry. You know that?"

"You haven't seen my ugly cry yet."

He laughed. "And what does that entail?"

"I get really puffy and red. And there's a lot of snot. More than what would be considered normal."

"I can't wait."

"Oh trust me. That's a show you want to miss."

"Beth."

We stared at each other, my pulse quickening with each passing second.

I knew that if this conversation continued, in my state, I would end up blurting out things that we'd both regret. I bit my lip. "I think I want to get out now."

He took a washcloth, added a dab of soap, and lathered it softly across my body. I closed my eyes, allowing myself to enjoy being cared for. After the day I'd had, I wanted to curl up with Porter and sleep into the next day.

I shivered as he toweled me off, taking extra care to gently dry my body, each touch deliberate and so damn soft, I wanted to cry at the way he treated me like royalty.

He helped me get ready for bed, then tucked me in.

"Aren't you going to come to bed?" I hated how needy I sounded.

He leaned down and gave me a lingering kiss on this lips. "I just have to make some phone calls."

———

I woke up to the sun streaming into my room and Porter cuddling me from behind. I groaned, loving how warm his big body felt wrapped around me.

"How are you feeling?"

To be honest, I felt like I had been tackled by a 220-pound man onto a cement sidewalk. "I feel great," I lied, not wanting to add to his guilt. "In fact, I feel almost back to normal."

"Liar."

I slowly rolled my body over, so I faced him, using most of my effort to stifle my pained groan. "Nope. I'm fine. I'm totally good."

He tapped me on the nose. "You know what we call that in the military?"

"What?"

"SEAL tough."

"You saying I'm tough?"

"Damn straight."

"Is it hard to be a SEAL?"

"No. Not really."

"What do you like about it?"

His eyes searched my face. "To be honest? I like fighting."

"Is that why you fought with Yates?"

He snorted. "That wasn't a fight."

"Did the military teach you to like fighting?"

"No one can teach you to like to fight, but I think the military just helped me focus that energy."

"What do you like about it?"

"I think when the bullets are flying, and there is a real risk to your life, that's when the world just slows down."

"What do you mean?"

"When you're in a real fight, the consequences are big. If you lose you die, and if you win you live. My mind becomes completely focused. My body can do these amazing feats — I have speed and strength that I don't have any other time. And all this adrenaline is pumping, so I feel amazing, but this sense of calm just washes over me. Those moments are when I'm the best version of myself."

I stared at him in fascination. "That's why you like to fight."

"Yup."

I thought about the video of him racing across the street, being narrowly missed by a speeding car and flying through the air to save me. "Did time slow down when you saved me last night?"

He paused so long I wasn't sure he was going to answer. "Time didn't just slow down. My fucking heart stopped."

CHAPTER 38

NINE DAYS LATER, I sat on a park bench during my lunch break, talking to Emily. I had promised Porter that I'd eat at my desk, but they'd closed the office for a private meeting, and I had no choice but to leave.

Plus, it was so gorgeous outside, I couldn't help myself. There were enough people walking around that I was reasonably sure I was safe.

"How are you feeling now?" she sounded so concerned.

"A lot better. My bandages have come off my hands, and I can actually move without crying."

"Have you told your dad yet?"

"I've tried, but my dad left on yet another business trip, and he's not returning my calls. Plus, this situation warrants a sit-down talk."

"What does Porter have to say about that?"

He's beyond pissed.

"He's fine. He said the minute my dad gets back, we're going over to my parents' house, and he's going to spell everything out for him."

"So, basically, he's livid."

"Why do you say that?"

"When Jackson says he's going to spell something out to someone, it usually doesn't end well for the other person."

I laughed. "Okay, he's not happy, but in my dad's defense, I haven't been exactly pushing the issue."

"What happened with Yates?"

"Well, the detective called me, and she told me that Yates admitted to putting some sort of tracker on my phone when we were dating!"

"What? That's so creepy."

"Right? Which explains why he always knew where I was. The detective told me I could press charges, but he's not the real enemy here. He's not trying to kill me. He only wants to date me."

"You don't think he's involved with this other stuff?"

I made a noise. "No. The other stuff is too big, too dark, for him to get messed up into."

"What did the detective say about the guy who was driving the car? The one who got murdered?"

"Apparently, he's known by the police, but that's all she'll tell us. She said she's still trying to determine if he was actually targeting me and how he ties into everything."

"Do you think your life is in danger?"

Yes!

"No, Emily, don't be silly. Come on."

"But this seems to be escalating."

"The detective can't even determine if any of this is related. Besides, nothing has happened in the last week."

"How is Porter dealing with this?"

He's losing his mind.

"Oh, he's become a bit more safety conscious, but at least with my dad being away, we haven't had any campaigning to do. It's fine, Em. Honest."

"Okay," she sounded unconvinced, "and how's the wedding planning going?"

"My mom is completely out of control, but she and Roo have planned the most gorgeous wedding."

"So...are you and Porter actually engaged?"

I could feel my face turn hot and red. "Emily! No!"

"Well, I don't know. With all that hot sex and him being so protective, I was thinking maybe this was becoming the real thing."

"Em, I coerced this guy into everything. He's probably counting the days until this mess is over. Trust me, Porter doesn't want to date me."

"I think you like him."

I couldn't lie. "Maybe, but my feelings don't count in this situation."

"I think you should tell him how you feel."

"Are you kidding me?"

"No. You know, sometimes honesty is good."

"He came to New York to get Felicia back."

"I know."

"And one night, as a quick favor, the poor bastard got called to a police station to bail my ass out of jail. I was in jail, Emily. *Jail.*"

"That wasn't your fault."

"I forced him to be my fake boyfriend to ward off the jealous ex-boyfriend."

"It was a spur of the moment thing."

"Just like the secret fake engagement? Which has led us to our big, fat fake wedding."

I could hear her smile. "You make it sound so bad."

I laughed. "It's bad, Emily. This is so bad, even you can't make rainbows out of this."

"He deserves to know the truth."

"He deserves a medal. His interactions with my mom, alone, warrants him receiving a purple heart. He's a damn freaking hero around her. But regrettably, the fun isn't over yet. We still have a public break up to face. And that's going to be ugly."

"I think he likes you."

"I think he likes you and Jackson. So, despite the fact that one little favor has turned into a full-time, life-altering, life-threatening public experience, he's still valiantly trying to hang in there. Because of you guys. But forcing him to face my unwanted emotional advances after he has expressed how he feels about Felicia would be cruel."

"Who says he'll let you down?"

"Right. Are we having the same conversation? I'm running for the Pulitzer of worst dating candidates right now."

"I vote that you talk to him."

"Emily, this is one of the reasons I love you so much—your unfailing belief in humanity and everything good. But Hell will freeze over before I burden him with that."

"Will you think about it?"

I snorted. "No."

"We can talk about this later."

"You're relentless. How does Jackson put up with your strong arm techniques?"

"He says I'm the boss."

"That I believe."

"I miss you."

"Not as much as I miss you."

I had experienced crushing loneliness when Emily and Jackson left. But I no longer felt lonely.

When had that feeling gone away?

Since the day Porter showed up.

I didn't want to think about the day he left. But that day was coming. It was coming fast.

CHAPTER 39

"OH, FUCK, BETH," Porter's voice was harsh in my ear.

My skirt was lifted up around my waist, and I sat on the edge of the kitchen counter with my legs wrapped around Porter's waist, his huge cock driving into me with intensity.

"I'm so close," I begged. "Please, don't stop."

His hand was fisted in my hair, pulling my head back while his other arm was wrapped around my waist, pulling me against him for better leverage. "Come on, gorgeous. Come for me. Come all over my cock."

My orgasm exploded, making me constrict tight around his hard dick. My entire body shuddered as wave after wave of mind-numbing pleasure rolled through me.

"My turn," he said through clenched teeth, and then he was pounding into me with ferocity. His forehead pressed hard against my neck, and he harshly swore as his body stiffened and he released himself into me.

We both breathed like warriors.

He eventually lifted his head, and his grey eyes stared into mine. "Was I too rough?"

"You know I love your savage mode."

"Savage mode?" Amusement colored his face.

"I'm going to miss this," I said truthfully, thinking about my conversation with Emily.

He lifted me down off the counter. "Oh, yeah?"

I pushed my skirt back over my legs and peered up at him, taking in his relaxed, post-sex face. "Not just the sex, though this is the best sex I've ever had in my life, but I'm going to miss you."

Grey eyes glanced at me. "We get along."

I swallowed, feeling more naked than I ever had in my life. "I just wish all of this had happened differently."

"What do you mean?"

"Just...this whole fake situation put a shelf life on this....on us. And I regret that."

He crossed his arms and leaned back against the counter. "You think this could have been different?"

Now that was a loaded question. A truthful answer would all but strip me down to my soul.

"I don't know. I just know that when this is all over, and you leave, I'm going to miss you. All of you."

He didn't speak. He just studied me.

Damn you, Emily, for making me believe in all your stupid romantic fantasies.

"We haven't plotted our big breakup either." I turned away in an attempt to hide how much his lack of response hurt.

"We'll sort something out."

"Okay." My emotions crushed me. "I should go change."

He moved with such stealth, I didn't hear him, but suddenly his arms were wrapped around me from behind. "You think I'm done with you?"

"What do you mean?" My voice shook.

"I can't get through my day unless you come on my tongue at least twice."

I can't get through my day...what did that mean?

I opened my mouth to ask, but his phone rang, ruining the moment.

"It's Jackson."

I dropped a kiss on his stubbled cheek and retreated to my room, but the question continued to occupy my thoughts.

What had he meant by that?

———

Three days later, after two mind-altering orgasms, Porter playfully slapped my ass and got out of bed. "I'm going to shower." He tossed me his phone. "If the pizza guy calls and says he's arrived, don't go down to the lobby by yourself. Come and get me."

I rolled onto my stomach. "You're not worried I'm going to snoop?"

He glanced back at me, a grin on his face. "You're curious about me?"

I shrugged. "Maybe."

"Snoop all you want. Just don't go downstairs by yourself." He walked into the bathroom.

"Don't you think the danger has passed?" I called after him.

He returned to the doorway. "Are you going to come and get me if the pizza arrives?" He had that don't-fuck-around look to him.

"I promise."

He stood there, studying me for a moment. "I mean it, Beth."

"Porter! I won't. I promise."

He disappeared back into the washroom. I heard the shower start, and I wasted no time opening his phone. I started with his photos. He didn't have too many. There were a surprising amount of pictures of Theo on his phone.

But the further back I went, the more pictures I found of Felicia. Fuck, she was gorgeous. She had that ethereal beauty that just defied logic. The more I studied her face, the more perfect looking she became.

There was a photo of her lying on a beach in a bikini. Another one of her cooking and laughing. One where she was lying on the couch, reading. But the one photo that ultimately hurt my stomach was a selfie of her and Porter.

They were on a beach. She had her arms wrapped around his big neck, and her head was on his shoulder, and she had the most content smile on her face. He was laughing up at the camera. He seemed so damn happy it hurt. And if you tried, you couldn't find a more beautiful couple.

What had their relationship been like? How could two people look so happy and end so tragically? Did he want her back? When this was all over, would he return to her?

I moved to skim his text messages, caring only about the ones between him and Felicia. I scrolled past dozens of messages from her, begging him to call her, and then there were three texts from him.

Porter: Felicia, where are you?

Porter: Felicia, I need to know that you're okay.

Porter: Felicia, just pick up your phone.

I could feel my heart pounding in my stomach. I checked the dates. These texts were just before the weekend of Theo's christening. Which meant he had come home, found her missing and sent those out.

The man did not resort to begging. He texted her three times and then nothing. He never reached out again. That didn't mean he hadn't tried to find her, but he hadn't bombed her phone with messages either.

I scrolled further back in time. Some messages showed me just how regular of a couple they were before she had left.

Felicia: At the grocery store, do we still have potatoes?

Porter: Yes. Can you pick up some more toothpaste?

Felicia: Got it already. Anything else?

Porter: I think we need pancake syrup.

Felicia: Okay. Home soon.

I kept scrolling. A few more texts that showed they were a typical couple that didn't always get along perfectly.

Porter: Some friends are going out tonight. Want to come?

Felicia: Again?

Porter: Come on, it'll be fun. The wives are coming, too

Felicia: I'm doing my nails tonight

Porter: Do them tomorrow

Felicia: No, thanks

Porter: I won't be late. Wait up for me

Felicia: Don't wake me when you get home

Wow. Her snarky tone shocked me. If Porter texted me to wait up for him, I'd be lying on the bed in something sexy, counting the hours until he got home.

I scrolled down some more and covered my mouth as I read what appeared to be a fight. About sex.

Porter: I'm sorry, okay?

Felicia: You know I HATE THAT

Porter: I didn't mean to take it that far

Felicia: You pulled out some of my hair extensions, do you know how expensive they are?

Porter: I did not know you had fake hair attached to your head

Felicia: My extensions are not fake!!! Okay?!? That is hair from a real person and pulling my FUCKING hair is not acceptable

Porter: I barely touched your hair. I was gentle

Felicia: You were not gentle. You were rough. New

rule. **Don't pull my hair, don't touch my hair, don't even look at my hair when we make love!!!**

Porter: Don't be mad

Felicia: I'm mad!

Porter: Don't wait up

That exchange shocked me. Exactly how incompatible had they been in bed? Porter never was overly rough when we were in bed, but damn, I loved it when he pulled my hair and showed me who was in charge.

I couldn't imagine ever complaining about anything he did in bed. The guy defied my wildest dreams in the bedroom. Honestly, I'd take anything he'd give in bed.

I heard the shower water turn off. I hurriedly scrolled through his phone calls. There were multiple phone calls from Felicia, and all of them were unanswered except the last one.

My throat tightened.

Two days ago, Porter had picked up one of her calls, and they had talked for over ten minutes. My heart buzzed in my throat.

"Did the pizza guy phone?" Porter called from the bathroom.

"Not yet." I quickly locked his phone screen and tossed it aside.

Worry washed over me. Three days ago, I had confessed to Porter that I was going to miss him when this was all over. I had told him that I wished this situation was different.

His indifferent response had cut me deep. Now, to find out that the very next day he took a call from Felicia and talked to her for ten minutes? That sent chills down my spine.

I watched through half-shut eyes as Porter walked into the bedroom, a towel wrapped around his waist, showcasing his perfect body off. Usually, I would be plotting how to get that towel on the floor, but instead, I rolled off the bed and began to pull some comfy clothes on.

"Feel free to stay naked." He wrapped his arms around my waist from behind. "You know I'm going to get you naked as soon as I have some sustenance."

"I'm a bit cold," I wasn't lying. My entire body felt cold, but not because of the temperature of the room.

"I can warm you up."

I turned and flashed him a sassy smile, even though my heart felt limp. "After pizza, you can do your best."

CHAPTER 40

A WEEK LATER, I stood outside work, looking for Porter's truck. Usually, if he couldn't get parking in front of my building, he parked and walked over to meet me.

He was running forty-five minutes late. I checked my phone for the tenth time. No texts, no calls.

And I had already sent him multiple texts.

Me: Are you tied up?

Me: Want me to take a cab home?

Me: Should I wait here?

Me: I'm going to take a cab home, okay?

I canvassed the street, wondering what had happened. This wasn't like Porter. He was meticulous about picking me up, making sure I was okay. He never let me out of his sight when I went out in public.

I thought his protective behavior was overboard, but now, when he wasn't around, with no word from him, I feared that something was wrong.

Maybe his phone had died.

Maybe he'd been in a fender bender.

Maybe someone had attacked him and hurt him.

Panic made my throat tighten to the point of pain. What if something had happened to him? I wondered what to do. Should I stay here and wait? Should I go home?

What if he was lying unconscious at home, unable to move? What if someone attacked him in the garage and he was lying there bleeding to death? I needed to help him, right?

My mind was going into overdrive.

I decided I couldn't stand, waiting around. I hailed a cab and checked for any accidents along the way home. I saw nothing, and the cab driver pulled up in front of my building.

I paid the cab and checked the garage.

Porter's truck wasn't parked.

He failed to pick me up.

And he had talked to Felicia two days ago.

Maybe he was with Felicia.

I squared my shoulders and went upstairs, wondering if I'd find his boxes still in my apartment. Is that how he'd eventually leave me?

Would he simply disappear one day?

My phone rang. It was Porter. "Beth, are you coming down soon?"

I frowned. "What do you mean?"

"I'm at your work. Waiting for you, but I'm about to get a ticket. You need more time?"

"What are you doing there?"

"An hour ago, you sent me a text telling me you'd be an hour late."

"I sent you no such text. In fact, I waited 45 minutes for you to pick me up. You didn't answer my texts, so I grabbed a cab."

"I haven't had a chance to check my phone, I've been driving, but I did get the text saying you'd be late."

"If you got a text from a woman telling you that she was running late, then you either got your texts or your women mixed up, because I didn't send you anything like that." I was breathing hard. I hated this. I wanted to cry. I didn't want it to end like this. With lies. And deceit.

"Where. Are. You?"

I walked into the bedroom and kicked off my shoes. "I'm at home."

"I need you to leave your apartment and go stand in the lobby. I'm on my way."

"Don't be ridiculous," I scoffed, hating that he was going to use my fear to cover up his lies, "I'm here, and there's no one here."

"Beth. I need you to get the fuck out of that apartment."

Someone grabbed me by the throat. It was a big arm, hauling me back. I screamed as my feet kicked and flailed in the air. He had a knife, and it was pressed against my throat. This was like that moment in the restaurant bathroom, only I knew the outcome would be much worse.

I was going to die here.

Of that, I was certain.

Something came over me. Something that said I wasn't going to die without a fight. Maybe it was Porter in the back of my mind, or the way his scent lingered in the air, but I felt him here, and it gave me strength.

I drew upon that strength and slammed the heel of my foot on the top of his foot. He grunted in pain. Then, with a scream that sounded borderline feral, I head-butted him back, hitting him in the nose.

I caught him off guard, and I stepped wide, catching him off balance. The knife waved dangerously in the air. I kicked him in the nuts and felt something warm burn my side.

My fingers clawed at his eyes, scratching, gouging, working to blind him. He howled in pain, staggering back. Someone was screaming, so loud, it was hurting my ears.

Was that me?

Was that sound actually coming out of me?

I jumped with all my weight back onto his foot and clawed down his face. His arms came up in self-defense, and one hand grabbed me by the throat. I was a wildcat. Kicking. Kicking. Kicking. Knees up. Scratching.

He bent over. I must have connected with his balls.

And then he tipped back, his face a bloody mess. "You're a crazy fucking bitch."

I glanced down. There was blood. So much fucking blood. Where was it all coming from?

"I'm just getting warmed up, asshole," I wavered towards him.

"Fuck you." He disappeared out of the bedroom.

I fell to my knees, looking down at my dress. A growing stain, so bright, so red, was spreading across my yellow dress.

Too much blood.

I held my side, looking around the room. Something was ringing. I could see the light of my phone. I felt so weak. So tired. I crawled to my phone and swiped to answer.

"Porter?" I wheezed.

"Oh, fuck, Beth," Porter sounded so intense. So angry.

"Hey," I said, falling onto my back, looking at the ceiling of my bedroom. I was pretty sure I was in shock. "Some guy attacked me in my bedroom. With a knife."

"The police and ambulance are on their way." Panic laced his voice, and so much emotion I couldn't decipher accompanied it. "Okay? Hang on."

I heard a horn blaring. "Get the fuck out of my way," he yelled.

"Don't get into an accident," I said slowly.

"Baby, I'm on my way. I'm three minutes out."

His horn blared some more.

"I fought," I said, fighting the blackness that was closing in on my vision. "I fought so hard, but nothing slowed down. It all sped up. Why didn't it slow down?"

"Sweetheart," his breath was harsh in my ear, "tell me you're okay."

I raised my head and peered at my stomach. My dress was drenched in blood. "I think he stabbed me. I think I'm dying."

"No, fuck that. You're not dying, okay? You fucking stay alive. That's an order!"

"I thought you were with Felicia," I whispered. "I thought you were leaving me, but maybe I'm the one leaving."

"Beth! Beth, baby, stay on the phone with me, okay? No one is leaving anyone."

"I did something stupid." I laid my head back, fighting to stay awake. "I broke the last rule. I don't think of you as a friend. I think I like you. A lot. Which is so stupid of me, and I feel embarrassed, but since this might be our last conversation, I wanted you to know." I started to cry. "I want you to be happy."

"Beth," he yelled in my ear. "If you leave me, I'm not going to be happy, so stay the fuck alive."

I tried to keep the phone by my ear, but I felt weak. I blinked, and then darkness came over me.

CHAPTER 41

BEEP. Beep. Beep.

I opened my eyes. I was in a bed in a strange room. A man in green scrubs stood at the foot of the bed, writing something in a chart.

"Hey," I said, my voice hoarse.

He put the chart down and moved to stand beside me. "How are you feeling, Beth?"

My body hurt, but my mind felt alert and awake. "Who are you?"

"I'm your surgeon."

"What happened?"

"You got stabbed."

"I know that. But what happened after that?"

He pulled the stethoscope from around his neck and began to listen to my chest. "Deep breaths, please. The blade of the knife slightly nicked your liver. We went in laparoscopically and stitched you up. Barring the possibility of an infection, I expect you to have a full recovery."

I swallowed. My throat felt dry. "Is anyone here?"

He stood back up and looked at the monitors above my head. "Your parents are here. And there is also a furious, terrifying guy, who has been raising hell since you were admitted. He's terrorized my nurses, and he threatened to kill me if I didn't save your life."

Porter was here!

"I don't think he actually would've killed you."

The doctor gave me a look. "I'm pretty sure he meant it."

"Good thing I lived then, hey?" I awkwardly joked.

"Tell you what. You can see them for five minutes, and for my own personal safety, you can show them that you're alive, but then you need to get some sleep."

***

Mom wept when she saw me. She sat beside my bed and held my hand while tears poured down her face. Meanwhile, Dad stood on the other side of the bed and stared down at me like it was his mission to look devastated.

"Beth..." He swallowed. "I'm so sorry. So sorry."

But the one person I was interested in leaned against the far wall. His arms were crossed, and he had the worst scowl on his face. He didn't speak. He just stared at me.

Porter was beyond pissed. I could feel the anger rolling off him in waves, and he was doing nothing to hide it.

"Mom," I said weakly. "I'm fine. Okay?"

She shook her head, unable to stop crying.

I turned to my dad for help. "Doctor said I'm going to make a full recovery."

He blinked at the ceiling as he fought tears. I had never seen my father show any emotion. Certainly not tears.

"Dad, come on," I said softly.

He struggled to gain composure. My eyes were drawn back to Porter, whose t-shirt was covered in dark brown stains. My blood. He hadn't moved an inch, and his eyes never left my face.

His stare was cold and hard. Fuck. I remembered Emily telling me that Jackson had two modes. One was normal, tough guy Jackson. And the other mode she called his SEAL mode.

She told me Jackson got this edge, this energy, that could clear rooms and make grown men shit their pants. I studied Porter. He was in full-on SEAL mode. He was edgy as fuck, and one wrong look, one wrong move, and a beast would be unleashed.

"Mom, Dad, can you give Porter and me a moment?"

They'd been dealing with Porter for who knew how many hours. It was telling what those hours had been like, because without saying another word, without looking at him, they stood and vacated the room.

I laid there and evaluated him. If looks could kill, I'd be dead a hundred times over. "You're pissed."

He stared at me, blinking, but other than that, he didn't move a muscle.

"I fucked up." I bit my lip. "You warned me, and I ignored your warning."

He swallowed but didn't even blink.

"Can you tell me what happened?"

His voice was cold and clipped. Emotionless. "I wasn't there to protect you. You dropped your phone, and I could hear your screams. You sounded like you were being murdered. And I had to hang up. I had to hang up on you to call 911. And when we got to you, you were no longer conscious."

"Do you hate me?"

He didn't move. He stood there, arms crossed, staring down at me.

"Okay, " I said, my voice cracking. "I understand."

The nurse pushed in the door. The moment she saw Porter, she stopped in her tracks and started to back out of the room.

"Is visiting time over?" I asked. I needed him out of here before he told me he was done. I didn't think I could handle it if he told me that. I needed to gain some strength before he told me he was done with me.

"Yes," she said timidly.

I looked back at Porter. He pushed himself off the wall and, without looking back, walked out. I started to cry, wondering if I would ever see him again.

The nurse rushed to my side and placed her cool hand on my forehead. "Are you okay?"

I shook my head, as tears squeezed out of my eyes. "I think he's going to leave me."

She looked dumbstruck at my reason for crying. "Why don't I give you something for the pain. It'll help you sleep, okay?"

I nodded. "Please knock me out. I don't think I can take this."

She thought I was talking about my wound, but I was talking about my heart.

I woke up, disoriented. I pushed open my eyes through the haze of drugs they had pumped into me. The room was dark. Something big and warm was holding me.

Was I hallucinating?

"Porter?"

Stubbled lips grazed my temple. "Go back to sleep."

I snuggled back against him. Porter had climbed into my hospital bed, and he was big spooning me. And it felt so damn good.

"Are you still angry?"

A long beat passed. "Anger doesn't cover it."

I fought sleep that tried to tug me back under. I had so much to say, but the words in my brain weren't escaping. Random, weird thoughts flitted around in my head, like fireflies buzzing in circles.

Time did not slow down when I fought. Ask Porter why.

That text wasn't from me.

What does a liver do?

Did they catch that guy?

Where was Felicia? Did he see her?

Did someone call Detective Christensen?

Would he stay?

"Please don't leave," I mumbled.

"I'm not going anywhere."

"Promise?"

"Go to sleep."

And then those fuzzy, buzzing thoughts faded and everything went dark.

CHAPTER 42

"FOR ONLY BEING four days post-op, you're healing at a remark-
able rate," my doctor said after examining my wound. "You've no sign
of infection, and your liver panel is perfect. I think tomorrow, if you
have a good night, we're going to discharge you."

Mom leaned forward in the chair. "We've hired a team of private
round-the-clock nurses."

The doctor glanced at me, unable to hide the fact that he thought
she was going overboard. "That's not a bad idea for the first day or
two. A nurse can help you change your bandages and help you
manage any pain, although, at the rate you are healing, you're going
to be fine."

"We've also hired a full security team," she added.

"Why?" I asked, baffled.

"Porter insisted on it, but your father agreed."

I observed my mom. She looked disheveled and tired.

I waited until the doctor walked out before I asked my mom, "Are
you okay?"

"It's been a strain. Your father feels horribly guilty."

"This isn't Dad's fault."

"He knows you tried to talk to him. He feels terrible that he didn't make time for you."

"I don't blame him."

She shook her head. "If it wasn't for Porter, I simply don't know how we'd have coped. That man has been an absolute rock."

You mean the man who hasn't come by to see me yet?

It confused me that Porter was still very much on the scene, working with my parents, planning my life for when I got out of the hospital, but except for that first night that he climbed into bed with me, I hadn't seen him.

When I wasn't sleeping or reassuring my parents, I spent the rest of my time thinking about him. My phone call with him after I had been stabbed was a bit fuzzy, but I was reasonably certain that I had confessed my feelings to him.

And I recalled him being pretty upset over me getting attacked, which could possibly be interpreted as him caring a bit for me, but now he was avoiding me. How many awful moments had I thrust him into?

Anyone else would have disappeared a long time ago, yet he continued to rise to the occasion. I couldn't figure out if that was because he cared or if he was simply a man of exceptional character.

Mom interrupted my thoughts. "Your apartment is much too small for all the staff, and I was hoping to bring you home to our place, but Porter made alternative arrangements."

"Oh?"

"Emily has offered you use of her penthouse until you make a full recovery."

Thank fuck.

"Mom, you should go home and get some rest."

She fought tears and shook her head. "Sorry."

"Mom, it's okay to cry."

"Porter said under no circumstances are we to upset you or bother you."

"It doesn't upset me if you cry."

She sniffed and stood. "I have to go to your apartment and supervise the team that's moving some of your stuff over."

"Mom, go home and rest. I can deal with that in a day or two."

"Porter said that he didn't want you to have to go back there until you're fully recovered. He thought the crime scene would be too upsetting."

"Is there anything he hasn't taken care of?" I joked to cover up my bewilderment.

She took my question seriously. "No, I think he's covered pretty much everything. He's... he's a good man, Beth."

Why did she choose to realize that when the end felt so near?

―――

"How are you feeling?" Dad asked, standing in front of the couch the nurse had settled me onto.

"I'm good." I looked around the vast sitting room in Emily's penthouse.

Roo and Mom sat on the opposite couch. Porter leaned against the wall, his arms crossed, his face devoid of expression. This was the first time I had seen Porter since I had been discharged, and he still looked as pissed as he did that first night in the hospital.

"I want to make a family announcement." Dad cleared his throat, glancing at Porter.

I furrowed my brows. "Okay."

"After careful consideration, I've decided to drop out of the race for mayor."

I couldn't believe it. It was not like my father to ever back down.

"Dad, I think Michael Renner is behind these attacks."

"And that's exactly why this is an appropriate decision. You almost died. If that isn't reason enough, I don't know what is."

"We all feel that way," Mom added.

I suddenly realized that I wanted my dad to run for mayor, and I wanted him to win. After everything that had happened, it would feel like defeat to give up now.

I struggled to find words to express myself. "Renner's corrupt, and he's a bully. And that's exactly why he can't continue as mayor," I argued.

"I'm not willing to risk your safety."

"And I'm not willing to be the reason you give up your dream."

He looked conflicted. "What if something happens to you?"

"Dad, nothing is going to happen to me. This place is like Fort Knox, and you've hired an impressive security team."

"And Porter is here, too," Mom added, glancing back at Porter.

I couldn't even process that, so I ignored Mom's comment. "Dad, I think you'd be an amazing leader for this city. New York deserves someone like you." Definitely not Renner.

"Porter, what do you think?" Dad deferred to Porter, who had been silently listening.

I froze, thunderstruck by how Porter seemed to be the new leader of this family.

"I've never quit a fight in my life," he said, his eyes on my face.

"Please, Dad." I turned back to my father. "I really want you to give this your all and go kick some ass."

"Beth, language!" Mom interjected.

My mom, despite herself, couldn't be anything but who she was. I don't know why, but that made me so damn happy. At least some things hadn't changed.

"Dad, it would mean the world to me."

"You really want me to do this?"

"Yes, Dad. More than anything."

The burden visibly lifted off his shoulders. "All right, then. Let's win this race!"

Roo clapped with glee, and he shared a hug with my mom. The pair looked close, thicker than thieves.

"Everyone out," Porter's voice was low.

My parents and Roo obediently stood like good little soldiers.

Mom came over and kissed me on the cheek, and then, within moments, the penthouse was quiet, and then it was only Porter and me.

Silence ticked between us. I studied him. Grey eyes studied me back.

"Hi," I said a bit lamely.

He continued to look at me. No expression. Just that intense stare.

"You're still pissed," I volunteered.

"Yes."

"Did you really get a text from my phone number telling you I'd be an hour late?"

His jaw tightened. "It was a fake SMS."

No one since I had been in the hospital had been willing to talk to me about what was going on. I craved information, and I hoped he'd give it to me. "Do they know who it was from?"

"An untraceable burner phone."

"Do they have any leads on who did this?"

"I'll find him."

That sounded ominous. I didn't even know what to say about that.

"Why are you mad at me?"

"Why do you think?"

I hated it when tough questions got volleyed back at me. "Because I took a cab home by myself."

"What else?"

"Because I didn't leave the apartment when you told me to."

"What else?"

I thought about that long and hard. I chewed on my lip. "Because I didn't trust you?"

"Because you didn't trust me."

I swallowed, remembering my state of mind before my attack. I had been so convinced that Porter had been delayed because he was with Felicia. I had been certain he was leaving me.

His voice was rough. "Have I ever done anything to warrant your lack of trust?"

No. He hadn't. Those had been my own fears, my own past prejudices coming into play.

"No."

"If you don't trust me, there's no point to any of this."

Cold fear drenched my heart. "What are you saying?"

"It's your choice. You either completely trust me, or we don't do this at all."

I didn't know if he was talking about him protecting me or if he was referencing us. I couldn't bring myself to call this a relationship, but whatever it was, it was becoming the most important thing in my life. The thought of him walking away terrified me.

"I choose to trust you. Completely."

He pushed himself off the wall and walked towards me. He grabbed my chin and forced me to look up at him. "Don't ever fucking scare me like that again."

Warmth flooded my heart. "You don't look like you scare that easy."

"I don't. But when I heard your scream on the phone..."

"I fought." Stupid tears filled my eyes as I remembered the terror of that moment.

"You fought like hell, and you survived."

"What if he comes back?"

"I told you I'd take care of it."

I stared up at this beautiful man. He was a master at sending mixed messages. If this was a different situation, the ambiguity of his feelings compared to how deeply I was falling would drive me to push him for answers. But under the circumstances, I felt pathetically grateful he was still around.

My mouth opened, but I snapped it shut in an instant, taken aback. At that moment, I realized I was falling in love with him.

CHAPTER 43

I *WAS FALLING* in love with Porter.

And I had no idea how he felt about me.

His actions told me he cared, but all my feeble attempts to move this sham into reality had fallen spectacularly flat. I mean, I'd all but confessed my heart to him on my deathbed.

If he felt anything back, wouldn't that have inspired some sort of conversation? Instead, in the same breath, he was asking me for absolute trust while threatening to walk.

Maybe that was the price for loving this man. You gave him your heart, and he responded by being the best man you've ever met without promises to stay. He still felt so distant, so far away.

I needed some reassurance. Having his body against mine would chase those fears away.

Hopeful, I asked, "Does this mean we can have sex now?"

He frowned. "You're still recovering from surgery."

"A blow job, then."

"When you're better."

"I feel loads better already."

A ghost of a smile traced his lips. "Get some sleep. Obey your security team."

He stepped back from me.

"You're not going to be here?"

"No."

I wanted to ask him where he was going and who he'd be seeing, but we'd just finished the trust talk. What if he was going to see Felicia? I hated how small and jealous I felt. The situation was infuriating, but I bit the question before it escaped my mouth.

"Talk," he demanded.

"If our situations were reversed, wouldn't you want to know where I was going?"

"You want to know where I'm going?"

I did, but I didn't want to admit that. It made me feel small and insecure.

He answered for me, "I have a meeting with Detective Christensen tonight, and then I'm going to do my own hunting."

"Oh." I felt stupid. "For my attacker?"

"For your attacker."

"But he's a dangerous person."

"I'm a hundred times more dangerous than his worst nightmare."

"What will you do if you find him."

"We'll sit down and have a talk."

Translation: there'd be no talking.

Should I be scared for him? I doubted he'd be able to find a man that the police force couldn't find. But maybe it'd make him feel better to look. Who was I to hinder that?

But what about Felicia? Was he back in contact with her? After spending time in my world, was he ready to go back to her?

He growled. "What's on your mind?"

I hated myself for even saying anything, but I couldn't stop myself from speaking, "Remember when I had your phone, and you were in the shower? The night we got pizza?"

"What about it."

"It showed that you had talked to Felicia. For ten minutes."

"So?"

Was he really going to make me ask this?

"So, are you two hanging out now?"

"No."

That should have made me feel better, but it didn't. It only made me feel stupid for asking. "Okay."

"Want me to help you to bed?" When I nodded, he easily lifted me into his arms and carried me to the California king-sized bed in the guest room. With infinite gentleness, he laid me into bed and pulled the covers over me. "Sleep."

"Will you kiss me?"

He hesitated so long, my heart began to pound, but then his mouth covered mine. I moaned into the kiss that had all the passion, all the lust and chemistry that I remembered. My entire body responded to that him, remembering what the kiss could lead to, remembering how good it could feel.

He pulled back, slightly breathless. His eyes were dark with desire. But without saying another word, he walked out of the room and shut the door, and suddenly, I didn't feel too desirable.

<hr />

Another week passed, and my body healed to the point of near normalcy. Except for the tiny row of stitches on my abdomen, you'd never know I'd been stabbed.

What hadn't returned to normal was my relationship with Porter. He was gone night and day, never telling me where he went. I barely saw him, and when I did, he was as intense and emotionless as he'd been the last two times I'd talked to him. I stressed about that. I mourned those easy-going days when he was light-hearted and fun. I missed being desired. I craved his body. Instead, this SEAL side of him intimidated and confused me.

Roo and Mom set up what they termed their 'war room,' which

was an entire room dedicated to the comprehensive planning of my faux wedding. Out of sheer boredom, I spent a lot of time with them, helping them fill party favors for guests, doing cake tastings and discussing floral colors.

To my profound shock, they'd switched the colors of my wedding theme to a soft, gentle pink. No more smaragdine. When I asked them what had happened to the emerald green, Roo didn't bother to glance up from his binder and said, "Porter happened."

Even when he wasn't here, he was here.

I woke up to a noise in the kitchen. Pulling my short robe over my body, I crept out toward the light. Porter sat on a stool beneath the light. He looked like hell. He had a black eye, and his lip was cut.

A very professional medical kit laid beside him on the counter. I approached him silently and covered my mouth when I saw what he was doing. His arm rested on a surgical towel, and he was stitching a deep cut on his forearm with a needle and a professional pair of medical forceps.

"Oh, no, Porter." I gasped, rushing forward.

He glanced up at me. "What are you doing up?"

"What happened?"

I stared in horror at his arm. The cut was deep, and he had put in five expert stitches. Blood trickled down his forearm.

He ignored me.

"We should take you to the hospital."

He expertly tied off the last stitch. "No need."

"What if your arm gets infected?"

"It won't."

"How do you even know how to do that?" I watched as he irrigated the wound with a syringe, ripped open a package of gauze with his teeth, and covered the cut before taping it.

"We stitch ourselves up in the field all the time." He was so casual about the fact, he could have been talking about a paper cut.

"What happened?" I stared at his face.

His bottom lip was marred by a nasty cut. He stood and stretched his arm, testing the bandage. Dark blood stained his t-shirt.

My eyes widened. "Your shirt. You're bleeding."

He shook his head in disgust. "Ah man, this is one of my favorite t-shirts."

"Where else are you hurt?"

"I'm not. That isn't my blood."

Whose blood was it?

I felt so much dismay over this turn of events, I almost couldn't take it. "Are you going to tell me what happened?"

He gathered the suture kit up and dumped it in the garbage. "No."

"Well, what can you tell me?"

He leaned over and dropped a hard kiss on my lips. "It's done."

"What's done?"

He peeled off his t-shirt and inspected it closer. "Do you think this blood will come out?"

Desperate to help with something, I stepped forward. "I can soak it for you."

He leaned down and pressed another hot kiss on my mouth, and a deep moan escaped me. "I'm going to shower."

I stood there, clutching his shirt and watched his retreat. Several black and green bruises marred his muscular back. I wanted to join him. I wanted to beg him for answers. Instead, I rinsed his shirt in cold water, then soaked it.

Who had hurt him? Why had he been in a fight? What did he mean that it was over? I knew this was related to my situation, and the fact that he was hurt over it, made me feel terrible.

I crept back into bed and muffled my tears in my pillow. What was happening? Why had he been in such an extreme fight? Where was he going at night? I couldn't stand the idea of him being hurt.

Especially because it was my fault.

CHAPTER 44

MY BEDROOM DOOR OPENED, and he stood in the doorway, a silhouetted shadow. He approached the bed and, without speaking, climbed in and wrapped his huge warm body around me. "Were you crying?"

I sniffed. "No."

I could hear the smile in his voice. "Liar."

"No one likes a crybaby."

"Was this the cute cry or the ugly cry?" he teased.

"It wasn't the ugly cry."

"When's that going to happen?"

"Hopefully never. Nothing good has happened if I'm doing the ugly cry."

He tightened his arm around me, pulling me harder against his side.

"Do you ever cry?" I blurted out.

"Last time I cried, I was ten."

"What happened?"

"My horse died."

"You had a horse when you were ten?"

"I got Billy for my birthday when I was five. He'd been Dad's horse and had been passed through all my brothers until he became mine. He was really old and slow. But he was my horse."

"What happened?"

"Old age. Billy was already a grandpa by the time I got him, but I loved him until the day he died."

The image of Porter as a kid, crying over his horse, made me choke up. "That's so sad."

His lips grazed my neck. "It was, but Billy had a great life, and he died a peaceful death."

I laid there, thinking about Porter and this mysterious life he had lived in Montana. I tried to imagine him growing up with five older brothers on a ranch where five-year-olds got their own horses.

Whenever he spoke about that time in his life, there was nothing but respect and reverence for his childhood. What had gone wrong? Why had he left when at 18? And why didn't he think he deserved to return and be part of that legacy?

"You're different," I blurted out.

"From what?"

"Just... you seemed so distant after my accident. And now, you seem like yourself again."

He waited so long to answer, I wasn't sure he would. "I was focused."

"On what?"

"When I'm on a mission, we can't afford distractions. Most of us are really good at shutting everything else out."

"What were you focusing on?"

"Keeping you safe."

I twisted in his arms to look up at him. "There's so much going on."

He bent down and winced, before kissing me. "We'll figure it out."

"Are you hurt?" I lifted my head in concern.

He shook his head, his eyes already shut. "I'm fine."

I knew he was hurting, but I also knew he'd never admit it. "What can I do?"

"Go to sleep. We'll talk tomorrow."

Detective Christensen whistled as she walked into the vast living room. "Nice place you have here."

I sat up from where I was lying on the couch, reading. "Detective Christensen."

"Is Porter around?"

I shook my head. "He's gone for a fitting for his tux."

"Right, the wedding. When is that happening?"

"Five weeks from now." I shifted uncomfortably at the lie. I had five weeks left of Porter, and then he'd no longer be part of my life. I couldn't quite process that.

"How's the wedding planning going?"

"My mom and Roo are working over time."

"Who's Roo?"

"Our wedding planner."

She raised her eyes brows and nodded. "Right."

Porter walked into the living room. "Hey, Lena."

My eyes widened at the use of her first name.

"Hey, Porter."

"What's going on?" He sat on the armrest of the couch beside me.

"I just came by to tell you that we've had a break in the case."

"Oh, yeah?"

"We found the perp who attacked you," she said, looking at me. "His name is Donny Patrino."

My hands flew over my mouth. "Thank you."

"Don't thank us. The police had nothing to do with catching him. Last night, Donny was found on the steps of my precinct. He was hog-tied and beaten to a pulp. Tortured, actually. He had a confession note taped to his chest that was in his own handwriting, and he said that he'd tell us anything if we'd protect him."

I stilled, thinking back to last night, and I knew that was all Porter. "Oh."

"We did a rush DNA test on him and found that he was an exact match for the DNA we found under your fingernails after you were attacked."

"Did Donny say who tortured him?" I whispered, suddenly terrified that Porter would get in trouble or go to jail over this.

She shook her head, her eyes on Porter. "No, the guy was too scared. He kept saying he'd be safer in jail. You know anything about that Porter?"

He crossed his arms, and he slowly shook his head. "No clue."

"Right." She rolled her eyes. "Well, at this point, we don't actually care how he showed up. This guy is one bad dude. He's been known to the organized crime team as a high-level hitman for one of the biggest mafia families here in New York. When his DNA hit the system, it popped up in association with four other unsolved homicides in the city for the past few years alone."

"What did his confession say?" I asked.

"That's the concerning part. He said someone, whose name he did not know, hired him to first threaten you, which he did in the washroom of the restaurant. Then, he was rehired to increase the pressure. He said he wasn't actually hired to kill you, but he was instructed to mess you up as good as he could without killing you outright."

Fear pressed me back against Porter's leg. His hand moved onto the back of my neck. The words stuck in my throat, "Who hired him?"

"Even he doesn't seem to know. The instructions came through a burner, which we've retrieved. The message was sent from another untraceable burner phone. The money was sent to him via Bitcoin. It's also virtually untraceable."

"Do you think they'll try again?"

She was staring at the bandage on Porter's arm. "I think it'd be wise to keep that security team of yours on high alert until we get more information."

"We'll take care of it," Porter answered.

Detective Christensen stood up. "Everyone at the station is talking."

"About what?"

"How Donny was all but begging to be arrested. He was scared. Real bad. I'm wondering what kind of person could actually scare someone like Donny." She scanned Porter's face.

He shrugged but didn't speak.

"Uh-huh." She turned to me. "How are you doing after your surgery?"

"I get my stitches out today."

She nodded. "That's good."

The three of us stood there for a moment.

"Well, I'll see myself out."

The moment I heard the front door shut, I turned to Porter. "Does any of this have to do with you needing to stitch up your arm last night?"

Those grey eyes narrowed on my face. "Would it bother you if it did?"

I thought about this man, who had taken on a violent hitman of the mob and brought him to justice. For me. To keep me safe. Yes, maybe he had taken the law into his own hands, but did it bother me? Not in the least.

"No."

He held out his hand. "Come on, I'll take you to your doctor's appointment to get those stitches out."

CHAPTER 45

AFTER MY APPOINTMENT, Porter drove us to a small Thai restaurant to celebrate. He held my chair when I sat. We ordered our food and talked. Not about our situation or hitmen or how we were going to break up. He steered the conversation to talk about real life things. Like movies. Travel. He told me cute stories about Theo and how he met Jackson.

It struck me that this felt like a date. This is what it'd feel like to be taken on a date by Porter. He looked so attractive, smiling at one of my stories, with those high cheekbones and those lips, and suddenly, I felt sick at the thought of the next woman that would be lucky enough to date him.

"What are you thinking?"

"Why do you ask?"

"You have that look on your face."

"It's stupid."

"Tell me."

I swallowed, not wanting to ruin the mood. "This felt like a date."

"You just figured that out?"

"Wait, what?" I stared at him in shock.

"We're on a date."

"This is a date?"

"You're acting like you've never been on a date."

"Not with you!"

"So, we're unconventional. First we get engaged then we go on dates."

I took a moment to process that statement. "Did you date a lot?"

"Not particularly."

I was so curious about this man. Who did he date before Felicia? Did he do conventional dating? Was he a romantic at heart?

"What's the most romantic thing you've ever done for a date?"

He teased, "I usually save talking about past relationships for second dates."

"Humor me."

"I don't do romance."

"Do you break out into hives?"

"Something like that." He nodded. "What's the most romantic thing someone's done for you?"

You, when you risked your life, saving my ass from getting run over.

You, when you cared for my parents when they needed help.

You, when you hunted down a hitman to protect me.

"I bet you've had your fair share of romantic getaway weekends with a lot of champagne and roses." Those grey eyes watched my face, a question in them.

I blurted out, "When you took care of Donny Patrino."

"Come on."

The teasing tone between us faded as we stared at each other. I lifted my chin. "That is, hands down, the most romantic thing anyone has ever done for me. Nothing before that or nothing after that will ever compare."

He stared at the table for a long moment. *Why* did I say these things? Why did I ruin moments by always speaking my mind?

He lifted his gaze to mine. "You need to know I don't put out on the first date."

"How's it going with Porter?" Emily asked via FaceTime.

I glanced over my shoulder, making sure I was alone. "Two weeks ago, he took me on a date."

"What? That's great." She looked over her own shoulder and whispered, "Did he rock your world?"

I shook my head. "We came home, and he made out with me like a horny high school boy, but I never got him past first base."

Delight flew across her pretty face. "And?"

"We've gone out for coffee, he's bought me dinner three times, and he meets me at my job during lunch hour to eat with me in the park. But he seems to have put on his chastity belt because I haven't gotten past second base with him."

Her mouth dropped open. "He's wooing you."

"What?" I leaned forward. "Wasn't that word archived in, like, the late 1800s?"

"I think it's sweet."

"We're going backwards," I wailed. "We started out fake-engaged, and then had scorching hot sex, and now we're going on lunch dates, and he's kissing me like I'm in grade school."

"He's obviously interested in you. He's spending time with you. What are the kissing sessions like?"

I planted my head on my desk and groaned. "I'm so damn hot after those sessions, I'm practically self-combusting. It's torture, Emily. Torture!" I paused. "Maybe they teach sexual torture in SEAL training. You think?"

She laughed but didn't answer.

I put my face to the camera. "Is he trying to slowly end this with me? Is this his way of letting me down easy?"

She scrunched up her face. "I kind of doubt it."

"How do you know?"

"The guys on Jackson's team are a different breed. They don't play games. They don't screw around. If they're into a chick, they're the most patient men alive. But if they aren't interested, they're upfront about it."

"How?"

"You simply cease to exist in their world."

I sat back, horrified. "That sounds terrible."

"I've seen it happen. They're honest about how they feel, but they're not like other guys. When they like a chick, they're confident and patient, and they do things on their own terms."

"Emily, please translate."

She sat back, satisfied. "I think he likes you, Beth. I think he's trying to have a relationship with you. One that is not about fake relationships or hot sex."

I put my heart on my chest. "If you're wrong..."

"I think he likes you."

"I've told him how I feel about him already. He's never said anything back to me."

"These guys don't talk about their feelings."

"What? Why not?"

"I don't know." A thoughtful crossed her face. "It was actually really confusing when Jackson and I were getting together."

I snorted. "Well, not for anyone watching."

"What do you want?"

"I want hot sex. Lots of it."

She smiled that cute little smile. "That's easy. You need to seduce him."

I gaped at her. "What?"

"Yeah, you know..." She trailed off. "Take the bull by the horns and make it happen, but make him think he's the one who's making it happen." She was devious for my innocent Emily.

I put my hand on my forehead. "You think it'll work?"

"Well, maybe don't make it obvious, so if he does shut you down, you can pretend you weren't actually trying to make it happen."

"Why do I come to you for advice?" I moaned. "That's like the worst advice ever."

She laughed. "It's not. And you know it. Now go get some sexy time happening and report back."

CHAPTER 46

WE HAD three weeks until the wedding. Only three weeks until Porter and I parted ways. I decided I'd regret it if I didn't try it Emily's way at least once. I brought Porter shopping with me at an exclusive dress store. I figured I could flash him a bit and give him a quick reminder of what he was missing.

I carried several sexy little dresses to the dressing room. I put on a slinky silver number that did wonders for my cleavage and skimmed my legs mid-thigh. I topped the outfit with high, strappy heels because the man had a weakness for heels.

"Porter, are you around?" I called out.

"Right here."

I opened the door and sashayed to the three-way mirror. Ignoring him, I struck a pose in the mirror, looking over the dress. "Be honest, what do you think?"

He was sprawled in the big comfortable chair, and those grey eyes were glued to my legs. "I approve."

"I'm not sure," I said, walking back to the dressing room. "Tell me what you think of this next dress."

I proceeded to model three more dresses, each one more revealing and tighter than the last. I didn't look at him, pretending to be wholly focused on the outfits, but when I checked his reflection in the mirror, I noticed that he shifted in his seat a few times to adjust himself.

When I walked by him, I noticed that there was a familiar, significant bulge in his jeans. I shut the door and stared at my own reflection. I could do this. Strategically placing the stool in front of the clothing rod, I decided I'd take one more step to remind him of what he was missing.

"Porter, can you come here for a minute?" I called. I opened the door.

He easily stood up and walked towards me. I grabbed his hand, tugged him into the changing room, and shut the door. The changing room shrank instantly with him inside of it.

"I can't get this zipper down," I lied, turning to give him my back and lifting my hair off my back. "Can you help me?"

His big hands brushed the nape of my neck, and he slowly pulled the zipper open.

"Thanks." I let the dress drop at my feet. "Just have a seat. You're going to have to help me with the next one, too." I bent over, giving him a good shot of my ass in my thong when I picked the dress up off the floor.

When I turned around, he was sitting on the stool, those grey eyes feasting on my body. I reached over his head to grab a hanger and stepped closer to him while I hung the dress, my breasts precariously close to his face.

"What are you doing?" his voice was low.

I feigned indifference. "What?! It's not like you haven't seen this all before." I reached over his head to pull the red dress off the hanger. It was skin tight with expensive, stretchy material that more than hugged all my curves. I stepped daintily into it and pulled it up over my shoulders. "Can you do this up, please?"

I sensed him stand, and his hands zipped me up. I dropped my hair and gazed into the mirror. I rocked this dress. If there was ever a fuck-me dress, this was it.

It barely reached mid-thigh, and the front dipped so low, it was nothing but miles of cleavage. I smoothed the fabric over my hips and adjusted the front, so even more cleavage worked its way into view. Porter stood behind me. His jaw was tight, and his eyes were taking all of it in.

"I think it might look better without underwear lines. Hang on." I shimmied the fabric up over my hips, and with two thumbs, slowly pulled my underwear down. I kicked them off and smoothed the material of the skirt back over my legs. "That's better."

His hand snaked around my waist, tugging me back against him while his hot mouth moved against my neck. Our eyes met in the mirror. His were dark with lust. "Are you trying to tempt me, Miss Stirling?"

"Wouldn't dream of it."

His other hand reached in front and slowly dragged up my thigh. Warm fingers slowly traced the soft skin of my inner thigh, teasing just above the hemline. "Because you should know I'm engaged to be married."

"Lucky girl," I said, pretending to ignore him. "What's she like?"

"Hot as sin," he whispered in my ear. We stood, looking in the mirror as his hand moved up, beneath the fabric, pushing it up, higher and higher.

"What are you doing?" I asked in my most scandalized voice. His fingers were so close. My knees almost buckled when his fingertip grazed my clit.

"I think someone's looking for trouble," his voice growled in my ear.

"I wouldn't dream of doing anything naughty in this very public dressing room." My eyes drifted shut as he slowly traced the very tips of his fingers through my folds. They circled my entrance.

"Spread those legs," he demanded.

I stepped my legs wider. The fabric of the dress pulled higher up my thighs, and his fingers lightly teased me, circling my opening in a tantalizing rhythm. I bit my lip, working to not make a sound.

All the while, my gaze focused on his hand moving between my legs.

"Someone is so fucking wet," he breathed, biting my neck hard enough that I knew it'd leave marks.

I arched my neck back, pushing my ass against his erection. He spun me around, pushing my back against the cool mirror. I watched, breathless, as he dropped to his knees and pushed the dress up to my waist.

"I want those legs spread," he instructed.

I stepped wide in my heels, and then he was feasting on me like a man starved. His tongue laved my folds and teasingly circled my clit while his fingers pushed inside me. I covered my face with my hands, trying not to make a sound. A knock sounded on the door. We both froze.

"Miss Stirling, is everything okay in there?" the clerk asked.

"Yes," I stuttered. "I'm trying to decide between some dresses."

"Do you need any other sizes?"

Porter began to again move his fingers inside of me.

"I think I'm good."

"The black dress you have, we also have in midnight blue."

Oh, hell, he found my g-spot. My hips thrust towards his face. "I really need a black dress." My head hit the mirror behind me when Porter's tongue began to explore my clit again.

"Okay, well, did you see that Marc Jacobs dress? It's a gorgeous black crepe."

"No, I didn't. But I already have too many choices here." My legs were shaking so hard, I was so damn close.

"Okay, well, you can stick your head out and holler if you need anything."

"Thank you." Oh, now he was doing something with his thumbs. I clenched my fists and squeezed my eyes shut as I felt my body prepare to come apart.

"Also, did you know that we have a sale on right now?"

Please, lady. Please just walk away.

"No. No, I didn't," my voice cracked. His fingers stroked my g-spot with such speed, I was sure I was going to faint.

"If you buy two t-shirts you get a third t-shirt for half price."

My hands covered my face. "I'll be sure to check that out."

"Okay, dear. I'll be right outside."

He pushed a third finger into me at the same time he began to suck on my clit. My entire body arched back against the mirror as my orgasm pulsed through my body like an electric shock.

My legs buckled as explosive sensations washed over me. I bit my lip to prevent any noises from leaving. From between my legs, those grey eyes, dark with desire, watched me come part.

I yanked on his hair, pulling his mouth off me, unable to take it anymore. The smile on his face was wicked. I was crumpled back against the mirror, legs spread wide, naked from the waist down. A complete hussy.

He pushed his fingers deeper. "You know what I'm going to do to you when we get home?"

"Tell me."

"You really want to know?"

"Oh, yes." I gasped when his thumb pressed on my clit.

"Get dressed. We're going home. Now." He stood and spun me around. He unzipped the dress and unceremoniously peeled it down my body. "And you're buying this dress."

My limbs felt like water. He sat back on the stool and watched in amusement as I worked to get dressed. My legs were shaking so hard, I could barely pull my panties on over my heels.

I was so flushed, and I couldn't stop trembling. "Tell me what you're going to do to me?"

He crossed his arms, his eyes taking in my bra-clad breasts. "I'm going to strip you down to only those heels, and then I'm going to show you who's boss."

I gave an unsteady laugh. "How will you do that?"

He grabbed my hand and yanked me towards him, pressing my hand against his monstrous hard-on. "I have some ideas."

CHAPTER 47

T-MINUS ONE DAY UNTIL THE FAUX WEDDING...

PORTER LAID PROPPED on my bed, looking sinfully hot in his suit and open white shirt. He watched me dress, his eyes so dark it made me want to rip my clothes back off and forget about the "friends and family" rehearsal dinner we had planned for tonight.

The last three weeks had been the best weeks of my life. It had felt like we both knew there was a shelf life to this relationship, so each moment, each time we came together, was more intense and more mind-blowing than the last.

In between preparing for the wedding and helping my father campaign, we stole away for hot dates and discovered a mutual love of public sex. The riskier, the better.

And I had never seen my parents so happy. To say they adored Porter was an understatement. Mom was his number one fan. She doted on him like the sun and moon shone out of him, fussing over him like he was her own son.

"Does Porter like Wellington beef?"

"Porter doesn't like cooked carrots. Please, steam some other veggie for him."

"Porter mentioned he likes to hike, so I bought you some hiking boots, Beth. And this thing they call a water camel."

"I bought these dress shirts for Porter. I think this blue would look fabulous with his eyes."

It felt so perfect, so magical, I couldn't believe it was all about to come to an end. Mom was going to be devastated when he was gone. I, myself, was in complete denial.

The thought of facing the rest of my life without him was too impossible to process. So, I'd immersed myself into this fantasy, not willing to face the truth of this situation.

This was the end.

I didn't understand how something so perfect could abruptly end. The whole thing felt surreal. We didn't talk about a future. We didn't talk about what would happen past today. I didn't even know if he'd still want to see me.

Unwilling to ruin the last few weeks I had with him, I had been too afraid to bring it up. And he certainly didn't talk about it. I think part of me had been hoping against hope that he'd bring it to the table.

I wanted him to tell me that he wanted to see me post-fake-wedding. But he never did. And now, in a few hours, in front of all our friends, we were going to announce our breakup. Not my idea of a good time.

I shrugged into my dress, turned around and lifted my hair. In a heartbeat, he was at my back, his lips at my neck while his fingers inched up the zip.

"Are you ready for tonight?" I asked, shutting my eyes as his warm lips nibbled on the sensitive skin behind my ear. We had decided as soon as everyone got adequately liquored up at our party, we'd drop the bomb that we had amicably decided to call off our wedding.

"You sure you want to do this?" his voice was low.

What???

Our eyes met in the mirror.

"Well, I'm pretty sure I don't want to be the bride left standing at the altar, so it's now or never."

Grey eyes studied me in the mirror. "Can we talk?"

Oh, please, tell me you actually want to marry me.

"Sure." I spun in his embrace and wrapped my arms around his neck. "What did you want to talk about?"

He swallowed hard as his gaze searched my face. A knock sounded at my bedroom door.

"Go away," I yelled, not even joking.

"Beth," Mom's voice sounded through the door. "We need to talk to you."

"Mom, come back later."

She persisted in a way only she could. "Beth, this is incredibly important. Please. Roo and I need to talk to you."

Porter kissed my forehead. "Go, but promise me we're going to talk before dinner tonight."

I nodded. "Okay."

My mom's emergency was more of a non-emergency, involving shades of pink for the bridesmaid's bouquet ribbon. I honestly couldn't see a difference in any of the shades of pink, but according to Roo, the wrong tone could be disastrous.

Once I had calmed them both down, I went searching for my fake groom. I heard Porter and my dad talking in the living room. Their words stopped me in my tracks.

Dad sounded anxious. "Of course, I'm giving you my blessing, but I'm begging you, one man to another. Please, don't tell her."

Porter's voice was firm. "I need to tell her. This isn't something I can pretend didn't happen."

"Porter, it'd ruin everything. After all these years, our family is finally where I've dreamed we'd be. I can't afford to let the truth come out."

I froze, wondering what they were discussing.

Porter's stubborn tone was all too familiar. "I know that, but I can't go through with this unless she knows."

"It's all working out the way it should've anyway. So why do we have to go there? Please, don't tell Beth. Promise me, Porter."

Before Dad could wrangle a promise out of Porter that Porter obviously didn't want to make, I stepped into the room. "Tell me what?"

Porter stood with his arms crossed and a scowl on his face.

Dad turned and pasted the weakest smile on his face. "Darling, you look gorgeous. Is that a new dress?"

"Tell me what?" I inspected both men.

"Nothing, sweetheart. There's nothing to tell," Dad lied to my face.

I glanced at Porter, who seemed grim. He shrugged, and whatever they'd been talking about, I knew, as long as Dad was present, he wouldn't tell me. I stepped further into the large room, about to push Dad for answers, but Mom approached from behind.

She sounded so damn happy it hurt, "There you three are. What are these long faces for? Come on, hurry up. The reservation is at 7 PM, and we should be there to greet everyone."

"Of course, darling," Dad said with false cheer. "Come on, now. Shall we all take my driver? The parking at this restaurant is dreadful."

I knew the only reason Dad wanted to drive with us was so Porter wouldn't talk to me. I glanced over my shoulder, catching Porter with his eyes momentarily shut. He looked tortured. I vowed that the moment we were alone, I would find out what they'd talked about.

The restaurant was one of New York's most beautiful dining spots. Mom had reserved the entire restaurant for the affair. As soon as we arrived, friends and guests started to join us.

It was standing room only, with dozens of different tapas, sliders, a sushi table and a carving station, all paired with the finest wine available. I was kept busy, meeting and greeting people.

I searched the room, trying to find Porter. He stood at the bar, talking to some of my father's friends. What didn't Dad want Porter to tell me? Was that the same thing that Porter had wanted to speak to me about earlier?

And what about announcing the end of our engagement? Would that still happen tonight? Porter had made me promise we'd talk before our announcement.

Our guests were more that liquored up. We were reaching the now or never point of the evening. If we didn't do it tonight, when would we do it? We were scheduled to get married tomorrow afternoon.

"I can't believe you're going through with this." Yates appeared beside me. "This was supposed to be us."

"I can't believe you're still my father's campaign manager," I replied, disbelief lacing my voice.

Dad had downplayed everything Yates had done up until this point, claiming they were too far into the campaign to replace Yates. Secretly, I believed it was because Dad was good friends with Yates' father and couldn't punt him without damaging his own friendship.

"Your father needs me. So do you."

I worked to refrain from rolling my eyes. "Have you always been this delusional, or is this a new, fun trait?"

"Something is going on," Yates assured me. "I don't know what it is, but I'm going to find out."

I sighed, and my eyes met Porter's eyes across the room. I tapped out the only Morse code I knew with one of my fingers, against my wine glass.

Short, short, short, long, long, long, short, short, short.

S.O.S.

"Yates, has it ever dawned on you that maybe you should move on?"

Porter's eyes narrowed on my tapping finger. I repeated the signal.

"We were the ones that were supposed to be engaged. And now you're marrying him?"

Porter put down his glass and started to make his way towards me. Yates was going on about something, and he was completely unaware of Porter, but the moment Porter stood in front of us, he stopped mid-sentence.

"Well, if it isn't the military monkey," Yates sneered, counting on the fact that Porter wouldn't do anything in front of a roomful of people.

Porter smiled one if his scary smiles. "How's the broken nose? Did you enjoy getting that re-set?"

Yates took a small step backward. "Don't think you can physically bully me. I know something is going on. I'm going to find out."

"Beat it." Porter's eyes shifted to my face.

Yates disappeared into the crowd.

"SOS?" he asked.

"Thanks for saving me." I stared into those beautiful eyes I loved.

He bent his head, so his lips pressed against my ear. "I need to talk to you."

"Right now?"

He pulled back and stared into my eyes. "Right now. In private."

My heart thudded against my ribs. His tone was so serious. "Okay. Let's find someplace to talk."

"Let's go outside." He took my hand and started to lead me across the room when he suddenly stopped so short, I almost bumped into him.

Five huge men, who all looked vaguely familiar in an unfamiliar way, stood in the doorway, staring at Porter.

CHAPTER 48

"HOLY SHIT," Porter breathed.

And then, like a hurricane, they descended on him, intense expressions on their faces. I stepped back, unsure what they were going to do to him.

Bear hugs.

They were pulling Porter into giant man bear hugs.

It was borderline roughhousing. One guy ruffled Porter's hair. Another pulled him into a headlock. There was a lot of backslapping and affection. The entire room watched in bemusement.

Friends? Army buddies? Guys from his SEAL team? I scanned the room for Emily. If that was the case, where was Jackson? Emily said they wouldn't be arriving until tomorrow morning.

One of the guys caught my eye. His eyes widened, he stopped moving, and he called out, "Guys. Guys!"

I stood silently as they all stopped short.

"This is the bride," he said in near reverence.

Six pairs of eyes, including Porter's, all turned and measured me. Six pairs of beautiful grey eyes. All fringed with the beautiful lashes. Holy shit. These were his brothers. His big brothers.

They stared at me, and I stared back. They all shared his same physique, but their hair ranged from caramel blonde to dark brown. My eyes found Porter's and he watched me with an expression I couldn't read.

"Hi," my voice cracked slightly.

One of them slapped Porter across the back of the head. "Are you going to introduce us?"

Porter stepped out of the bear pack and wrapped his arm around my waist. "This is Beth. My fiancée."

The first guy stepped forward and gave me a devastating smile. "My name's Jordan. As you might have noticed, I'm the best looking one in the bunch, but don't hold that against Porter."

They roared with laughter, and I snickered as he shook my hand.

Jordan.

Brice.

Calvin.

Forrest.

Miles.

One by one, they introduced themselves to me, all the while razing each other or Porter. They were funny. They liked to joke. And they all held deep affection for Porter.

"I can't believe you're here." Porter looked like he'd woken up in some sort of dream.

"Well," Brice—or maybe it was Miles—said, "Weddings are about family, aren't they little brother?"

A female voice, soft and so full of emotion, spoke, "Porter."

The boys parted, and there stood an older woman, looking at Porter with her hands over her mouth. An older man in a wheelchair sat beside her. He had the same grey eyes of the man I loved. Porter had gone completely still, his eyes moving between the couple.

"Mom. Dad." His Adam's apple bobbed as he repeatedly swallowed.

"Oh, my baby." She rushed into his arms.

They hugged for a long time, his face buried into her neck. It felt like a reunion hug between two people who hadn't seen each other in a very long time. I didn't know why, but I was fighting tears. Looking around the room, I was pretty sure I wasn't the only one.

And then Porter stepped back and focused on the man in the wheelchair. "Dad." Emotion coated his voice.

"Come here, son," the man said.

Porter crouched beside him and gave him a long hug. Pure joy and love cross that man's face while he hugged Porter tightly.

Roo sidled up to me and gave me a sideways smile. "Do you think Porter likes his surprise?"

"You did this?" I gawked at Roo in shock.

"When I asked Porter about his family, he told me that they wouldn't be interested."

No shit. Because this was a fake wedding that wasn't supposed to happen.

"Wow, Roo," I was at a loss for words, watching as Porter crouched beside his father to talk to him.

His father surreptitiously wiped tears from his eyes. Eyes that never left Porter's face. I was fascinated with all of this. Fascinated with these people that made Porter's identity. This was his family.

"You must be Beth." Porter's mom approached me.

"Hello." I was terrified to face this woman without Porter at my side.

She pulled me into the warmest, softest hug imaginable. "Thank you so much for inviting us. I can't tell you how much it meant to us."

I was about to explain that it had nothing to do with me, but Roo stepped in, "Beth knew how much Porter would want you guys here. She killed herself to find you guys."

Porter's mom beamed at me. "Thank you so much. I've been worried sick about Porter for years. And this..." she choked up. "This is so special for us."

"Oh, yes," I pretended to know what she was talking about, but I wondered why Porter's mom had been worried about him for years.

How much time had passed since he'd seen his family? "I'm so glad you could come."

She pulled me into another wonderful hug. "I can't wait to get to know the woman my son has fallen in love with." She had a warmth to her.

I liked her. "Are you hungry? Can I get you something to drink?"

She tucked her arm in mine. "Maybe some wine, but first, I need to meet your parents."

Three hours later, I watched as four of Porter's brothers, Dad, Roo, and six other men, arm in arm, tried to perform some complicated circle dance that involved a lot of Hungarian kicks and laughter. A dozen other people gathered around, cheering and clapping.

It took the arrival of Porter's family to shake this party loose. Now, instead of a formal, staid affair, in which everyone stood around and quietly talked, it actually felt like a party. Jackets and ties had been shed. People danced, drank, laughed, joked and fell down drunk.

I glanced over at Mom, who was stared lovingly at Calvin doing a full-on demonstration of a story that involved what appeared to be a horse. Porter's mom stood beside mine, sipping a glass of whisky as—I couldn't believe it— Mom burst out laughing. Now Calvin was pouring out two shots of amber liquor, and it appeared he was trying to teach Mom how to do a shot.

My eyes scanned the room, trying to pick Porter out of the crowd of sweaty, happy, drunk people. As if he could sense that I was looking for him, his eyes pinned mine across the room and he walked towards me.

"Porter."

He looked fucking delicious. His jacket had been shed. His dress shirt was rolled up at the sleeves and untucked from his pants. His hair was rumpled.

He stated the obvious, "My parents and brothers are here."

"I noticed. They really know how to liven up a party."

"I didn't invite them."

"Roo did."

Porter paused and gave a short nod. "Roger."

"He thought it'd be a nice surprise for you."

He didn't respond.

I stared at Porter. I could see concern and tension in his eyes. "Porter."

"Can we hold off on our announcement?" he interrupted.

I looked around the room of so many happy people, "We might cause a riot if we called it off now."

A sad smile teased his lips. "I need to talk to you. And with my family being here..."

"I get it."

He rubbed his eyes with one hand. "My brothers want to take me out drinking after this party. Can I wake you when I get home?"

I stared up at him. "Won't you be drunk?"

"No. I'll keep it under control. I might be late, but I really need to talk to you."

"Does this have to do with that conversation you had with my dad?"

"Yes. No. Part of it does, but this is another part." His stress was palpable.

I reached out and grabbed his arm. "It's going to be okay."

He nodded, but I could tell that he didn't think things were going to be okay at all.

CHAPTER 49

I WOKE UP TO A CRASH. Lifting my head from my pillow, I peered into the darkness of the room. It was 5 AM.

"Porter?"

"I'm here," he said from the floor.

I turned on the lamp. Porter laid on his back on the floor. His white shirt was streaked with blood, and he had a fat lip that suggested he'd been in a fight.

"What happened?" I shot out of bed, crouching beside him.

He worked to focus on my face. "You waited up for me," he enunciated really slowly, in a way that only drunk people did.

"What happened to you?" I grabbed his hand, examining his bloody knuckles. "Were you in a fight?"

"You know I'd do anything to protect you, right?" He struggled to sit up.

"I know that."

"Beth, I really need you to know that. I'd do anything for you."

I put his face in my hands. "I know that." I kissed him, and he pulled away to focus on me.

"You're so beautiful. You dazzle me."

I half-laughed and stood, using all my muscles to bring him to his feet and guide him to bed. "Come let's get you on the bed."

"Things are going to shit, Beth." With a gentle push, he went down to the mattress like a felled tree.

"Things are just a tiny bit complicated."

He caught my hand and tugged me, so I sprawled over him. "Promise me you won't leave me."

"Porter, please," I begged. "Tell me what is going on?"

"I want to, but I should get sober first."

I pulled a pillow down and tucked it under his head. "We need to talk."

"I have something I want to ask you."

I froze, staring down at this beautiful man. "You do?"

"I'd do anything for you," his words were getting slower.

"When are we going to talk?" I was a bit desperate.

"Tomorrow," he managed to say before he slipped into a drunken slumber.

Would he remember this conversation in the morning?

———

The next morning, I got up and left Porter to sleep off the alcohol in my bedroom. I fretted about our impending marriage—in eight hours. Emily appeared in the kitchen.

I yelped in delight. "Where are Theo and Jackson?" I hugged her hard.

"Jackson took Theo to the park. After the flight, Theo had some pent-up energy." She grinned. "How are you?"

"Still engaged." I explained how his entire family had shown up and taken over the party.

Her eyes were wide. "So, you didn't call it off?"

I shook my head. "I don't know what's happening. We still have to talk."

A member of my security team interrupted us. "There's a Detective Christensen here to see Porter?"

"Did she say what it's about?"

He shook his head. "I seated her in the living room."

Emily and I exchanged glances before I went to my bedroom to find Porter. He was passed out hard on my bed.

"Hey." I sat next to him. "Detective Christensen is here to see you."

He cracked open his bloodshot eyes. "Right now?"

"Yes."

He sat up, wincing, "Okay, tell her I'll be right out."

His dress shirt was covered in brown blood stains. "You might want to change your shirt."

He grimaced. "Yeah, okay."

"What happened to your face?" Detective Christensen said the moment she set eyes on Porter.

He leaned against the wall and crossed his arms. It was amazing how he could be hungover and probably even drunk yet present himself as entirely in control. "What brings you here today?"

She sighed and glanced between the two of us. "Porter, where were you between 3 AM and 4 AM last night?"

"Why do you want to know?"

"Michael Renner was beaten up last night, and then he was shot."

My head jerked back. "What do you mean, shot?"

She eyeballed me. "With a gun. He took one slug to his arm and another one to his chest."

All I could think about was how Porter had shown up at 5 AM, covered in blood, talking about how he'd do anything to protect me. "Is he alive?"

"Renner's alive and out of surgery. But the bullet wounds are the least of his concerns. Someone took one of his own golf clubs to his head, and he currently remains unconscious and in critical condition."

"You think I had something to do with that?" Porter asked.

"I prefer to think of this as me clearing you, but I need to know where you were last night between 3 AM and 4 AM."

Porter's eyes flickered to me. "I'd rather not say."

"We can do this two ways, Porter," Detective Christensen advised him. "But to be honest, I'd rather not drag you down to the station."

"If I wanted to kill Renner, he'd be dead."

"You're not helping your cause," she warned.

He sat beside me on the couch. "I didn't have anything to do with this."

Relief hit me hard. If Porter said he didn't do it, I trusted him. "I believe you. Just tell her where you were."

"You promise you'll let me explain?" His eyes were on my face.

"Of course."

He gave a short nod and said to Detective Christensen. "I was with my brothers until the bar closed. About 3 AM, I left the bar to go talk to my ex-girlfriend, Felicia."

W.T.F.

I'm pretty sure I'd stopped breathing.

"We're going to need her address." Detective Christensen opened up her pad of paper.

He rattled off her address while I sat, frozen. Unable to move.

"And how did you get that fat lip?" she asked.

"My brother and I got into it at the bar."

I moved further away from him on the couch while my mind raced. Porter had been with Felicia? Last night? I felt cold, then hot. I couldn't even look at his face.

"Beth," he said calmly. "Let me explain."

Detective Christensen stood. "Sorry for this. I know this is your wedding day. I'll be in contact with your ex-girlfriend with the purpose of clearing you from this crime. Don't go far." She let herself out.

"Beth," he said in a soft voice. "Let me talk."

I turned on him, feeling so much right now, I couldn't even distinguish my emotions. "So, after you got into a bar brawl with your own brother, you decided, in the middle of the night, that you needed to go see Felicia."

"I needed to talk to her."

"You needed to talk to *me*. That's what you told me."

"I needed to talk to her first."

"About what?"

"It's a long story."

"You want her back," I accused him, standing up.

"No." He grabbed my hand.

I was close to yelling. "No one goes to see their ex in the middle of the night unless they have feelings. Feelings that come out when they're drunk. And you were stinking drunk."

"You said you'd listen."

"Not right now." I yanked on my hand.

"Come on."

"I know I have no hold over you. I know this isn't a real relationship, but right now, everything I feel is real. And I'm too pissed to listen to you. I need to calm down."

"We have to talk."

"We will talk when I'm ready."

I fought tears.

Fought emotion.

Fought the panic and fear threatening to bubble out of me.

Fought *him*.

CHAPTER 50

EMILY SAT beside me in my car, and we both peered at the big brick building. My phone was going off like a bomb. All the calls were from Roo and Mom.

"Is this where she lives?" Emily whispered.

"Yes."

"What are you going to do about your wedding?"

My fake wedding that was scheduled to take place in five short hours. Fuck.

"I have no idea."

"Do you want to talk to her?"

I tried to explain what had possessed to me to drive us here. "No. I'm here because I need to think."

"What are you thinking?"

I avoided Emily's eyes. "I thought when Porter said he wanted to talk to me, part of me was hoping..."

"Hoping that he wanted to marry you."

"Yes." I sighed, giving her a regretful look. "Stupid, right?"

"No. I've been hoping the same thing."

We shared identical sad smiles.

The front door of the building opened and out stepped Felicia. She wore a cute little navy jumpsuit, and her long hair was pulled into a ponytail.

"There she is." I sunk a bit lower in my seat.

"Go talk to her," Emily encouraged.

I was about to refuse, but my body was already half-way out of my Corolla. I met Felicia on the sidewalk.

Her blue eyes widened when she saw me. "I've already told that detective everything I know." She put her hand on her slim hip.

"Was Porter here last night?" I asked in a pleading voice.

"Yes."

My heart sunk. "Okay. Thanks." I started to turn away.

"It's not what you think."

I spun. "So, why was he here?"

"He showed up here drunk, looking for his ring."

"What ring?"

"His grandmother left him her wedding ring. And I took it. Out of his boxes. I never gave it back to him."

"You did?"

"He showed up here last night, ranting about it."

Wait, what?

"I gave it back to him."

I worked to say something. "Oh."

She seemed genuinely regretful. "I'm sorry for ruining your engagement party and your cake."

I didn't give a shit about that. All I cared about was that Porter had shown up to get a ring!

"That's okay."

Her big blue eyes pensively studied the street behind me. "I needed Porter. I needed him to take care of me and act like he gave a shit. And he did take care of me. He never let me down. But it was never enough. I always wanted more from him. He did everything I asked, but he could never feel for me what I needed him to feel."

I was humbled by her honesty. "I've been jealous of you since I met you."

She tilted her head. "Don't give up on Porter. I've never seen him like this."

"Like what?"

"Like he actually has a heart? He's a hot mess."

In a daze, I walked back to the car. I got in and stared unseeing through the windshield. Porter hadn't wanted Felicia back. He'd shown up here, in the middle of the night, to get his grandmother's ring back.

"Tell me," Emily demanded, interrupting my befuddled thoughts.

I started the car, "I need to talk to Porter."

———

The second I walked back into the penthouse, Mom and Roo were all over me. "Beth, the hairdresser and makeup artist, are here. We need to get you ready," my mom snapped.

I turned on both of them. "No. I'm not doing anything until I talk to Porter."

"He's not here."

Apprehension squeezed my heart. "Where is he?"

"I'm assuming he went to the church to get ready. What is this about? Was Porter in a fight last night? Doesn't he know we have to take pictures today?"

I held up my hands. "I need to talk to Emily." I yanked her into my bedroom and shut the door. We stared at each other, wide-eyed. "What do I do?"

"Try calling him."

"I knew you were the brains in this operation." I hit dial on my phone. "Went to voice mail," I said as I hung up.

"Are you going to leave a message?"

I paced back and forth across the room. "I don't know what to do."

"You need to show up at the church. In a wedding dress."

"Emily," I wailed. "What if he doesn't show?"

"Isn't that what you originally planned?"

"Yes!"

"So, what's the issue?"

"The issue is I actually want to marry the guy now."

"You've always wanted to marry him."

"Fine. Rub it in."

"I think he wants to marry you too."

"You don't know that."

"He got his grandma's ring back last night from Felicia!"

"That was before I refused to listen to him."

"Well, you have three scenarios. You can possibly leave him at the altar, or he can leave you there."

"That's only two. What's the third scenario?"

"You both show up, and you get married."

I stood there completely still, for a moment and then I yelled over my shoulders, "Mom! I'm ready for the hair stylist."

CHAPTER 51

EMILY'S EYES glistened with emotion. "You're a stunning bride."

I turned and studied my reflection in the mirror. My $60,000 Vera Wang sleeveless wedding gown showcased my diamond choker and bare shoulders, falling into yards and yards of wispy tulle. My blond hair was pinned up. My make-up was as perfect as I've ever seen it. I looked dewy and soft. It was probably the best I've ever looked.

"All dressed up and nowhere to go." I regretted the impulse to show up at my own wedding. "Which means I need more champagne."

"You get two glasses." She topped my glass. "And then you're cut off."

"I'm about 99% certain my groom is going to be a no-show. You can't withhold the booze."

She grabbed the bottle and topped her own glass. "One of us has to drive the getaway car, and since I never get a babysitter, this is my day to get drunk."

I forced a laugh. "We can take a cab."

"Fine, but if he does show up, you're going to be upset if you're falling down drunk. Maybe we should reserve the hard-drinking for after the fact."

We clinked glasses, and I downed my champagne in one go.

Trying not to sound desperate, I asked, "Has anyone seen Porter?"

"Not yet."

"Is Jackson here?"

"He's not answering my texts."

"Do you think Jackson will be Porter's getaway man?"

"He never mentioned anything."

I was so nervous I wanted to puke. "Have you see any of my bridesmaids?"

"Roo has them all corralled in the next room. Their dresses are gorgeous."

"Porter made them change our colors to pink."

"That's very un-Porter of him."

"He told Roo and Mom that every decision for the wedding had to be run through me."

"How romantic!"

I grabbed the bottle and drank straight from it. There wasn't enough champagne in this world to get me through today.

Emily pulled it away from me. "Are you going to be okay?" Concern filled her blue eyes.

"I don't know why I thought he'd show up."

"Don't think about it."

"My mom is going to be crushed."

"What about you?"

"I won't lie. This one's going to hurt. But I'm prepared."

Someone knocked on the door. I wrapped my arms around my waist, feeling sick. "Here's the moment Roo tells me they can't find Porter."

She winced with pity. "You ready?"

"Let's get this over with." I called over my shoulder, "Come in."

Roo stuck his head in the door. "You look perfect."

My throat felt like sandpaper. "Thank you."

He had a headpiece on his head, and he wore a tux. This was Roo in full-blown wedding mode. He touched his earpiece and spoke to someone, "Right. Thank you." His tone was surprisingly authoritarian. "Guests are seated. Bridesmaids are lined up, ready to go. Your father is waiting for you, and the groom and groomsmen are waiting for their cue to walk. Are you ready? Should we cue the music?"

My skin tingled, and I felt dizzy. Disoriented. "The groom is ready?"

Porter was here?

Porter was here!

His eyes narrowed on my hands. "Where is your bouquet?"

Deranged laughter barked out of me. "I don't know."

He stepped into the room, picked up the pink and white trailing bouquet and thrust it into my hands. "Can I give them the cue?"

Emily cut in, "Yes. We're ready."

"You have exactly three minutes to make it to the back of the church. Don't be late." He disappeared from sight.

I clutched Emily's arm. "Am I hallucinating or did Roo say Porter is here?"

She giggled. "He did."

I stammered, "He showed up?"

She gave a happy shrug. "I knew he would."

"We haven't had the talk yet."

"Take a deep breath."

She started to walk out but turned to look back at me. "Are you coming?"

"Give me a second."

CHAPTER 52

PORTER WAS HERE!

I walked around the room in a circle. Did that mean he wanted to marry me? Is that why he showed up?

A tightness banded across my chest when another dark thought passed through my mind. What if he planned to literally leave me at the altar?

If that was his plan, I would kill him.

Would he actually do that?

Since I didn't know what else to do, I followed Emily to the back of the church where Dad waited for me.

He reached out and put both hands on my shoulders. "Beth, I've never seen you look more beautiful."

"Dad." I watched as my bridesmaids disappeared one-by-one through the double doors into the cathedral. I could hear the faint strains of the string quartet play. "I'm freaking out."

Understatement of the year.

He chuckled and patted my hand. "You know, I've never been so proud of you."

Emily looked over her shoulder at me, a cute smile teasing her face. She winked, and then she moved out of sight.

"Our turn." Dad tucked my arm in his and tugged me to the doorway of the huge cathedral.

The thunder of feet echoed through the massive church as eight hundred guests stood to honor my walk up the aisle. My eyes flew to the front of the church.

There he was. Standing straight and tall, looking like a million bucks in his tux. The man I loved.

Holy fuck. He'd actually shown up.

I couldn't take my eyes off his handsome face. Why was he here? What was he thinking? Did he actually want to marry me?

My trip to the front felt like an underwater dream. Hundreds of face peered at me, as we moved up the aisle. And then Dad helped me up the steps toward Porter. Behind me, Emily adjusted my dress. I couldn't bring myself to face those grey eyes. Instead, I stared blindly ahead and concentrated on bringing air into my rib cage, but despite my efforts, I wasn't sure any oxygen reached my brain.

A small children's choir stepped forward, and their high sweet voices began to sing. With courage I didn't feel, I peeked up at Porter. He stared down at me, but what he was thinking was anyone's guess.

"You showed up," I whispered.

"So did you," he breathed back.

Why was he here? I needed to know.

"Did you lose the memo?"

"What memo was that?"

"The one that said, if we failed to plan a breakup, you were the one who needed to leave me at the altar."

"It went against my policy of always having your back."

What did that mean?

"So does that mean you're not going to leave me at the altar?"

He regarded me with a mild expression and shrugged. "Nope."

I nodded and stared, unseeing, as the choir finished its song. I didn't know how to respond. Was this some a joke to him? Did he not grasp the fact that we were standing at the altar about to be married?

The minister announced a congregational hymn. The organ started, and eight hundred people stood behind us. Questions spun my mind in a hundred different directions. We were here. About to get married, but that still didn't mean he wanted to marry me. And that fact was killing me. We listened to people sing behind us. I worked to gather my scattered thoughts.

I pinched my lips together, "Do you think we should talk about this?"

"I wanted to earlier, but you took off."

"I was pissed."

"Where did you go?"

"You want to have the talk right now?"

"Do you have a better time?"

The minister cleared his throat and chastised us with a pointed look.

My wedding, I can talk if I want to!

But we fell silent and watched as a soloist made her way to the front.

She started singing Ava Marie. I started to get pissed.

"We're about to get married," I reminded him.

"You're free to walk."

His casual tone frustrated me.

"Why do I have to walk? My mom would kill me."

"Well, my parents are here now, too."

"So?"

"If my folks are here, I can't leave you unmarried at this alter."

"But if you stay, that means we're getting married."

"Doesn't matter. I can't do it."

The last chords of the harp sounded.

"That's a terrible reason to get married."

"If you don't want this to happen, you're free to leave," he offered.

"Do you want to marry me?"

"I'm not opposed to the idea."

My gaze snapped up to him, too shocked to speak.

His shrug was unapologetic. "We get along."

And there it was. The most unromantic thing anyone has ever said to me. If I wasn't so pissed, I'd be crushed.

"We get along?" I hissed. "That's what you have to say?"

"What do you want me to say?"

Again with the out of body experience. Without remembering moving, I found myself walking to the side of the church. Loud whispers of hundreds of people ricocheted off the stone walls.

Porter caught up with me. He pulled me behind a huge planter of flowers, away from prying eyes.

"You're leaving?" His grey eyes flashed with intensity.

I blinked up at him, finally allowing myself to ask the question I really wanted to ask. "What are we doing?"

"Would it be so bad?"

No, it'd be fucking great. But only if he actually wanted to marry me.

"Are you asking me to marry you?!"

His eyes never left my face. "I'm shit at this kind of stuff. This isn't how I wanted to do it."

"Do what?"

"Ask you if you'd be interested in not canceling our wedding."

My mouth dropped, as shock rippled through my body. "You want to marry me?"

"I don't not want to marry you."

"Why are you suddenly using double negatives?"

He ran both his hands through his hair. "I can't imagine not doing this."

Disbelief, shock, and joy washed through me, but mostly joy. "That's still a double negative."

His lips twitched in amusement, "When did you become the grammar police?"

"Semantics matter."

"Fine. Beth Stirling. I feel things for you that I've never felt before."

"Why didn't you say something earlier?" I half-whispered, half-wailed.

"I wanted to."

"But?"

"I wasn't sure what you'd say."

Disbelief. "You thought I'd say no?"

"I don't know."

Our eyes locked. "Is this real?"

"I'm the one who told Roo to invite my parents," he added.

"What!?"

"But I didn't think they'd show. There's a whole lot of stuff there that I need to tell you."

"Why didn't you talk to me?"

"Because you're the only thing in this world that scares me."

"I'm in love with you," I whisper-shouted, "So stupidly in love with you, I can't even take it."

He crushed me into his arms, and his kiss was so passionate, so intense, I swooned. He lifted his head. "Is that a yes?"

"Yes, I want to marry you."

"You look hot as fuck in that wedding dress."

"You should see the negligee Roo forced me to buy."

He groaned and kissed me again. "Sorry for the shit proposal."

Porter wanted to marry me!

My arms clung to his neck. "It kind of suits how we came together."

Determination crossed his face. "Let's get this show on the road. I want to make you mine."

"Stay bossy," I instructed.

"Oh, I plan on it."

When we reappeared, the entire congregation clapped.

Porter led me to the front. We exchanged goofy smiles, and the minister asked with a dry tone. "Are you two ready?"

Porter didn't look away from my face. He looked so damn happy. "We're ready."

CHAPTER 53

IN FRONT of eight hundred people, we stood at the front of that massive church, to come together as man and wife. Porter listened to the minister's message with serious intent. I didn't hear a word the man said. I was too busy trying to wrap my mind around the fact that Porter wanted to marry me.

Not out of obligation.

Not because he felt trapped.

The man said it himself.

He felt things for me he never felt before.

Porter was becoming my husband. And I was becoming his wife.

I still had a lot of questions. But they were good questions, and I wanted to savor his answers. Like what moment had he realized that he loved me? When exactly did he know he wanted to marry me? But all that could wait. His family. His history, all of that, would eventually be shared.

What I did know was that I loved him. With all my heart.

I let out a happy sigh, when the minister said, "Time for your vows."

A considerable bang sounded at the back of the church.

"This wedding can't happen!" Yates stalked up the aisle.

What the living hell?

Porter turned with a growl, his entire body stiffening. Too stunned to do much else, I watched Yates' approach.

"What might your reason be?" the minister's voice called out.

Yates cleared his throat. "I know this isn't a real marriage. This whole thing is a fraudulent plot to promote Mr. Stirling's political campaign."

The entire church gasped. My eyes swept over the blurry faces of the congregation. My body tipped against Porter's hard frame. I put my hand on his arm. He hadn't moved a muscle. I glanced at him. His jaw was so tight, his neck corded.

Yates continued, "I have evidence that proves Beth's father paid Porter to be part of her life, to marry her for his campaign. This wedding is a sham."

It kind of felt like I was under water. Without oxygen. Struggling to breathe. My eyes flew to my father. His expression was a mask of guilt. Roo sat collapsed on the pew with Mom bent over him.

I glanced up. Grey eyes held mine. I couldn't read his expression.

"Tell me this isn't true, Porter," I whispered.

Why was there so much regret in his eyes?

"I can't."

I swallowed, and my ribs expanded and contracted as each shallow breath rushed through my body. "This was your secret? My father paid you?"

"At first. But then things changed."

I took a few steps away from him in complete disbelief. This was not happening to me. Not to me. My mind tried to process what was going on. "My father paid you? To love me?"

"Beth..." Pain painted his features. "It's complicated."

I couldn't even process this. "So this is a big joke? I've been set up by another one of my father's elaborate plans?"

"No. I really love you."

I wasn't a violent person, but suddenly I was hitting Porter with my bouquet. Pink and white flowers exploded between us. He didn't even move. He took every single blow.

I realized I was crying. Hard. Everything ran. Tears. Snot. Make-up. I couldn't catch my breath. As far as ugly cries went, this one was epic. My bouquet was now nothing but stems and a ribbon. I tossed it aside. Emily put her arms around me.

I glared at him and managed to say, "I trusted you."

He swallowed. "I'm sorry."

I shook my head, and then I was running down the aisle.

CHAPTER 54

I STOOD in the bride's room at the back, my chest heaving.

Emily stood beside me. "Oh my goodness."

I paced the length of the room. "My dad paid Porter."

Bewilderment traced her voice. "How did he even know Porter?"

I tried to think of our beginning. "When I was arrested, what did Jackson do?"

"I called my lawyer. Jackson called Porter."

The door opened, and Dad stepped in. "Beth, please. Let me explain."

Rage nearly blinded me. "When are you going to stop meddling in my life?"

"I thought I did what was best for you."

"Best for me." I stopped in my tracks. "You thought that paying someone to love me was the best thing for me? Everything about you is about control. This is my life. My happiness!"

"It's not like that."

"When did you met him?"

"Beth, listen to me."

"WHEN DID YOU MEET PORTER?!"

"The night you brought him to Bayswater for dinner."

I covered my face with my hands. "You took him for an after-dinner drink."

"Yes. I used that chance to talk to him."

That night on the balcony of Bayswater. I tried to remember what Porter had said to me. He'd asked me what I wanted, and I told him I wanted space from Yates. And to pretend that we were dating.

"How much did you pay him?"

"Is that important?"

"How much am I worth? Tell me how much your daughter's happiness is worth."

"Five hundred thousand."

That sucker punched me. "You paid him half a million dollars to what? To date me? To marry me? Sleep with me?"

"He gave me the money back."

"I don't care," I cried.

"Please let me explain."

"How can I believe anything that comes out of your mouth?"

The door burst open, and Yates stood with a pleased expression on his stupid face. "Beth."

"Get out," I gritted at him.

"I love you. I want to marry you. We can still do this. Today."

"That's enough," Dad yelled at him. "Get out of here!"

Yates waltzed up to Dad and pointed his finger in his face. "I've done everything you've asked. I'm basically your slave. You have no idea what I did for you. You don't appreciate me."

"You were in on this too?" I asked in disbelief.

"No," they both said at the same time.

"I would never hurt you, never betray you the way these two men did," Yates boasted.

My dad punched Yates in the chin. As far as punches went, it wasn't very effective, but Yates still crumpled to his knees.

My dad seethed. "Yates, my daughter doesn't want to have anything to do with you. Neither do I. You need to leave."

The door flew open, and Porter wrestled with two of his brothers. They fought him, but he was a crazy person, trying to get into the room.

"I'm going to kill him," he grunted. "Give me five seconds."

Yates crab crawled backwards across the floor. "Don't let him near me."

Miles, or maybe it was Calvin, shouted over his shoulder. "Can we get some help here?"

Emily pressed against the wall beside me. Our eyes met. Jackson stepped into the mess and put his arm around Porter's neck. It was a cross between a hug and a choke hold. He spoke to Porter, but no one could hear what he said.

"Fine," Porter ground out, "Get off me."

Jackson turned and spoke to his brothers, "Let him go."

With extremely reluctance, they let go of Porter, who straightened. For the first time in my life, I saw fear on his face. Grey stormy eyes found mine. "Beth, I need you to listen to me."

"I think I've heard enough of your lies," I shot back.

"You really should hear him out. This is all my fault," Dad added.

"Be quiet. Just stop. I can't take any of this anymore."

"What is going on here?" Detective Christensen appeared in the doorway, surveying the scene.

"Nothing," four of us said at once.

Two officers crowded the room.

"Michael Renner woke up," she said. "And he told me what happened last night. Yates Bennet, you're under arrest for the attempted murder of Michael Renner. You have the right to remain silent. Anything you say can and will be used against you in a court of law. You have the right to speak to an attorney, and to have an attorney present during any questioning."

In shock, we stood and watched as the officers hauled Yates to his feet and handcuffed him behind his back.

"This is a mistake," Yates yelled. "I didn't do anything."

Dad stepped forward. "Yates! Shut up. Don't say a word until your lawyer is present."

"This isn't my fault," he begged, looking at me. "Beth. You have to save me. Please. Tell them we were together last night. Tell them the truth."

I remained silent and watched as Yates was half-carried, half-dragged out of the room. "Everyone get out," I said, my voice low.

The men assessed me. Jackson. Porter. My father. The brothers.

Emily spoke this time, her voice ringing clear and fierce. "You heard her. All of you need to clear out of this room right now."

CHAPTER 55

AT THE DOORWAY of the penthouse, I grabbed Emily's arm. "Is he gone?"

"He did what you asked, and he left."

Knowing Porter wasn't here, made my heart ache. At the church, Emily had gone into a mode I'd never seen before. She placed Jackson and my security team at the doorway of the bridal suite and banned anyone else from coming in.

She sat beside me on the floor and held me while I wept. When I could no longer cry, she helped me get out of my dress. I wanted to talk. I wanted to tell her that my heart was breaking. I wanted to get angry and throw things and curse his name. I wanted to beg her, ask her how I could possibly live the rest of my life without him in it.

But the words remained stuck inside of me. For the life of me, I couldn't speak. So, I sat on the chair like a statue and watched as she pulled every pin out of my hair and brushed my hair out. I lifted my face to hers as she used a warm facecloth to wash my face. I sipped the glass of scotch she'd placed in my hand, unable to help as she packed up the room.

At my request, she'd sought out Porter and told him I needed space. She told him to leave the penthouse. Apparently, he had obeyed. Now, we stood in the penthouse, alone.

"Do you want something to eat?".

"Not really." This place felt so empty, so quiet without Porter. "Where are Jackson and Theo?"

"I sent them to a hotel."

"Emily." Her kindness would be my undoing.

"I'm going to order Thai food. You don't have to eat, but I'm starving."

I ate the Thai food. We sat at the big island in the kitchen and ate in silence. Yet another reason I loved Emily. Anyone else would talk or try to make me feel better or ask too many damn questions. Not Emily. She quietly sat with me.

"You'd be good at a wake."

"Awake?"

"No, a wake. Two words. Like when the family sits around the coffin and holds a vigil for the person who has died?"

"Oh, a wake. Why?"

"Because you're so comfortable being quiet."

"This is your time."

"Did you know it would end like this?"

She dangled noodles into her mouth from her chopsticks. "Well, up until this morning, I thought the plan was to call your fake wedding off in a very amicable fashion. You'd either be locked up here doing dirty things with Porter or you'd be alone and sad. Either way, I figured you'd need some space."

This.

This was why Emily was my best friend.

"How was my mom?"

She shrugged. "I thought she'd be more upset, but she focused her attention on Roo which I think took her mind off everything."

"Is he okay?"

"An ambulance was called and he was treated for fatigue and

dehydration. They gave him an IV while he sobbed like a baby, and those two things seemed to restore his spirits."

"My mom loves Roo. I think if she could, she'd adopt him."

"What about you?"

"He suits our family." I couldn't bring myself to talk about Porter. The words were there, choking in my chest, but I couldn't say his name out loud.

"I love Virginia, but man do I miss New York food."

New York. This city would never feel the same. Neither would my apartment. How would I go back to my old life? What had I done before Porter had been in my life? Had I laughed? I had spent so much time alone.

I didn't know how I'd bear it.

I pushed my plate away. "I need to sleep."

If I didn't shut down my brain, my thoughts or this massive crack that was opening in my heart, I wasn't sure I'd survive. Sleep was my only option.

"You're mom gave me her valium."

"Give me." I held out my hand.

She shook out one blue pill into the palm of my hand. "I'll be here all night."

I crushed her in a hug. "Thank you."

And then I crawled into the bed that still smelled like him, and I sobbed myself to sleep.

CHAPTER 56

SIX WEEKS LATER, I showed up at Emily and Jackson's place without warning. They welcomed me without judgement, without questions, and made me feel at home.

Emily and I sat on her deck, watching the lazy fireflies buzz around the yard. Theo was down for the night, and with Chloe panting at my feet, I silently sipped from my wine glass while Emily patiently waited for me to talk.

"You look thinner," she broke the silence.

"I've lost my appetite."

"What happened with Yates? How did he get tangled up with Renner?"

"I guess he owed some big gambling debts to the wrong people. People tied in with Micheal Renner."

"I read in the newspaper that Micheal Renner is being charged with corruption."

"Apparently, he's been under investigation for over a year for having strong ties with the mafia. He scratched their backs, and they scratched his. And they were all anxious to make sure that my father didn't win the election."

"So, Renner's mafia friends were the ones that attacked you?"

"Detective Christensen thinks that coming after Dad would've been too obvious. So they came after me with warnings and accidents, hoping it'd persuade him to drop out."

"How was Yates involved?"

"Renner used the fact that Yates couldn't pay off his debts. He told Yates that he could work those debts off by getting intel from my dad's campaign. That's why Yates convinced my dad to hire him as his campaign manager."

"So, Yates was a double agent?"

"Essentially. I guess the night Renner got shot, Yates was in his office, trying to find something to blackmail Renner with, and Renner walked in on him. They got into a fight, and Renner pulled a gun on Yates. Yates is claiming he wrestled the gun away from Renner and accidentally shot him. Twice."

Emily sat back, a dismayed expression on her face. "Poor Yates."

"My father is furious, but he's also hired him a brilliant lawyer, with the condition that Yates never talks to me again."

"Have you talked to your dad?"

I drained my glass. "No. I'm too pissed at him."

"How's your mom doing?"

"She's also pissed at my dad. Like, really pissed. But she handled everything like a pro. Her and Roo sent back all the gifts."

Chloe stood, stretched and pushed her cold black nose into my hand. I stroked her face, staring into her beautiful brown eyes.

"And how are you doing?"

How could I tell Emily how I was doing? It felt like my life had no meaning. I didn't laugh. I didn't cry. I went to my shit job and slept. I missed Porter so much, I thought I might die, but somehow my heart kept beating. Somehow I kept waking up and pushing myself to get through yet another meaningless day.

"I'm okay."

"Porter didn't come back to work."

I swallowed hard, staring into my empty wine glass. Part of me

MY FAKE FIANCÉ   329

had almost been hoping I'd run into him here. Stupid, right? But the heart wants what the heart wants. I'd kill for a mere glimpse of him.

"Do you know where he is?"

"No. He told Jackson his head wasn't in the game."

"What did Jackson do?"

"He told Porter that he'd keep his job open for him for as long as he needed him too."

"How did Porter seem?"

She shook her head. "Not good."

"Am I being too harsh on him?"

"You know I'm a bleeding heart."

"So, yes."

"I'm on your side."

"But?"

"But he seemed so sad. Maybe you could hear him out."

"He took money from my dad."

"He did."

"And he didn't tell me."

"Nope."

"You think I should talk to him?"

"I think you're in love with him. And I think he loves you, but whatever you decide, I totally support you.

"Thanks." I felt more conflicted than I ever had in my life.

CHAPTER 57

TWO DAYS LATER, I sat on the beach and watched the waves crash against the shore. I'd never admit it to anyone, but I regretted not hearing Porter's side of things.

What had actually happened? When I asked him to leave, he did exactly that. And I never saw him again. But he also told me that he loved me. I felt heartsick. It was the kind of pain that never went away. From the moment I opened my eyes in the morning until I closed them at night, I ached.

Someone sat beside me. Without looking, I knew it was Jackson. We sat there in silence.

He cleared his throat. "You're hurting."

I traced patterns into the white sand beside me. I didn't speak.

"He was hurting, too."

I glanced up at Jackson. Any story, any tidbit, any news about Porter felt like a drop of water after an endless trek across a desert. I would take anything he could give me.

"I met Porter in BUDs, and man, that guy was a serious shit disturber." He gave a short laugh, not looking at me. "If the instructors asked him for ten, he'd give them twenty. If they pushed him, he'd shift into another gear and go harder, faster, stronger. At first, I thought he had something to prove, but after awhile, I realized there was no punishment great enough for Porter. Anything that involved danger or pain he was the first one to sign up. He's the only one I saw in BUDs that the instructors backed off on. They were used to pushing men to their limits, but it's like they knew they could push him past all his limits and he'd keep going. And eventually, it'd be his heart that'd explode, or he'd drown, or his lungs would blow. I think, at that point in his life, that was his end goal."

My eyes met his green gaze. "Why?"

He shrugged. "Not my story to tell, but Porter has carried around guilt for years. And no one is harder on Porter than Porter is."

I swallowed. I knew it had to do with his family.

Jackson continued, "Porter's one of the best operators I've ever met. He's fearless, ruthless and unbelievably protective. He's the only one I considered to be Theo's godfather. Without a moment's hesitation, he'd sacrifice himself for anyone."

I knew that about Porter. He'd risked his life diving in front of a car to save me.

"He and Felicia worked until they didn't. She was needy in all the wrong ways, and it fit into exactly what he thought he should be. He was protective. He took care of her. He was patient with her. He did all the heavy lifting in that relationship, but he could never give her the one thing she wanted."

"What was that?" my voice sounded like a rusty nail.

"He couldn't give a fuck."

Our eyes met again.

"Your relationship with Porter is the first time I've seen him give a fuck. And you know what?"

"What?"

"He kind of sucked at it. He's lived his entire adult life a certain way. And when you came along, he didn't know how to make that work."

"You talked to him when this was all happening?"

MY FAKE FIANCÉ 333

"He'd tell me different things, without actually telling me things. But he wasn't himself. From the get-go, you threw him off his game so hard."

"I did?"

He smiled down at me. "Was it this painful to watch me and Emily get together?"

"It was excruciating."

"Have you talked to your dad?"

I shook my head.

"Some friendly advice—start there."

"You think?"

"When we're in the field, we don't always have the benefit of seeing the entire picture. We get bits of intel coming in, and we make the best decision based on that intel."

"You think I need more intel."

"Don't you?"

I sat there, staring at the waves. "I think I need to get my ass back to New York."

—

I stepped into Dad's office.

He stood behind his desk, looking nervous. "Beth."

"Dad, I need you to be honest with me."

"Have a seat."

I sat down across from him. Deep lines on his face indicated his exhaustion. "I need you to tell me what happened that first night when you talked to Porter. Don't spin this to suit you. Tell me the truth."

He sighed. "One night Yates came to my office and told me you'd been arrested and that you had a new boyfriend."

I bit back my response, letting him speak.

"It didn't take much to figure out who Porter was. What I did, I'm not proud of. I had him investigated. And I found out something from his past to hold against him."

"Dad!" My fingers flew to my parted lips.

"Things were already starting to heat up with the campaign. I had reason to believe those drugs were deliberately planted in your purse. A raid was called. They wanted to have you arrested. That was the start of a smear campaign."

"What does that have to do with Porter?"

"I wasn't sure if he was part of that smear campaign."

I shook my head in denial. "What did you do?"

"First, I told him I knew you two weren't real. He didn't budge. Then, I offered him a lot of money to walk. He refused. That's when I got a bit dirty."

"What?"

"I knew that he was a SEAL. And I also knew he had some sort of agreement with you. If there was one person who could keep you safe, it was him. So, I offered him half a million dollars to stay with you and keep you safe until I said so."

"What did he say?"

"He told me to go fuck myself."

I sprung out of my chair and walked blindly to the window. "But you got him to accept the money."

"I threatened him. I told him if he refused, I would reveal his secret to the media, and it'd be front page everywhere."

I spun around to face him, "So, he really didn't have a choice. He either protected me for money and continued to protect his secret, or you'd blow up his life if he didn't accept."

"Yes. He told me he'd take care of you for free, but I forced him to take the money."

"You wanted him to take the money, so you had something over him." My heart raced in my chest.

"Beth, I'd do anything to keep you safe."

"He said he'd do it for free." My voice accused. "Why is everything about control with you?"

"I don't know," his shoulders dropped.

"I loved him. I still love him. He was the one, Dad."

"I know. I know that. And he loved you. Porter came to me and told me he loved you, and he wanted to marry you for real. I couldn't have been happier."

"But?"

He couldn't meet my eyes. "He wanted to tell you the whole truth."

"The night of the rehearsal dinner, you begged him not to tell me."

"I thought you'd never forgive me."

Big, rolling waves of pain pushed through my body. "He stuck with me."

"He did."

"He protected me, and he loved me, and I was...I was so awful to him."

"Beth. I'm so sorry. I've tried to find Porter."

"You have?"

"His phone has been disconnected. No one knows where he is. I wanted to apologize to him and fix this. What can I do?"

"He's never going to forgive me. He did everything right by our fucked up family and me, and look how we treated him."

"Your mom is so angry at me."

"Does she know?"

"I told her the entire thing. She threatened to divorce me if I didn't make this right." He stared down at his hands. "Can you forgive me?"

I was tired of feeling angry. So tired of being the wronged party. I didn't want to hold onto any of that any longer. "Dad, you have to let me live my life."

"I know."

"Please. You need to take a big step back. I can't go through this again."

"I know."

I picked up my bag and paused, unsure what to do next.

"What are you going to do?"

I needed to find him.

"I'm going to find Porter."

━━

Roo and Mom bent over a binder, heads almost touching as they murmured, two little peas in a pod. I stood in the doorway and watched. I realized I'd never seen Mom connect with another person quite like she had with Roo.

Had she ever had a friend like Roo? They were real friends, who actually cared about each other. She had told me recently that Roo has asked if she wanted to come and partner with him at his wedding planning company. I was truly happy for her.

I wished it had been me who had bonded with her, but right now, I felt glad she had such a close friend in her life.

"Hi," I said from the doorway.

Mom rushed to me, pulling me into a hug. "Darling girl." She pulled back to look at me. "I've been so worried."

"I talked to Dad. He told me everything."

A cross expression marred her face. "That man. I swear, I'm so angry with him."

I shrugged. "I wasn't exactly innocent in all of this either."

"What can we do? How can we help?"

I shifted my attention to Roo. "How did you find Porter's parents?"

He cocked his head to the side. "Porter gave me their address and phone number."

"Do you know where they live?"

"What's going on?" Mom rushed.

"I need to apologize to Porter, but I don't know where he is. I thought I'd contact his parents and see if they know where he is."

She covered her mouth with both hands. "Oh, that's perfect."

"I need to talk to Porter."

"They live in Montana," Roo offered.

That was going to be problematic. I had exactly $400 to my name. "Mom, can I borrow some money? I think I need to take a flight."

She crossed her arms. "I think I can do better than that. It's time your dad stopped holding your inheritance over your head from your grandmother."

I didn't give a shit about the money. But it would help. "Are either of you interested in helping me book a trip to Montana?"

CHAPTER 58

AFTER A SEVEN-HOUR CONNECTING flight to Helena, Montana, I swore as I set the GPS in my rental car. How could I still be a five-hour drive away from my destination? I debated getting a hotel in Helena for the night, but I was anxious to get there. The sooner I could talk to Porter's parents, the sooner I could find Porter.

Let me tell you about Montana. There's a whole lot of distant, mountainous ranges and even more rolling green hills. It didn't get any more beautiful, but I was bewildered by how wild the country seemed and how civilization seemed to have ended on the outskirts of Helena.

Things went from bad to worse when it started to rain. Not a sprinkle. Not a downpour. Sheets of rain cascaded down making the drive treacherous.

Five hours later, my GPS started to beep. I peered through the windshield. The only thing around was a lone wooden ranch gate.

I couldn't see a house. For miles, there was nothing but wild ranch land. With trepidation, I drove the car over the bumpy cattle gate and started up the driveway that was more slippery clay than gravel.

How long was their driveway, anyways?

The rain pounded my crappy rental. Unlike my trusty Camry, it fishtailed on every greasy bend.

My windshield wipers frantically flapped, but still, my vision was limited. Out of nowhere, a suicidal squirrel, with a death wish, appeared in the middle of the road.

I honked as I drove towards it, but it stood there, beady-eyed and frozen.

"Get out of the way," I yelled.

In a game of chicken, he bravely stood his ground.

I am not a squirrel killer.

With gritted teeth, at the last second, I twisted the wheel. The car slid off the road and bumped hard into the small ditch.

I watched the squirrel scamper away in my rearview mirror.

"I hope you're happy," I grumbled, putting the car in reverse.

It didn't budge. Reverse or forward, the car did nothing but spit gallons of mud high into the air behind me.

I'm from New York. In public, at any given time, there are dozens of people around. Here, there was no one. Not for miles. I felt like I should know what to do, but I was at a loss. I picked up my phone, but it had no cell service.

Holding a plastic bag over my head, I stepped out of the car. My Calvin Klein boots sunk ankle deep into the thick black mud. The back wheels were ground into the mud up to the rim. I knew enough that retrieving my car would require a tow truck.

And there was nothing but rolling grassy hills, the occasional tree and the winding driveway surrounding me.

In the middle of the downpour, I debated my options. I could sit in the car and hope someone drove by, but since I hadn't actually seen another human being in the last two hours, that was unlikely. The other option was to walk, through the rain, sans umbrella and coat, to Porter's parents' house.

I cursed my stupidity. Instead of phoning them, out of an irrational fear that they wouldn't talk to me, I had decided that showing up, unannounced, would give me the best chance to be heard. In my wildest imagination, I never imagined they lived on the edge of civilization. I thought I'd show up, have a quick chat and be back on my way to the airport.

Instead, I would show up on their doorstep, soaking wet, and without a vehicle. If they didn't want to talk to me, it'd be extremely awkward.

Twenty minutes later, a huge house came into view. Drenched and chilled from the rain, with a wet thong that was rubbing my ass in all the wrong ways, I stopped and re-weighed my options.

I'd ask to speak to Porter's mom. At the engagement party, she had exuded warmth and kindness. Even if she refused to tell me where Porter was, even if she didn't want to speak to me, I was certain she'd call a tow truck for me.

My boots echoed on the wide, wooden veranda. I pushed my wet hair off my face.

I knocked.

And waited.

And waited.

It hadn't crossed my mind that they wouldn't be home.

I knocked again.

An older woman swung the door open wide.

We studied each other. She looked no-nonsense. There was a sturdiness to her, a strength in her stance. In her expression.

"Sorry to drop by without calling first, but is Mrs. Lyons home?"

She held the door opened even wider. I stepped into the massive foyer. The place felt majestic yet homey.

"Come," she instructed and started to walk.

I pointed at my wet clothes and muddy boots. "I'm filthy. I can't mess up your floors."

"Floors can be washed."

I wiped my boots off on the mat as best as I could, before following her down the long hallway. I could hear voices. Laughter.

The sound of kids giggling. The woman stopped and pointed towards a door.

"You want me to go in there?"

She had to be joking.

"Do you think maybe you could see if Mrs. Lyons wants to come out and talk to me?"

She grabbed my arm and pushed me through the double french doors.

CHAPTER 59

HOLY HELL. It was a dinner party.

For about a million people.

A long dinner table lined the length of the entire room, and everywhere I looked was Porter's family. His brothers. Parents. Kids. Women. And a whole bunch of faces I didn't recognize. Another shiver wracked my body.

The entire room fell silent as they all took note of me.

And then I saw him.

Porter.

He sat beside a little kid. Grey eyes met mine, and suddenly I couldn't breathe.

Oh, *my*.

Porter was here. My heart sang as I drank in his appearance. He seemed different. Additional stubble and even longer hair made him look tougher than I remembered. Those slate grey eyes surveyed me back.

I tried to wipe the longing off my face but failed.

What was he doing here?

Why didn't either of us say anything?

Drip.

Drip.

Drip.

The silence in the room was so deafening, you could hear the water dripping off my clothes.

I cleared my throat, more than conscious of the dozens of eyes that watched me with varying degrees of shock and curiosity.

Why hadn't I phoned?

The irrationality of my actions was only exacerbated by the fact that I was covered in mud and completely soaked. I prided myself on never overstepping my boundaries with any of my ex-boyfriends, but at that moment, I realized that I probably looked like some crazy stalker chick.

Maybe I was.

If I had a working car that wasn't a twenty-minute walk away and stuck in a ditch, I would have bootlegged it out of there, but right now, my only option was to say something.

"Why are you so muddy?" a small boy saved me from speaking first.

My eyes dropped down to my pants that were caked in mud.

"There was a squirrel on the road."

The kid's lip started to wobble. "Did he die? Did you run him over?"

The entire room's gaze volleyed back to me.

"He's fine. But to save him, my car hit the ditch."

Miles, no maybe it was Brice, hunched over his plate, his eyes cast down, while his shoulders shook.

It took me a second before I realized he was trying to not laugh.

Someone else snorted.

And then the entire room exploded in laughter.

Porter's mom, with amused concern, spoke over the laughter, "That was very thoughtful of you, Beth."

Porter stood. He walked towards me, took my arm and steered me out of the room. At first, I wasn't sure if he was guiding me to the door to boot my ass back into the rain, but it became apparent that he was leading me up the stairs. He pushed me into a bedroom.

He crossed his arms and leaned against the dresser. He didn't need to speak, his expression told me that he wasn't impressed. Still, my greedy eyes soaked in the sight of him. His presence was larger than life. So strong and muscular. Stupidly hot.

Fuck, I had missed him. Down to the core of my soul.

"I didn't think you'd be here," I finally said.

"Why'd you come then?"

"I was hoping your family could tell me where you were." A shiver wracked my body.

"Go shower. You're freezing."

This clinical conversation was opposite of how I had imagined our first conversation.

"Don't you want to talk?"

"We can talk when you're not dripping wet."

It felt like an imposition, but I obediently moved to the bathroom and stared at my appearance in the mirror. I almost didn't recognize myself. My face was streaked with dirt, and my hair was plastered to my head. After a flight, five hours of driving and a rainstorm, my make up was non-existent.

My throat convulsed. This wasn't how I thought our talk would go. I hadn't been expecting hearts and flowers, but I thought I'd get more than what he gave me. Which was exactly nothing.

Now what? After I showered, would he listen to my apology? If he kicked me out, I'd still need someone to tow my car out of the ditch.

I soaped myself off and wrapped myself in a towel. I looked at my dirty, wet clothes lying on the floor and realized I didn't have anything to replace them with. My suitcase was in the car. I didn't even have clean underwear.

I tugged the big fluffy towel tighter around my body and took a bolstering breath before opening the door. Porter stood by the window, looking out at the rain. I felt nothing but relief seeing him still in the room.

At least he was willing to talk.

Now. Now I'd beg him to forgive me. For not trusting him. For not believing in him. For not hearing him out.

He didn't turn around. "I betrayed you."

I took a moment to gather my thoughts. "No, my dad betrayed me, and he blackmailed you. He forced you to protect me, and he forced you into an uncompromising position with your secret."

"I would have protected you. I didn't want his money."

"I know that. He knew that, too. The only reason he wanted you to take the money was so he had something to hold over you."

"It wasn't my secret that I was protecting."

"I don't know what that secret was, but I know you acted honorably."

"I told him I wanted to marry you for real, but you needed to know the truth."

I clung to the thick post of the four-poster bed. "Dad told me that, too. He told me everything."

Finally, he turned around, his face puzzled. "Why did you come here to apologize? You did nothing wrong."

"I should've trusted you and believed you. And at the very least, I should have listened to your side of the story."

"Why didn't you?" he walked towards me. Reminding me of a big cat, moving towards his prey.

I lifted my hand in a helpless gesture. "First, we were going to announce that we were not getting married. And then your family showed up. And then you were gone all night. And Detective Christensen came, and you revealed you were with Felicia. And I was so jealous."

Porter's arm wrapped around my waist and yanked me hard against his warm body. His mouth crushed down on mine.

Yes. Fuck, yes.

I moaned and wrapped my arms around his neck.

He lifted his head. "Why would you be jealous of Felicia?"

"Because she's gorgeous, and I saw your photos with her on your phone. And the day after I told you how I felt, you talked to her for ten minutes."

"I told you I'm a one-woman man."

"But you didn't tell me who your woman was."

"You didn't know? Not even when I did this?" His hand moved between my legs.

My knees almost buckled as I felt his fingers rim my opening. "Why did you talk to her for ten minutes?"

"To tell her it was over. To ask her to stop calling me."

I moaned, as I felt his fingers push into me. "I didn't know that. But then you went to see her in the middle of the night."

"I needed to get my grandmother's ring from her. I wanted to give it to you." His fingers were punishing, but my body couldn't get enough.

I rode those fingers like my life depended on it. My voice rasped with pleasure, "I didn't think you'd come to the church. I was such a bitch to you."

He bit my neck. "You know it makes me hot when you get all feisty."

I panted as those big fingers teasingly tortured me. "And then you showed up to the church. And I wasn't sure if you were there because you wanted to be or because you felt obligated."

His thumb circle my clit. "I told you at the front of the church how crazy I am about you. I told you I wanted to marry you."

"And I was so happy. Deliriously so, but then you were accused of only pretending to love me for money, and both my father and you wouldn't deny it."

His fingers had slowed, and now he stroked my g-spot until my legs shook. "I wanted you to hear my side of things." His thumb moved so lazily, I thought I was going to die. "I wanted to tell you the truth."

"I'm sorry," I gasped. "So sorry."

"You think that maybe you need to be punished a bit?"

"Yes, I totally think that'd make me feel better." I was so close. So close to coming all over his hand. I shut my eyes as my body prepared itself to come apart.

Knock. Knock. Knock.

Porter's hand stilled. "What?" he called.

"We're heading down the road to tow Beth's car out. Want to help?" a male voice called through the door.

"Be right out!"

I whimpered as his fingers slid out of my body. I was so close to having an orgasm, I saw double. "You can't leave me like this," I gasped.

"You heard them. I have to go." The amusement rang clear in his voice.

"I hate you," I said weakly.

He pressed a hot kiss to my lips. "Come downstairs and have something to eat. We can finish this conversation later."

"I don't have any clothes."

"Find something of mine to put on."

CHAPTER 60

I PULLED on a pair of Porter's sweats and a baggy sweatshirt. I swam in his clothes, but since I wasn't wearing a bra or underwear, I was okay with that.

Downstairs, his mom waited for me in the kitchen. It seemed like everyone else had left. "I have some dinner for you." She gently put her arm around my shoulders. "Come and sit down."

I obediently sat down. The steaming bowl of soup and bread that she set before me smelled incredible. "Thank you."

She squeezed my shoulder. "I'm thrilled you're here."

"I am, too."

She sat across the table from me. "Please, eat. You look like you need a few hearty meals."

Obediently, I picked up the spoon.

She watched me eat for a few moments and spoke, "You know, I wanted a girl more than anything. When I was pregnant with Porter, I knew six kids were more than enough, and I prayed that my last baby would be a girl."

She had my attention. "It was like Porter knew that, and he came out squawking mad, red-faced and pissed off. I wasn't prepared for all of his emotion. All of his passion. His older brothers are like me. Calm and patient. Slow to anger. Slow to feel. Porter's exactly like my husband. Passionate with the ability to feel so deeply."

She laughed as she played with her teacup. "He's also the youngest. He couldn't keep up with his brothers simply because he was so little. When he was a toddler, with these tiny chubby legs, he couldn't stand that he couldn't keep up with them. Can you imagine a three-year-old angry because he can't keep up with a twelve-year-old? He was always so determined. He never saw his size or his age as a limitation. From the day he could crawl, he's been working to catch up and pass his older brothers."

Her eyes met mine. "Porter is exactly like my husband. They both have that fiery passion that can outshine anyone. Those two love harder than anyone else. But Porter had some losses early on associated with that passion, and now, he equates love and that intensity with something bad."

"He hides it. He hides how he really feels," I blurted out.

She nodded. "I know. He's changed a lot since he joined the military. When he was 18, he wore his heart on his sleeve. He was either laughing or fighting but either way, he was the light of the party. These days, the only thing I know about him is that he's desperately in love with you."

My throat thickened. "I love him, too."

"You know, the whole family took bets on how long it'd take him before he went searching for you."

"Really?"

She patted my arm. "I got the sense he was giving you as much space as he could, but it was only a matter of time until he couldn't handle not seeing you."

Was she speaking the truth?

I chewed on my lip and stared at my empty soup bowl. "Thank you for dinner."

She waved my hand away when I tried to pick up my dishes. "Go now and sit near the fire in the living room. Porter will be back in in a few minutes."

I wandered into the massive living room that overlooked the endless yard. I watched as a tractor towed my car up the road. Behind it, two men in yellow rain jackets walked behind the car.

I instantly recognized Porter. He laughed at something his brother said and shoved him. His brother shoved him back, and they were suddenly in a full-on struggle, both laughing, both pushing against each other like two bulls in the rain.

The guy in the tractor stood on the back of it and shouted something at them. Still laughing, they walked to the end of the tractor to unhitch my car. My heart beat solid in my chest, watching him with his brothers. He seemed so at home here. This place suited him.

He waved goodbye to them. They moved off, and he pulled my suitcase out of the backseat and walked towards the house.

Without speaking, he sat down on the couch beside me. I couldn't keep my focus off his face. That mouth. Those cheekbones. Those grey eyes that focused on me.

"Are you still mad?" I asked.

"Beth, I was never angry with you."

No. It had been me who'd been angry.

"What happens now?"

"I need to tell you the whole truth about me." He fixed his gaze at the flames that flickered in the fireplace. "But if you don't want to have anything to do with me after I tell you, you have to promise not to leave tonight. The roads are too shitty."

"Porter, I'm not going to leave."

Grimness defined his features. "You might want to after you hear this."

I swallowed and waited.

He stared into the fire. "When I was 17, I got Mandy, my 16-year-old girlfriend, pregnant."

Wow.

I blinked and didn't move a muscle.

"I was such a cocky kid. When she told me that she was having my baby, I was overjoyed. I wasn't even in 12th grade, but in my mind, it was just life, and we were living it. I got on my knees and proposed right there."

I worked to bring air into my lungs and fought all the questions that threatened to push out of me.

"My parents weren't happy that they had a grandkid on the way, but along with her parents, they signed papers, giving us permission to get married. On the condition that we both finished school. I was so arrogant, so certain I could take care of shit, I got careless."

"Mandy wasn't the most experienced rider, but I wanted to take her to the top of this mountain ridge. I told her it was the best view in the entire world. And she trusted me. We were heading up there on a narrow trail, and her horse got spooked and reared back."

His eyes dropped down at his hands. "She was five months pregnant, and she fell 50 feet and landed on a tiny outbreak of rock."

My hand covered my mouth, my eyes never leaving his face.

"My dad, he'd warned me again and again about that ridge, but I never listened to him. I didn't listen to him about anything. By some miracle, my dad was in the pasture below, and he saw the entire thing." He took a deep breath. "Using a rope and his horse, my dad lowered me down to that ledge. Mandy was lying there. So silent. So quiet. Like she was sleeping. I cradled her in my arms, and my dad and his horse pulled us back up."

"Porter," I whispered.

"I had just gotten Mandy back up to the path when his horse saw a snake, probably the same snake that spooked Mandy's horse, and his horse came rearing back, fighting to get away from it. It came straight for us. My dad shoved us out of the way. His horse should have landed on me, but it landed on him, which is how he ended up in that wheelchair."

I reached out and grabbed his hand, squeezing hard.

"The fall caused Mandy to lose our baby and her ability to have any kids. She divorced me a week before my 18th birthday. All of that happened because I was too stupid, too cocky, and too immature to follow simple instructions."

"That's why you left. That's why you joined the military."

He shook his head. "You know what the worst part was? They all forgave me. My entire family. My dad. No one blamed me, and they should have. I couldn't take it."

I thought about what Jackson had told me. How Porter showed up, wanting to be punished, to the point of torture. "You punished yourself."

"Two people I loved more than anything in this world, and I ruined their lives."

A voice spoke from behind us, "You know, I've never stopped blaming myself for what happened up there on that ridge." His dad wheeled himself in front of the couch.

"Dad," Porter started.

"Everything that happened to you was my fault. I should have been a better parent. I wasn't, and because of that, I ruined your life."

"You've got it backwards."

"You think I didn't know what you and Mandy were doing? Hell, the whole county knew what you were up to. Your own mother was terrified you'd get that girl pregnant, but you want to know what my response was? I told her that choices had consequences, and the sooner you learned that, the better. Now, what kind of father says that about his 17-year-old son?"

Porter's voice remained low. "I knew what I was doing."

"You were a kid. A young, dumb, stupid kid, and I spoiled you. I let you do whatever you wanted. You ran wild, partying beyond your years, keeping up with your brothers when what you needed was a parent to give you boundaries."

"You told me not to go up there," Porter said between clenched teeth.

"Oh, yeah. I told you, and you did exactly as you pleased when you should have had a parent, safely teaching you life consequences. I should have taught you that if you disobeyed me, you'd get your truck privileges taken away. Or if you didn't do what I asked, you'd be given extra chores. But instead, the first consequences you ever learned ruined your life."

"You're the one in the wheelchair. I'm the one who ruined your life."

"You know what my regret is? It isn't this damn chair, because these are only legs, and I get around just fine. My biggest regret is not being the one to teach you responsibility or consequences. The military did that for me. They parented you in ways I should have."

"You can't take the blame here."

"Son, I was the parent. And I let this shit happen to my kid. And then worse, I let you carry that burden of guilt for another ten years because I was so damn ashamed of how I failed you."

"That's not how that went."

"And now all my mistakes are being thrown in my face because every day you continued to punish yourself for my mistakes feels like torture."

"Stop! Please stop."

"I had to grow up, son. You think your five brothers would've have made me grow up, but you're the one that made me become the man I am today. But I'm begging you to forgive me and stop carrying my burdens for me. Because if I have to watch you suffer one more day, I'm not sure I can take it."

"Dad," Porter sounded tortured.

"Son, I'm begging you to forgive me. Can you do that for me?"

I watched as Porter moved to his dad and kneeled before him. Then, they were hugging each other. So tight. I silently crept up the stairs. Tears squeezed out of my eyes as I climbed naked into his bed.

Suddenly, everything made sense. His mission in life had become about protecting others. About sacrificing himself. How many years had he tortured himself over an accident he'd been part of as a young teenager? He'd isolated himself from his family. Feeling too guilty to come home. Feeling too ashamed to face his parents.

I prayed that after he talked to his dad, he'd be able to find some peace and forgive himself.

⸻

I woke up to Porter kissing my neck. He was so gentle. So patient. His fingers were like silk, teasing soft sighs past my lips, his mouth hot and warm, coaxing me to arch and moan.

And then, when I couldn't take it any longer, he slowly pushed himself into me.

Missionary style.

Who said slow was boring?

Slow felt like pleasure drizzled over my body like warm honey.

Slow made me feel wanton and drugged.

Slow was surrendering with each breath.

Slow blew my mind.

When my body tightened and convulsed around him, I cried out into his mouth. Only then did he allow himself to gather me into his arms, crushing me as he called out my name, releasing himself into me.

We held each other while our racing hearts slowed.

"I missed you," he kissed.

"I thought you didn't do it slow." I kissed back.

He pushed my damp hair off my face and sucked my bottom lip into his mouth. "The complaints department is now closed."

"I was promised a proper punishment." I was drowning in his gaze. There was so much love coming at me, I thought my heart would burst.

"Come back tomorrow for what you've been promised."

"Oh, I plan on it."

"You ready for the bonus?"

"You going to try and cuddle me now?"

"I thought I'd give it a go."

I rolled over and sighed happily as he tucked his body around me. "You advertised that you didn't like to snuggle."

"I don't. Just you. You're the only one."

Another content sigh escaped me. "Well, good thing I like cuddling."

He kissed my shoulder. "Thank you for coming to find me."

"I got impatient."

"I was coming."

"You were taking your time."

He laughed.

"Are you okay?" My question hung there, in the dark, loaded with so much meaning.

"Yeah. I have a lot to think about."

"You were protecting Mandy. That was the secret my dad held over your head."

"She's been through enough. She didn't need her name splashed in the papers, nor did she need to re-live that part of her life."

"I like that you did that for her."

"I couldn't hurt her again."

"Do you ever talk to her?"

"No. My mom said she's married and has adopted two little girls."

"That's nice."

He pulled me tighter. "Yeah. That made me happy."

"I'm sorry that whole thing happened to you."

"If I could go back in time, I'd change it, but now I need to learn to accept it."

"And move on."

He pulled his arms tighter around me. "I love you, Beth."

I swallowed down all the emotion, that threatened to bubble out of me. "I love you, too."

CHAPTER 61

I SAT ON A HORSE, with Porter's arms around me. As far as my eyes could see, there was lush, hilly land. We stopped at a trickling creek that sparkled blue. It was so pretty, it almost hurt my eyes.

"Is this all yours now?"

"Yup."

"How much land are we talking?"

He got off the horse and lifted me off. "A hundred square miles, give or take." He removed a pack from the back of the horse and let it wander off to graze.

"Won't she run away?"

"He'll just snack a bit, but he won't go far." Porter spread a blanket on the grass next to the water and sat down on it. I sauntered towards him when his words stopped me cold, "Take off your shirt."

"Excuse me?"

His eyes burned dark beneath his cowboy hat. "You heard me. Take off your shirt."

I swallowed hard. "Any chance your brothers or dad will come galloping by?"

"I know for a fact they're working on the south-east fence today."

"Where is that?"

"About 75 miles away from here."

I double-checked over my shoulder, making sure no one was around. As far as I could see, there was nothing but blowing grass and hills.

I slowly unbuttoned my blouse and slid the fabric off my shoulders.

"Now your pants."

"That doesn't seem fair."

"I promised you a proper punishment."

"Does it involve spankings?" I kicked off my sandals and pushed my jeans down my hips and stood there in my underwear.

"I think you'd enjoy that too much. This is all for my pleasure," he said. "Come sit down."

I dropped to the soft flannel blanket and watched as he fished for something in his bag.

"Take off those cute little panties."

I lay on my back, lifted my hips and slid them down. This was going to be fun. With a wicked glint in his eye, he pulled a rolled towel out his bag, unrolled it, and presented it to me.

My mouth dropped open as my eyes took in a vibrator. "Are you serious?"

He slowly drizzled lubricant over it. "You see, I can't get this one image out of my mind."

"What image would that be?"

"The image of the first time you orgasmed in front of me."

He clicked the vibrator on, and we both watched as the bunny ears started to vibrate. Another click and then the head of the beaded vibrator slowly spun. He turned it back off.

"That's a bit of an upgrade from mine."

"Only the best for you."

I gave a nervous laugh. "I thought you didn't like toys."

"I've had a change of heart on a lot of things."

He knelt and then yanked my legs, so I was spread open to him with my feet planted on the ground.

Laughing grey eyes met mine. "Are you ready?"

"I'm nervous."

"Not as nervous as me."

I laughed even harder. "Why are you nervous?"

He touched the tiny rabbit ears. "Who can compete with this?"

"This doesn't seem like punishment to me," I gasped as he slowly inserted the vibrator into me. It felt cool and smooth.

"Wait until you're begging me to stop." He waited for my body to adjust around it. "Ready?"

"As I'll ever be."

He turned it on, and the vibrator slowly rotated within me. I half-shut my eyes as the beads massaged my entrance and the head slowly skimmed my g-spot.

"Oh, yeah." I bit my lip.

His eyes were glued to the show between my legs. "What do you think about when you pleasure yourself with your little toys?"

"Public sex," I gasped.

He undid his jeans with one hand while holding the toy between my legs. "What kind of public sex? Do you have a favorite fantasy?"

I lifted my head and watched as he pulled out his beautiful erection. "Yes."

"Tell me." He fisted his cock and started to stroke himself.

The vibrator endlessly spun inside of me. "I'm in a dark bar, and everyone is dancing."

"What are you wearing?"

"A short dress with high heels."

His lips curled. "Like that red dress?"

"Exactly like that red dress."

"Fuck me. Then what?"

"You get tired of me teasing you with my dancing, so you yank me down a hallway. It's dark, but there is a big risk anyone can walk down and see us."

He flipped a switch, and those tiny rabbit ears started dancing on my clit. My hips jerked and our eyes met.

"Then what?"

I lifted my head to watch him move his hand up and down his hard cock. "You spin me around, so my face is against the wall. You push up my skirt, and your fingers are inside of me."

"Teasing you."

"Yeah." I was breathless. "It feels so dirty but so right."

"Are you wearing panties?"

"Yes, but they're fragile and lacy."

He flipped a switch, and the vibrator began to swirl faster inside of me. "So, my fingers are deep inside of you. Do I rip off your panties?"

I moaned, and my legs shook. "Yes. Because they're getting in the way."

"What else?"

"You're so overcome with desire, you undo your pants and pull out your cock."

"What is my cock like?"

"Hot. Big. Hard."

I cried in protest as he pulled the vibrator out of me. Then, he flipped me on my hands and knees. My body ached at the loss.

"What happens next?"

I pushed my ass back and spread my legs wider, looking over my shoulder at him. "And then you're pushing your hot cock into me."

"Do I push it in gently or rough?"

"Rough. I like it rough." My teeth clenched. My body felt empty. I needed him so bad.

He pushed his hips forward, and he roughly thrust his cock deep inside me. "Like that?"

I groaned hard as I felt him fill me more than any vibrator ever could. "Yeah, exactly like that."

I could hear him breathing hard. "Am I missing anything?"

"You're pulling my hair."

He wrapped his fingers around my ponytail and tugged my hair, so my neck pulled back and my back arched in a delicious way. "Then, what?"

"Then, you start to fuck me like your life depends on it."

"Can you be more descriptive?"

I panted as he pulled out slowly and pushed himself all the way back in. "You use a lot of force to thrust your hot cock deep inside of me. I like it really fast. And hard."

"You're bossy." He was out of breath, but he started to move. Just the way I liked it.

He thrust deep and hard with a steady rhythm while simultaneously yanking on my hair. His big cock stretched me, hitting all the right spots, sending impossible shivers of addictive pleasure through my body. There was no hesitation in his movements. He was fucking me like he meant it.

My entire body trembled, welcoming each time he plunged into me. My heart hammered in my chest, my core clenched and twitching around him, and I was drowning in desire.

I panted.

He groaned.

I twitched.

He thrust.

I whimpered.

He moved faster.

"You need to come," he growled. "Because I'm about to lose it here."

"I'm close," I sobbed.

His hand reached around me and circled my clit. My orgasm violently shuddered through my body. I could feel my body pulsing, milking his cock as he shouted and buried into me with one last savage push.

We collapsed breathlessly beside each other, and I stared unseeing at the blue sky above us.

"I almost embarrassed myself there," he said, still breathless.

"Funny how my punishment doesn't seem that bad."

He gave a laugh. "Oh, just wait. I've got extra batteries for that rabbit."

CHAPTER 62

AFTER MULTIPLE ORGASMS, we played in the water. I clung naked to Porter's hard body as he dog-paddled through the cool deep water wearing only his beat-up cowboy hat.

"Does a cowboy ever take off his hat?"

"Not if he can help it."

"So, is that what you are now? A cowboy?"

He wrapped my legs around his waist and carried me up to the blanket. "I'm not quite ready to give up being a SEAL, but one day I want to retire here, come back, and be a ranchman. My brothers are going to take care of the land for me until I'm ready to come home."

I stretched out my naked body, loving how the sun felt on my skin. "It's perfect out here."

His eyes locked on mine. " Do you think you'd ever want to live out here?"

"I'd need to learn how to ride a horse."

"Obviously."

"And I'd need to get some cowboy boots."

"That's a given."

"And this ass does look pretty decent in a pair of jeans."

"It's the best looking ass I've seen."

"I could live out here."

He pressed his cold lips against mine. "And how do you feel about living on a military base?"

"That depends."

"On?"

"Would you come home in those hot military fatigues and force me to do dirty things?"

"What kind of dirty things?" He gave me an interested look.

"Like maybe you'd be wearing your uniform, and you'd bend me over the table and take me from behind, moments before company came over."

"Yup. That sounds like me."

"I'd consider it."

"What if I gave you this?"

I froze as he opened his hand to show me the most beautiful ring I'd ever seen. It was a large ruby surrounded by a dozen diamonds. Porter knelt in front of me, wearing only his cowboy hat.

"Are you proposing?"

"Do you think I'd be on my knee for any other reason?"

"You better mean it."

"I meant it the first time."

"Say it."

"Beth, will you do me the honor of becoming my wife?"

"Yes." I laughed, and happy tears sprung from my eyes.

He slipped the ring on my finger. It fit perfectly. Our kiss was long and hot, and then he was flipping me onto my back. His chin rested on my chest as he watched me study the ring.

"There are some rules."

I grinned at him. "These I have to hear."

"You need to learn Morse code. More than SOS."

"Why?"

"Cause I like your dirty Morse code messages."

"Deal."

"And we start *Grey's Anatomy* from the beginning."

I laughed. "I knew you were hooked."

"I admit it. But this is one closet I'm not coming out of. This is our secret."

"Fine. What else?" I smiled into those perfect grey eyes.

"No more secrets. No more stalkers."

I leaned down and pressed my lips against his. "Those are a lot of rules."

"And I get to use the rabbit on you whenever I want."

I laughed again—he was always making me laugh. "You're incorrigible."

"You want me to keep on going?"

"Yes, please."

"I want lots of babies."

My eyes widened. "How many babies?"

"Well, we can start with one."

"You like babies?"

He smiled at me. "Love them."

"Let's see. A hot cowboy, Navy SEAL husband who enjoys kinky sex and loves babies. I think I can live with those terms."

"You sure?"

"Pretty sure."

"Say it."

"I want to marry you, Porter. I want to be your wife."

"And my sex slave."

"I thought I already was."

"Say it."

"And I want to be your kinky little sex slave."

"Deal."

"Deal."

EPILOGUE
PORTER

STATESIDE.

Home.

I waited with impatience for the big back doors of our bomber plane to open.

"See you for beers this weekend?" Jackson asked as he lifted his canvas bag over his shoulders.

"Yeah, for sure."

"Emily told me that Beth found a job."

"Yeah, she got hired at the hospital doing PR for their fundraising team. She's pretty excited."

"Good for her." A satisfied expression crossed his face.

I smiled in memory of exactly how we celebrated her good news. Involving FaceTime and my favorite rabbit.

"How are you and her parents?"

We were healing. We had a ways to go, but we all wanted the same thing. To get along. "We're working on it. Her dad was recently elected mayor of New York."

"No kidding." He grinned. "You going to make an honest woman of her anytime soon?"

"Working on it."

"What's the hold-up?"

"A small Asian man named Roo, who insisted that he needed an opportunity to redeem himself."

"Do I even want to know?"

I laughed. Damn. Why was I always laughing? It was ruining my tough guy image. "Nope."

"MacDog." Someone called Jackson away.

Could these doors open any slower?

Finally, they lowered. I slung my heavy canvas bag over my shoulder and picked up my Sig P266, before walking down the ramp.

And there she was. Tall. Leggy. That gorgeous blond hair blowing in the breeze. She stood beside Emily and lifted her hand to smooth the hair off her cheek. I couldn't take my eyes off her.

My girl-next-door.

So mischievous.

How I got so lucky, I had no idea, but her presence in my life filled me with so much fucking happiness I almost couldn't breathe.

She paused, and her entire smile radiated joy when she caught sight of me.

Right now, I looked rough as hell and had an attitude to match.

It took a couple days stateside to turn off my inner warrior. After being deployed, I came back too intense, too wound up, too focused. But Beth didn't seem to mind. Her exact words were that my intensity was 'hot as fuck'. Which worked out in my favor. My last trip home we fucked so much, I thought my dick would break.

It didn't.

I studied her, as my long strides ate up the distance between us. She was my second chance.

At happiness.

At living.

At feeling alive.

Maybe I didn't deserve her, but fuck if I wasn't going to spend my life doing everything I could to make her happy. As happy as she made me.

A soldier whose name I didn't know, walked beside me. He gave a low whistled. "Who's the hot blond?"

"Her name is Beth."

She ran towards me, and those sweet arms, wrapped around my neck. I tugged her lithe body hard against mine.

Fuck she felt good.

I buried my face into her neck, breathing in all her sweetness.

She lifted her face back. We technically weren't supposed to engage in sexual affection on the deck, but I stole a hard kiss from those lips.

"You're home," she smiled into my eyes.

"Yup," I kept all the expression off my face.

"And you're wearing your uniform."

"They're called fatigues," I growled low.

Her pink tongue played with her upper lip, and that small action gave my dick ideas. A lot of dirty ideas.

"Whatever they're called, your soldier clothes make me hot," she breathed dramatically. "So hot."

My huge fucking grin ruined my tough guy act. We both laughed.

Her warmth, her heat, her passion and her fire had melted the ice wall I had built up around my heart.

How did you even thank someone for doing that?

I never could find the right words to tell her how much she meant to me. I tried, but I failed wide in that department. So I tried to show her in a hundred other ways. A lot of those ways involved my dick, but in the end, my goal was her happiness.

Was this normal?

I had no idea, but it was my new normal, and I loved every second of it.

Her gorgeous face beamed up at me, "I missed you."

I wrapped my arms around her waist and crushed her back against me. "I missed you too."

"Take me home?"

I held her hard against my body. "I'm already home."

BOOKS BY ODETTE

THE NAVY SEAL SERIES

My Fiancé's Brother: Duet Book 1

My Fiancé's Brother: Duet Book 2

My Fake Fiancé

My Donut Princess: Novella

THE VANCOUVER WOLVES HOCKEY SERIES

Puck Me Secretly

Home Game

The Penalty Box

High Risk Rookie

Hook My Heart: Novella

THE VANCOUVER MAFIA ROMANCE SERIES

Dark Russian Angel

FOLLOW ODETTE

ODETTE'S FACEBOOK GROUP

Come join the fun in Odette's exclusive Facebook group, "Odette's Hot Alphas". This facebook group offers exclusive giveaways, cover reveals, sneak peaks, and is the best chance to chat with odette.

Facebook Group: Odette's Hot Alphas

ODETTE'S VIP ACCESS - NEWSLETTER

Join Odette's VIP newsletter for exclusive access to free novellas and bonus chapters, exclusive to this group only. Participate in free giveaways, and get all the latest news on Odette's releases!

https://www.odettestone.com/odettes-vip-newsletter/

FOLLOW ODETTE ON BOOKBUB

Follow me on Bookbubs and get alerts for my Bookbubs deals and exciting new book releases.

Bookbub: @OdetteStone

ODETTE'S INSTAGRAM PAGE

Instagram: odette.stone

ODETTE'S WEBSITE

www.odettestone.com

Made in the USA
Coppell, TX
02 January 2024

27189472R00207